GW00385395

MIDNIGHT OIL

THE 1991 IAN ST JAMES AWARDS

Judges

TERRY MAHER
Chairman and Chief Executive, Pentos plc

EVE POLLARD
Editor, *Sunday Express*

KATE FIGES
Literary Editor, *Cosmopolitan*

KATE PARKIN
Editorial Director, HarperCollins

IAN ST JAMES

MARIE FITZGERALD
Manager, Waterstones, Dublin

DAVID ROSE
ITN journalist

MIDNIGHT OIL

The winners of the 1991 Ian St James Awards

Fontana
An Imprint of HarperCollins*Publishers*

Fontana
An Imprint of HarperCollins*Publishers*
77–85 Fulham Palace Road,
Hammersmith, London W6 8JB

A Fontana Original 1991

1 3 5 7 9 8 6 4 2

A catalogue record for this book is
available from the British Library

ISBN 0 00 647181 1

All royalties from the sale of this book will be paid to the Ian St James Trust and used for the furtherance and expansion of the Ian St James Awards.

All events and persons represented in these stories are fictional, and any resemblance to actual events or persons living or dead is purely coincidental.

Set in Sabon by Rowland Phototypesetting Ltd
Bury St Edmunds, Suffolk

Printed in Great Britain by
HarperCollinsManufacturing Glasgow

Foreword

Burning the midnight oil! What a vivid picture this phrase conjures up. No doubt you have your own picture but to me, as Administrator of the Ian St James Awards, the image which springs to mind is of thousands of authors throughout England, Scotland, Ireland and Wales working deep into the night to craft, polish and perfect the stories which will eventually compete for these Awards.

Here are the twelve magnificent stories which won the 1991 Awards – introducing very talented and *now professional* writers, some of whom will become established stars of the future. When Ian St James created these Awards, he sought to provide access for aspiring writers to the world of professional authorship. We now know that Ian acted as a catalyst to a movement which has taken on a life of its own. Thankfully this movement has many friends. On behalf of the charity which administers the Awards, it is my pleasure to pay tribute to literally hundreds of people who together create these unique opportunities for new writers. Our friends at Parker Pen play a major role, not only by supporting the charity with badly needed finance, but with ideas and encouragement. The same is true of our publishers, HarperCollins, whose involvement is fundamental. Thanks are also due to our panel of judges who donate so much of their time and expertise to selecting the twelve winning stories and to our team of professional readers who shortlist the fifty finalists from thousands of entries. Beyond these are even more people – established authors, booksellers, literary agents and literary editors – one hundred of whom band together as Friends of the Awards to select the overall winner, the second and third placed authors. Finally, we must never forget our friends in the retail booktrade who make entry forms to these Awards available in bookshops thoughout the land.

These then are the hundreds of people who have stretched out a helping hand to thousands of aspiring authors and, in so doing, made this book possible. My thanks to them and, of course, to Ian St James who continues to give of his time and efforts in a thousand and one ways.

To the winners of the 1991 Awards, I offer congratulations. To our friends, I offer grateful thanks. To our readers, I confidently wish every enjoyment, and to those who may be inspired by these stories to put pen to paper themselves* I wish every future success.

GRAHAM TAYLOR
Administrator
The Ian St James Awards

* Details of how to enter these annual Awards appear at the end of this book.

Contents

Small Beginnings 1
Faith Addis

Kenny 23
Richard Clarke

French Kisses 41
Alan Dunn

Me and Renate 69
Stephanie Ellyne

Adidas 87
Sarah Gracie

'Arry 'ad an 'Orse 105
Louise Lear

Shreds 125
Marion Mathieu

The Admiral's Daughter 155
Michael Morris

Missionary Endeavour 177
Patricia Mowbray

A Crack in the Glass 195
Dr Frances Peck

Life with the Farmers 219
Lesley Tilling

Night Shift 247
Patricia Tyrrell

SMALL BEGINNINGS

Faith Addis

Faith Addis has had such a varied career that to try and describe it would require far more space than is possible here! Briefly, she has at one stage or another worked at London Zoo, taken a diploma course in commercial photography, worked as a photographer's assistant, married and raised a family, fostered children, tried small scale farming and has run a riding school. She now writes part-time.

SMALL BEGINNINGS

David wandered along the pavement looking for feathers. His mother had told him to play in the garden until tea but she didn't know about the hole in the fence. Anyway he'd only be gone for a little while. The man in the next-door-but-one house kept chickens in his front garden and sometimes you could find a feather or two lodged in his privet hedge.

'What's up, Sunshine? Lost a tanner?' It was the chicken man.

'No. I want to be a Red Indian but I haven't got any feathers.'

'Oh dear, that's not very good is it? Got any war-paint?'

David said firmly: 'I don't want any war-paint, thank you. I'm going to use peace-paint.' It was 1942 and although David had been born before the war he couldn't remember that time at all. His world, like that of many London children, was narrow. His mother defined 'Is Your Journey Really Necessary?' to mean no further than the local Co-op, so apart from a twice-yearly duty visit to some ancient aunt, David's life was strictly confined to house, garden and school.

Peace-paint indeed. Poor little devil, said the chicken man to himself, and to David: 'Help yourself to feathers, mate.' He opened a wire-mesh gate and David slipped into the chicken run. Six fat hens, mildly disturbed, stood up and shook themselves. David laughed at them and inhaled the lovely smell of their enclosure – sun-baked dung and dust, mingled with poultry-feed spices. He said 'Excuse me' to a hen sitting in one of the nest boxes and grasped her tail. With a squawk of outrage one very cross hen took off in a flurry of sawdust.

'Oh, I'm sorry.' David looked helplessly at the bunch of feathers in his hand. 'I only wanted one.' The chicken man shook with laughter and said next time David must collect feathers from the ground not from someone who was still using them. 'You'd better run along now, son, or there'll be fireworks from your mum. Does she know you're out on your own without your gas-mask?'

'What's a firework?' asked David.

'Sodding, sodding Hitler,' said the chicken man, from which David guessed that a firework was something like a banana or chocolate, something you couldn't have because of sodding Hitler. Of the war itself he knew that the Allies were good and the Jerries bad. Daddy was somewhere in Europe. Messerschmitts sounded exactly like wasps but Spitfires sounded kind, like bees, so obviously they were on our side. Spitfires had Merlin engines and the Brylcreem boys said wizard when they meant nice. Uncle Mac, Stuart Hibberd and Mr Churchill were the most important men in the world.

'Where have you been? I've been calling you for ages. And what's that awful smell? Honestly David, you look like a gypsy. I don't know what people must think.' His mother attacked the grime on his hands and face with a damp flannel. David screwed up his eyes tightly and pretended he was a lion cub being rasped clean by the mother lion's tongue . . .

'. . . moving in next door tomorrow so I want you to be extra nice to her little girl.' With an effort David brought himself back from the jungle, half glad half sorry that his mother's furry paws had become her familiar pink capable hands. 'Poor woman,' his mother continued. 'Bad enough to have her husband a POW but this business with the grandmother going off has left her homeless so she's rented next door for the duration.'

David thought the business with the grandmother going off sounded interesting. Had the old lady exploded? He filed the promising picture away to be brought out and savoured later. Meanwhile he concentrated on his tea, spam, potatoes and greens. He hated greens but finished them nonetheless because the starving children in Europe were mysteriously made happier by people who ate up nicely.

The next morning Big Chief Reindeer was hard at work in the garden composing a rain spell when a small girl appeared in front of him. David stared. Although he had implicit faith in the powers of magic he couldn't think where he had gone wrong. 'I asked for rain,' he said accusingly, 'and you're – um, you're a person.'

'Your mother sent me,' said the person and David remembered that his mother had said he must be extra nice to someone's little girl because her grandmother had exploded. He said politely and not without a degree of morbid curiosity: 'Did you see your granny go off?'

'No,' said the newcomer. 'Mummy says it's disgusting at her age. She's fifty-six and her boyfriend's sixty.'

'Disgusting,' agreed David. 'I expect all the gizzards and things fell out. Come and help me with my rain spell. I'm Reindeer so you'll have to choose another name and you can have a feather to wear.'

'Reindeer's a very good name for making rain,' said the girl. 'I'll be Big Chief Spaniel.' She took the proffered feather and stuck it in her hair. 'Shall we make thunder and lightning while we're at it?'

Common sense told David that while a summer shower was one thing, a full-blown storm was quite another. 'We'd get into trouble,' he said with a certainty based on experience.

'Then we'd have to get married.'

'Married? Why?'

'People who get into trouble have to get married. Didn't you know?'

'Gosh,' said David, impressed at his companion's depth of knowledge. Then he had an idea. 'If we got married,' he said hesitantly, 'if we got married *before* we make our thunder and lightning, would it keep us out of trouble?'

'I don't know. We could try. What's your name?'

'David.'

'I'm Liz – Elizabeth, same as the princess but Liz for short.'

David said: 'Have I got to give you a ring?' and his fiancée, sensing his inexperience, decided to forgo the ring. 'You can build me a house instead,' she said.

'Then what?'

'Then we exchange vowels.'

'What's a vowel?'

'I don't know,' Liz admitted. 'I'll go and ask.' She ran indoors where the two mothers were getting acquainted over a cup of tea and reappeared a few minutes later clutching a scrap of paper. 'It's five letters out of the alphabet,' she reported. They studied the document closely. 'It's nice and short,' said David.

Their marriage ceremony was equally nice and short. Each in turn chanted 'a-e-i-o-u' followed by 'I give thee my vowels' (the 'thee' being insisted upon by David who liked archaic words in his rituals) followed by a formal handshake which they both felt was appropriate to the occasion.

'Are you six yet?' asked Liz. 'I'm six and two months.'

'Six and a week,' said David, 'but I'm taller than you.'

'And very handsome. Do you think I'm pretty?'

David examined her face. 'No,' he said and added kindly: 'But people change. I like your yellow dungarees. Mummy won't let me wear things that show the dirt.'

'Shall we let our children wear what they like?'

'*Children?*' Fleetingly David had second thoughts about his marriage.

'Why, would you rather have puppies?'

'Yes, I would. But we'll have children too if you like.' David was acutely aware of the age gap between them and was determined not to be thought too young for his responsibilities. 'How many would you like?'

'Ten, please. You can choose their names.'

David thought for a moment. 'Jack,' he said, 'we'll call them Jack.'

'What, all of them?'

'All of them,' said David firmly. 'It'll save having to remember ten different names. When their lunch is ready we can shout Jack and they'll all come in . . .'

'. . . and eat condensed milk out of the tin with their fingers,' added Liz with relish.

And so the ten Jacks were born, androgynous and of indeterminate ages. Housing for such a large family could have proved difficult but David, inspired by his new status, found the answer. 'They can live in a raspberry house. I've often made one for myself – it's easy. We'll make a really big one.'

Their mothers called them in for lunch. Before going indoors they swore an oath of secrecy, a hybrid oath, part Arthurian, part Enid Blyton.

'Seems a dear little boy from what I could see of him through the window,' said Liz's mother. 'Were you playing Lexicon with those letters?'

'Mm,' said Liz through a mouthful of sausage.

'That's nice. I think I'll put our garden down to vegetables and fruit, same as theirs. You must have David back here to play next time – fair's fair.'

'He's dark,' said Liz.

'Touch of the tarbrush somewhere back probably. I always think curls are wasted on a boy.'

David was jubilant when Liz told him they now had the run of both gardens. 'Smashing,' he grinned. 'Oh Liz, I am glad to have you next door.' Liz felt a wriggle of pleasure at this, short-lived when it turned out that it was her garden tap that was the attraction. 'We can canoe up the Nile to the Canadian Lakes,' he said gleefully – his own house did not possess an outside tap – 'Shoot the rapids with savage crocodiles coming out of the swamps –'

'What about our house?' Liz reminded him.

'I haven't forgotten. We'll make a house today and tomorrow we'll canoe up the Nile. OK? Now we need some big stones or bricks.'

They collected some stones and laid them in a row parallel to the row of raspberry bushes which David's mother had planted the previous year. By bending the tip of each raspberry cane down to the ground and anchoring it with a stone they soon had a snug tunnel literally dripping with ripe fruit. For the rest of her life Liz never forgot the enchantment of their first home; the smell of earth, the dappled sunlight, and best of all the roof, so cleverly designed to provide both food and shelter. Lost for words she picked a fistful of raspberries and crammed them into her mouth. The purple juice ran down her chin. 'A bearded lady.' David giggled and soon they were both helpless with laughter as they painted each other's faces with squashed raspberries.

All too soon they discovered that marriage was not after all an insurance policy against calamity. But it certainly helped – a trouble shared, etc. Lying in bed that night, still smarting from the smacking he had received, David relived the glorious afternoon. Having a wife and children next door was a lot more fun than being single. He drifted off to sleep, well pleased with the change in his fortunes.

For the rest of the summer David and Liz managed to stay more or less out of trouble. There were a few setbacks – like the night they forgot to turn off Niagara Falls, an oversight which transformed Liz's mother's brassica bed into a paddy field – but on the whole they climbed Everest and swam the Channel and scored centuries at Lords without too much adult hindrance. But when winter drove them indoors to play it was a different story. The mothers found out about the ten Jacks and forbade any more of 'that nonsense'. With nerves already stretched to breaking point by air-raids, rationing and absent soldier husbands, they simply could not cope with a houseful of invisible children, each of whom had by now acquired a puppy of its own, not to mention mannerisms and catch-phrases.

Liz and David dug their heels in; they refused to get rid of their precious Jacks. 'Want them to be refugees, do you?' David stormed at his mother. 'Living on Red Cross parcels?'

'But David, they're not *real*,' his mother pleaded. 'It's just a silly game and it's time you grew out of it.'

'If they're not real why do you keep tripping over them?' said David. His mother looked at him uneasily. To her, being 'different' was practically a capital offence. She decided to seek professional guidance.

The doctor at the clinic listened patiently to her outpourings: 'Ten of them, Doctor . . . there's never an empty chair to sit on . . . these blasted puppies now . . . it's not healthy, is it?'

'That depends,' said the doctor, who privately thought it sounded extremely healthy for a lonely child to create for himself a large cheerful band of companions. 'I'll see David on his own now.'

If he was surprised to learn that his young patient was a married man with ten children and ten puppies to support, the doctor was careful not to show it. 'The puppies *were* a mistake,' David admitted at the conclusion of his story. 'They bark a lot.'

'Good God,' said the doctor with a momentary pang of sympathy for David's mother. 'Look David, it seems to me that it's high time some of your elder children started to earn their own livings.' He consulted his notes. 'Big Jack for instance. Isn't he old enough to go in the navy?'

'Big Jack is going to be a circus acrobat. It's Jack Tar who wants to go in the navy. I did tell you.'

'Sorry. But surely acrobats are small and thin? How about sending Smallest Jack to circus school to learn how to be an acrobat?'

David said witheringly: 'You didn't listen. Smallest Jack is a cripple. We have to carry him everywhere.'

'No problem,' said the doctor. 'Bring him to the clinic and we'll make him better.'

'He's here now,' said David. 'He's sitting on your foot.'

Liz liked the idea of sending the Jacks out to work. 'We can give them going-away parties,' she said. 'Dress them up and play Pass the Parcel and things.'

'But we'd miss them,' David objected.

'They'll write to us and they'll come home on leave sometimes.'

The mothers proved surprisingly cooperative with the going-away parties. Preciously hoarded tins of pineapple chunks appeared, sacrificial offerings to speed things up. David and Liz rationed the parties to one a fortnight. Their mothers thought the time would never pass. Eventually Smallest Jack (now miraculously cured) was waved off, his puppy at his heels, to start his circus training.

'Goodbye, Smallest Jack. Please write to your old mother.' Liz sobbed happily and melodramatically.

'Don't cry, Liz.' David put his arms round her. 'He'll come back one day. Listen, do you like cobras and pythons? I've had a good idea what we can do tomorrow . . .'

When the war ended the children's fathers returned, not the hoped for conquering heroes but khaki strangers, ill at ease in their own homes and unprepared for domestic life. Liz's family moved house, only a bike-ride away but it meant the children saw less of each other. David's mother was relieved. 'That Liz was a bad influence,' she said, and tried to describe the difficulties of bringing up a boy who lived in a world of books and fantasy. Her husband, who had spent five years trying to avoid getting killed, was less than sympathetic. He was bitterly disappointed in David who, he predicted glumly, would turn into a pansy if Something Wasn't Done. Fortunately for David the hardships of the austerity years left his father little time or energy to do whatever it was that prevented people turning into pansies. Apart from being exhorted almost daily to get his hair cut David was able to make the transition from boy to youth – teenagers had not yet been invented – without undue influence from his jaundiced parent.

Secondary school came next, boys' grammar for David, girls' grammar for Liz. Being at separate schools was not the great divide that both sets of parents had hoped for and the youngsters continued to meet, sometimes just the two of them but more often in a crowd. Everyone had bikes, and expeditions were the fashion with tennis whenever they had enough money to get a court and swimming when it was hot enough. *The Goon Show* was required listening.

The Festival of Britain with its Skylon, fireworks, music and crazy buildings proved to be a turning point in Liz's and David's lives. The first time they went they had to stay with their respective school parties – the boys' headmaster being convinced that his pupils would all turn into raging sexmaniacs if they were let loose among girls – but despite this restriction they and most of their friends were poleaxed by the South Bank wonderland. For a generation which had been brought up to regard drabness as the norm (bottle-green and brown indoors, grey public buildings, beige classrooms) the colours alone were intoxicating. Geranium-red railings, poppy-red seats, blue stairs, cascades of jewel-bright flowers in hanging baskets, this was more like a dream than a school outing.

David started his week's essay on the subject of the Festival: 'A fanfare of trumpets has sounded in my head', which did not please his English master ('I thought you were taken to Battersea not the Albert Hall'). Liz, similarly affected but of a more practical nature, went to the Post Office and drew £3 out of her savings. 'We're going again,' she informed David.

For the second visit they sought out Battersea's infant Mafia. Coppers changed hands and they were shown how to bunk in through some bent railings thus saving several precious shillings. Hours later, money spent, they flopped down on some grass, bewitched and transformed.

'Liz,' said David at last, 'did you ever read Plato's *Republic*?'

'Mm, of course. Why?'

'Well, I think I'm just beginning to understand things. This place – the colours, the architectural anarchy – it makes my mind giddy. I could ravish the universe.'

Liz made a mental note to put herself first in the queue if any ravishing was on the agenda. 'I know,' she said. 'It's as though we've been at the bottom of a murky pond and now we've come up into the real world.'

'That's it. We've had a mystical experience. Do you feel converted?'

'I feel different. Not converted, more sort of privileged. When we were watching that colour film in three dimensions – you remember we had to wear those funny little goggles – I felt privileged that whoever had thought up the idea was prepared to share it with me. The same feeling you get when you read a good book.'

'I felt that about the Skylon. Someone with the vision to break the rules invented that.'

'Smallest Jack would have loved this place, wouldn't he?' said Liz. They often referred to their old 'family' casually and without inhibition. 'He was the one for colour and noise.' They giggled and went home on the bus quoting from Smallest Jack's repertoire of catch-phrases; side-splitting to them but mildly irritating to their fellow passengers who were not accustomed to being greeted: 'Hello, Humans.'

At David's school he was not the only one to have seen the

light at the Festival and by the time they entered the Upper Sixth half the class were wearing green corduroy trousers and saving hard for velvet jackets. Their fathers reacted in various ways, from apoplexy to ridicule – pointed references to Oscar Wilde. David's mother, still fighting her own private war against dirt and what the neighbours might say, kept her head down. She washed David's fuchsia shirt separately from the family laundry and dried it indoors safely out of sight. Meanwhile Liz had locked horns with her parents over the matter of her future. They wanted her to go to secretarial college, she wanted to go to art school. Stalemate.

'We need money of our own,' said David when they met at their favourite coffee house to discuss their problem parents. He handed Liz a pencil and paper and asked her to write down all the ways of earning money she could think of. He would do the same. They sipped their coffee. Liz wrote: Saturday jobs, baby-sitting, bank robbery, football pools, while David stared into space. Eventually he wrote one word on his paper and pushed it across the table.

'Ideas,' she read. 'What on earth does Ideas mean?'

'Well, it's all I can think of that I've got to sell. My call-up will come as soon as I'm eighteen so I can't get a normal job until after my National Service. But they're not calling up my *mind* – they only want my lovely body – so I'll use the two years to sell ideas.'

'Such as?'

'Such as the one I had at breakfast this morning. Have you noticed how boring cereal packets are?'

'Can't say I have. I read the *News Chronicle* at breakfast.'

'Precisely. You don't notice the cereal packet because there's *nothing interesting on it*.'

'Christ!' Liz was immediately on his wavelength. 'You mean games and puzzles and –'

'Little cut-out figures for kids to collect and swap. What do you think?'

'I think you're a genius. Let's make a prototype game and send it off to one of the cereal manufacturers.'

Next day their first idea, a cut-out puppet theatre, neatly drawn up on white card and with a typed (laboriously with one finger) letter was on its way. They never had so much as an acknowledgement but not long afterwards they were incensed to see their idea adopted and reproduced on the cereal packets. It was a hard lesson to learn. David, vowing he would never be caught out like that again, spent a morning in the library boning up on copyright laws, a useful morning's work. The next time he had an idea to sell he took it in person to the firm of his choice and asked for a receipt. To his astonishment he was given not only a receipt but a cheque for £25.

'Twenty-five pounds?' said Liz, open-mouthed. 'But David, it was only a weeny idea – something to do with perforations wasn't it?'

'Yes, I showed them how they could save acres and acres of cardboard just by redesigning their boxes. They seemed awfully pleased. All I had to do was sign something promising not to tell anyone else about it.'

Fired by the success of their first sale the young entrepreneurs set themselves a firm objective: to earn enough money to buy Liz her independence. After 'A' levels they had just eight weeks to achieve their goal, September being the month when David would have to go into the army and also the start of the secretarial college term. By mid-August they had amassed £61.1s.0d, the odd guinea coming from a friend of theirs called Michael who had bought the idea of setting up an agency to provide single shoes to disabled ex-servicemen. Michael flatly refused their offer of a free name for his agency. He felt Hoppalong Happily did not convey a caring image at all.

Then came an unexpected stroke of luck. David categorized his ideas into first, second and third class and it was one of his thirds that hit the jackpot. The cheque came by the same post that had brought him two rejections (special mazes for hamsters and garden dog loos were anticipating the market by some twenty years but David was not to know this) and he opened the envelope without optimism. He stared. Two hundred pounds? For what Liz called one of his weeny ones? He stared again and nearly fainted. He had missed a nought off. Stuffing the cheque into his pocket he leapt on his bike, flew round to Liz's house and hammered on the door until Liz's father opened it. 'Bugger off, you young lunatic, filling her head with your rubbish.' David pushed past him calling hoarsely for Liz. She was having a bath but hearing the commotion downstairs got out and peered over the banisters. David took the stairs three at a time, grabbed her wrist and dragged her back into the bathroom. 'David – my parents,' Liz protested.

'Fuck your parents. Look.' He showed her the cheque – 'Two thousand pounds.' They hugged each other and Liz deliberately pulled David fully clothed back into the bath with her. Alternately laughing and crying they were making such a noise they didn't hear Liz's parents. Her father's rage gave him the strength to haul David out of the water, box his ears and march him out of the house. 'I'll get you certified,' he snarled, and slammed the front door. David retrieved his bike and rode to the bank, leaving a spoor of bath water behind him.

They bought a secondhand Pickfords removal lorry with some of the money and a course of HGV driving lessons for Liz. Two of David's friends converted the interior to living and sleeping areas, a galley kitchen and a tiny shower room with a chemical closet. Now they had a mobile home which could be parked anywhere at any time without attracting attention. As long as Liz was careful to park unobtrusively each evening she could live rent- and rate-free for the whole of her time at art school. In September she drove David to Norfolk where he was to begin his army training and then made her way back to London. Parking was easy, relatively little traffic and traffic wardens not yet even a gleam in a bureaucrat's eye. She began a game of spending one night in each district on the Monopoly board starting with Park Lane and Mayfair. Art school was wonderful, everything she had hoped it would be.

David headed his letters 'Somewhere in England'. He didn't much care for army life at first, all that shouting and marching about in rows bored him, but after the initial six weeks' training the new recruits were given more interesting things to do and life became quite tolerable. He made some new friends and had one or two mild flirtations with the local girls.

Liz too had a few flings, medical students from the London Hospital (this was when she got up to Whitechapel on the Monopoly board) whom she found fun but immature compared to David. They called her Mary Pickford and stole a park bench for her with 'LCC' carved in the back rest. She had no use for a park bench but it proved a devil of a job to get rid of. As she wrote to David: 'Every time I try to leave it on the pavement some well-meaning person bangs on the cab door to tell me I've forgotten some furniture. It has become my albatross.' David replied: 'Change the L to an M and *deliver it openly* to Lords. If the groundsmen stop you all you need to say is that it's a present from an anonymous cricket lover.' The ruse worked so smoothly it made Liz wonder why all criminals didn't take to removal lorries since, like milk floats, their appearance never aroused suspicion.

The lorry once saved her from the unwelcome attentions of an admirer. He was a French student called Gerard, an intense lad who shared her table one lunchtime and then pestered her for a date. Liz didn't like to hurt his feelings so she told him in her atrocious French that she had to stay in and wash her hair. What she actually said was 'wash my horse' which Gerard took to be a joke until he followed her home and watched her climb into what looked to him like a horse-box. Mon Dieu! Mama had always said English girls only ever fell in love with their horses . . .

David came out of the army fit, hard and a dab hand at sticking bayonets into straw victims. There were very few vacancies for trained killers in central London at the time so he and Liz decided a debriefing holiday was called for. They drove across France and camped in the Pyrenees for a month, after which time Liz was pregnant and David's ability to daydream their livelihood restored to normal.

Returning to London they parked in Soho and David sold fabric designs (painted by Liz) to Heals, Habitat and Selfridges. On the proceeds they hitch-hiked to India, returning this time mind-blown by all the new sights and scents. Until they saw Goa they had not known that sea could be so blue or sand so white or people so beautiful. Carnaby Street shops beat a path to their door – or strictly speaking, tailboard – to buy their ideas. Liz would draw or paint impressions of India then they would both think out how best to use the work. Sometimes a simple line like a single flower on a whiter than white background would suggest its own solution, and that one would be earmarked for high-class bone china. Or tendrils of jungle foliage pierced here and there with brilliant flashes of humming-bird colours would make them think it would look great as curtains or wallpaper. They experimented with cane, raffia, leather, wood, clay and silk. Curiously neither of them ever had an interest in plastics. They used Sellotape and polythene bags, finding these new inventions useful and hygienic but for their own creative work they stuck to natural materials. Not all their ideas found favour, even in Carnaby Street and the King's Road. The world was not yet ready for leather shoes in primary colours or reusable containers of any sort. Britain's youth wanted the freedom to throw things away – the Save It generation could Stuff It.

Their home became a bit crowded now that it was doubling as a workshop so just before the baby was due David and Liz bought a tall house in the then still slummy Camden Town. It had a large garden gone wild and plenty of room in the street to park their much-loved lorry.

Liz went into labour and David sat in the hospital waiting room with two other expectant fathers. Five hours passed. Ashtrays overflowed. The other two were called out, leaving David to pace up and down in traditional fashion. There was a health poster on the wall advising people to eat a balanced diet. Little pyramids of meat, fish and eggs sat under the word protein, likewise vegetables under vitamins, bread under carbohydrates and butter under fats. David added a bottle of gin and a packet of cigarettes and labelled them 'Essentials'. More hours dragged by. He gave the Queen a monocle and a pipe, then his patience ran out. Finding his way to the labour ward he opened the door and walked in. There was a gasp from the attendants round Liz's bed and a nurse bustled over. 'Are you the father?' David said he would kill the milkman if he wasn't and could he please see Liz? The nurse hesitated. 'It isn't really allowed, but in the circumstances –'

David's heart thumped. 'What do you mean? What circumstances?'

The nurse made him put on a sterile gown. Then she said, 'Your wife's having twins.'

David was at Liz's side in a flash. 'Twins – oh Liz, how *marvellous*, how efficient. We never thought of more than one at a time, did we? Could you manage a few more while you're at it? Have a litter?'

Liz looked up at him, her face pinched with exhaustion. 'Hi.' She smiled weakly. 'I wish we'd settled for puppies instead.' Then David had to leave because this was going to be a forceps job.

Both sets of parents, who had steadfastly refused to speak to Liz or David ever since they left home to live in the lorry, now wanted to bury the hatchet. The lure of grandchildren was powerful, the babies themselves perfect. At ten days old they were huge, healthy and beautiful. David's mother said tearfully, 'At least you got something right' as she cuddled the boy twin close. (The fact that David earned more in a month than his father did in a year was never mentioned.) Liz's mother, similarly clutching the baby girl, asked, 'What are you going to call them?'

'Felix and Daisy,' said Liz.

'*Felix and Daisy?*' chorused all four grandparents in horror. David's father said, 'Felix is a cat's name.'

'There's an actor called Felix something,' said his wife, hoping to defuse the situation and realizing too late that she had put her foot in it.

'Daisy's quite nice,' said Liz's mother. 'I used to know a Daisy before the war. Housemaid she was, had a hare lip, poor thing.'

'Mum,' Liz groaned.

'I don't care if they have got horrible names,' said David's mother. 'They're Granny's little cherubs and that's all that matters.' Liz and David escaped to the kitchen where they collapsed in giggles while the coffee percolated. 'Oh Christ – Granny's little cherubs.' Liz mopped her eyes. David said, 'Did you see my father's face when Mum said actor?' This set them off again and Liz was still dabbing her face with her hanky when they carried the tray of coffee back to the family. 'Post-natal depression I daresay,' whispered Liz's mother. 'After all, you did have a Bad Time, didn't you?'

The twins thrived but, sadly, although Liz and David were fond of them they didn't enjoy them as they had expected to. As babies they were not very lively and seldom laughed. They didn't throw their food about or scribble on the walls; at a year old they were toilet trained without any effort on Liz's part and by the time they were three they had never quarrelled. It was unnerving. It was also very hurtful to hear them referred to by friends as 'your bourgeois babies'.

But it was true, David and Liz had to admit one evening after they had been ferreting around in the twins' playroom to see if they could find some clues as to the children's remarkably boring personalities. The playroom was painfully tidy. Teddy bears and golliwogs segregated like South Africans sat on one shelf, with miscellaneous soft toys on a shelf below. Down on the farm all the animals had been tightly penned-in according to species. David groaned and released a herd of Friesians into a green felt field. Liz let the pigs out. David, getting carried away, laid a milkmaid tenderly under a tree and placed the farmer on top of her. 'We won't tell,' he whispered. They opened Lego boxes which contained Lego and domino boxes which contained dominoes, ditto Plasticine and marbles. There was a bridal doll still in her gift tissue paper – she was immediately taken out and set to work grooming the rocking horse, while sailor dolls were issued with rum from the plywood shop and left to sleep it off in the streets of Toytown. David and Liz felt a lot better after the revolution. But this was only the start.

'Something will have to be done,' said David. 'Good God, they'll end up working in a bank if they carry on like this.'

So for the next few years they took the twins camping, rock climbing, sailing and swimming. (On their travels they looked up Liz's exploding granny, an old lady now, blissfully painting at Newlyn with her boyfriend.) They showed them the sky at night, sunsets, sunrises, minnows in ponds, elephants at the zoo. But it was as though Felix and Daisy had been blinkered at birth; to them autumn leaves were autumn leaves, not fairy gold or something to run through shouting at the top of your voice.

When David found they had discarded Mozart and the Beatles in favour of Max Bygraves singing 'I'm a Blue Toothbrush' he took them to the Child Guidance clinic. The psychologist there said he did not think Max Bygraves was an aberration. David had one more try, this time with the twins' headmistress.

'Look.' He waved their reports in front of her. They never varied: cooperative, polite, punctual, neat, a credit to the school. Never creative, amusing, original or wayward. The headmistress, who had not quite recovered from a spate of fourth-form arson, suggested coldly that if David wasn't satisfied with her standards he should send his children to Dartington.

In their teens, hope flickered briefly when all the boys in the neighbourhood developed a craze for Ben Sherman shirts in pastel colours. All except Felix. He stayed loyal to the school outfitter's white nylon regulation garment. Daisy half-heartedly bought herself some platform-soled shoes because her friends were wearing them to parties but she managed to lose them on a bus and didn't replace them.

David and Liz tried hard not to show their disappointment. They accepted philosophically that you really can't make a silk purse out of a sow's ear. They worked hard and saved hard, planning to travel round the world once the children were grown up. Meanwhile they took short camping holidays leaving the twins (at their own request) with one or other of the grandparents. The only serious row that ever occurred was when David asked Felix to fetch his and Liz's passports from the desk. Felix handed them to him and asked why they didn't have a joint passport. David said, 'You have to be married to get a joint one.'

Felix went white. 'You mean – you mean you're not *married*?'

'Not officially. Why? Does it matter?'

'Matter? Of course it matters you, you *artist*,' Felix shouted. 'What does that make *us*, I'd like to know?'

'Bastards,' said David mildly. Daisy sided with her brother and the row raged for two days. David and Liz were quite glad to get away to France for a bit of peace.

Ten years passed. Felix became a vicar and Daisy married a branch manager of Freeman Hardy and Willis. David and Liz rented out their house and took off to hitch-hike round the world.

They were exploring the foothills of the Himalayas when the letter came telling them that Daisy had had a baby boy and was going to call him Charles after Prince Charles. As everything had gone smoothly they saw no reason to cut their Grand Tour short, so they sent congratulations and a lovely bolt of silk and carried on travelling for another three years. Daisy wrote to them regularly *poste restante* of whatever place they were visiting, keeping them up to date in the matter of the baby's weight and her husband's golf handicap.

Eventually it was time to go home. Daisy wrote to say they had rented a holiday cottage in Berkshire ('*Berkshire?*' said David) for two weeks and would be so pleased if David and Liz would come and stay. The letter went on: 'It seems a nice place from the brochure, four bedrooms and all mod cons even though it is rather old. And something I'm sure will interest you – a mulberry tree in the garden that's reputed to be 150 years old!! I expect we shall have to watch out that Charles doesn't get them in his mouth!!'

'Better than sticking them up his arse,' muttered Liz, who didn't like the sound of the mod cons or Charles or the golfing husband.

They landed at Heathrow and took a taxi to the address Daisy had given them. Opening a wicket gate they walked up a brick path towards the cottage which they could see was of lovely mellow old brick like the path. A huge gnarled tree with crusty bark dominated the garden. 'This must be the mulberry tree. What a lovely –' They stopped, blinked and looked again. The genes of Liz's exploding granny mingled in with Liz's and David's own were only too apparent in the little figure before them. He had painted his naked body with mulberry juice from head to toe and now swung upside down from a low branch whooping like a monkey. ‘Hello, Humans,’ he shouted. ‘You’re upside down. Are you from Australia?’

‘We’re from Mars,’ said David, stepping towards his grandson with outstretched arms.

Liz’s eyes filled with tears. It had been a long wait. ‘Hello, Jack,’ she said.

KENNY

Richard Clarke

Richard Clarke was born in Market Harborough. After obtaining a BA in Economics and Philosophy at the University of East Anglia, he joined the Foreign and Commonwealth Office in 1977. Currently First Secretary (Defence and Arms Control) at the British Embassy in Washington, Richard's previous postings have included a five year spell in Caracas. His interests include Modern Art, English Medieval history, the American Civil War and football (Leicester City).

KENNY

'Here, Kenny . . . Give it here.'

The flame dipped and was gone. Colin leaned forward and prised the man's fingers apart.

'Look,' said Colin, 'like this,' and the flame came back, yellow and long-pointed this time. Kenny watched it flare, his gaze drawn deep into its palpitating blue heart, his jaw suddenly slack, his mouth dropping open. His hand came up, reaching for the lighter's twitching tail, and then he grunted, a syllable chopped at both ends, as the flame retreated back into its metal shell.

Colin swore and shook the lighter hard. He sparked it up again, clicking his tongue against the inside of his cheek.

'I'm getting low on gas, Ken. Tell you what.' He tore a strip from the newspaper that was spread out in front of them on the carpet. 'Let's give the little bugger some encouragement, eh? A bite to eat, to make it grow.' And with a cackle that rattled in Kenny's ear, he lowered the paper towards the flickering yellow point until the flame jumped up and raced towards his fingers.

Kenny's chin circled in the air. The fire had escaped at last from the thin prison block of polished metal and he was eager to see just how high it would climb. But his inner mischief wasn't about to let him, jerking his head upwards and then back, not once, but several times before it gripped his jaw and began to ratchet it slowly towards his shoulder. Kenny tried to cry out against it but the words wouldn't fit together, the pieces dissolving in a low gurgle that boiled in the back of his throat. Then his hands began to twitch, clenching themselves into fists which suddenly flew upwards, exploding past his shoulders like rockets of gaunt flesh.

'Kenny! Don't do that. Just watch.'

Kenny's jaw was jammed right up against his left shoulder-blade. Colin was talking to him from beside his other shoulder and the flame was there as well. With an effort that narrowed his eyes, Kenny managed to jackknife his gaze back to Colin's face.

'That's it, Ken. You can do it. Look, I'll help you.' Colin pulled down an outstretched arm and fitted the lighter into the man's hand, closing the fingers around it. Kenny watched as Colin worked something into his palm and then the boy pulled away and there was a hardness in the space between his fingers and palm. Only the silver head of the lighter was visible, cold and lifeless now that the fire was captive within it. Kenny eyed it suspiciously, as if this wasn't the one he'd just been looking at, the one with flame pouring out of it. He looked over at Colin, seeking reassurance, and then his jaw went hard and jutted forward.

'Go on, Ken,' said Colin softly, 'make the flame.'

Kenny squeezed his fist, tightening his grip until his arm trembled. At first nothing happened, and then his whole arm shook as if in spasm. Moments later, his body followed suit, shooting forward, his fists beating at the air around his head. Amid the windmilling arms the lighter came loose, spinning up in the air behind the man's armchair and clattering down against the fireplace.

'You daft bugger!' shouted Colin. 'You're never going to get it right.' He slipped off the sofa and slid across the carpet towards the fallen lighter. 'How can you expect to carry on smoking if you can't even use a lighter?'

Kenny moaned behind clenched teeth, his body still doubled up, his head hanging low between his knees. His hair was dangling down, lightly brushing the carpet as if it was growing upwards into his scalp. Colin crawled back to the armchair, the lighter gripped between his teeth, and slid sideways until he was crouched at Kenny's feet, staring at the man's pendant head. Colin lifted a tassel of the long black hair, held it up for a moment, then let it fall back down to the carpet again.

'I don't know why I bother sometimes. I really don't. Not when you're acting like this.' Colin spat out the lighter and pushed the man's shoulders back against the chair. Kenny's body resisted at first, then gave way completely, settling deep into the back of the armchair like a deflating bag.

'Come on. You just take it easy for a minute. That flame gets you going too much.'

Colin got up and went over to the sideboard by the window, one hand deep in the pocket of his jeans. With his other hand he squeezed at his nose, pinching at the bridge and then blowing it, nostril by nostril. He glanced down at his fingers as he pulled them away, wiping them across the thighs of his jeans. On top of the sideboard was an array of ornaments, all carefully separated, as if in a particular order. Colin delved his hands into them, bunching them together and turning them over.

'Where's she gone to today then? She had a new frock, like she was off somewhere special.' Colin picked up a small marquetry box and shook it. 'Never stays still, does she? Always busy, like life's a maypole she's got to keep running round.' He lifted the box up and turned it over, releasing a long string of jagged black beads. 'I only hope she's keeping her nose clean, for your sake.' He snivelled once more against the inside of his wrist. 'Your mum looks like the type of woman who's got a secret life, the sort you read about in the Sunday papers. To you and me, she's just an old dear who potters round the town on a Saturday, who comes back at teatime with a basket full of bacon and tinned carrots and long-grain rice. Whereas it's not like that at all, in all probability. As soon as she's round the corner she dumps that old woollen coat with the big round buttons and she's off go-go dancing in some sleazy drinking club.' Colin paused, glancing over at the back of Kenny's head. 'I can just see her now, in white plastic knee-boots and silver lamé hot-pants.' He sniggered, the jet beads clicking against each other below his hand. 'Three nights ago . . . I was at a disco . . .' And Colin began to bump his hip against the sideboard, the china ornaments tinkling.

Kenny groaned. The sound seemed to struggle up from dark and viscous depths, as if someone had been poking around down there with a long stick. His head lolled to one side and his eyes rolled back under their hooded lids, as if they were trying to look back at the boy dancing behind him.

'It's all right, Ken. No panic. Look. The china leopard's still in one piece.' He held it up for a moment, then put it down again on top of a silvered tray. He turned and looked out of the window to the street, his fingers snaking the necklace around his wrist.

'Christ! I don't believe it!' he cried out. 'Avert your gaze, Kenny! 'Tis the snake-headed monster, the Gorgon woman!' Colin raised his hand and pointed at the window.

Kenny's head was too far back to see anything but the ceiling.

'Quick, Kenny, get on the blower. Ring up the abattoir and tell them Lorraine's on the loose again.' He jabbed at the window with his finger. 'They're going to need the big lorry this time, it's no use them just bringing the van.'

Outside, a woman was pushing a pram past the house. She had rust-coloured hair that had settled, like a dead weasel, on the collar of her coat. Her cheeks had a just-slapped crimson glow and she was ambling by as if in a trance, a spell abruptly broken by Colin's accusing finger.

'She's seen us, Kenny! Quick, turn your shield the sunny side up.' The woman in the street was staring in at them, still pushing the pram past. 'That woman's on maps of the Midlands these days. And what's that she's pushing? It can't be a pram, surely?'

Kenny couldn't see, not from where he was sitting. But he managed to twist himself to one side, as though he wanted to try.

'It is, you know, it is. I wonder what's in it. Must be a dog or sack of King Edwards, it can't be a baby. I mean, I know that for certain,' said Colin as the pram was pushed out of sight. 'There's laws against that, as well as good sense. Besides, her tights squeak when she walks.'

Colin shook his head and poured the necklace back into its box. He crossed his arms once and then again, swinging them heavily across his body as if he was cold. The unspoken frustration snagged at Kenny and he began to bleat like an abandoned lamb.

'It's all right, matey,' said Colin, moving round smartly so as to face the man. 'I didn't mean to upset you, you know I didn't. You've done nothing wrong, not a bit of it. It's just, well, look.' He drew up a chair and sat down next to Kenny. 'Let me try to explain it to you again.' Colin picked up the sheet of paper that was lying on the low table in front of them. 'Now this box here, yes, that's it, put your finger on it, this box here is our town. This is where we live, you and me. And this' – Colin drew another box several inches to the left of the first – 'this one here is the University of East Anglia, in Norwich. Yes, that's it, that box. Now from our town here to the university there is about a hundred miles. That's the length of this line. And the university is where I'm going to be next week. See?' He rubbed at Kenny's arm, corrugating the sleeve of his pullover.

Kenny moaned, a gob of saliva spilling out of his open mouth. It oozed down his chin, thick and milky, like venom, and then his head rocked forward and back again, smashing hard against the chair.

'C'mon, shhhh . . .' Colin jumped up and pushed Kenny's jaw shut, his other hand reaching for the back of the man's head. But Kenny broke free, his arm reaching upwards, his hand bent back double at the wrist.

'Kenny. Please. Just listen to me. This is important. Look. One hundred miles.' Colin stretched out his arms, Kenny's eyes following the path of the pencil in his left hand. 'That's it. Now let's try it again on the paper. This dot, this dot is your chair. Dot, chair, dot, chair. Now if this dot is your chair, then this line, this one, Kenny, this line is a hundred miles. Eh? You see? Oh fuck it!'

Kenny twitched his left hand up from his lap, throwing it forward so as to catch hold of Colin's shoulder. It rested there, limp, like a glove, and then the fingers stiffened and began to bite into Kenny's flesh.

'Kenny!' Colin twisted his shoulder free and glared at Kenny, just as the man's broad, bleached face was turning away. Crab's eyes, the man had, small points of impenetrable darkness standing out against the soft white shell of his face.

'We're getting nowhere, are we?' Kenny turned aside,

straining, as though the voice was too loud for him to bear. 'I've got to get through to you somehow. I've got to.' Colin sighed and looked down at the floor. 'I know what. Why don't we bring cake time forward? That'll get you interested again.' Colin stood up. 'I'm just going to go into the kitchen, Ken.' He pointed to the door. 'I won't be long.' He patted the man on the shoulder. 'Oh, and watch my seat for me while I'm gone, will you? You know how this place gets on a Saturday.'

Out in the kitchen Colin opened the door of the refrigerator and crouched down. While he was poking around under the bottom shelf, he drank from a carton of milk that was standing on the rack inside the door. He moved a lettuce aside and brought out a couple of foil-wrapped bundles, sniffing at each of them in turn before putting them back. And out in the living room Kenny began to whimper.

'It's OK, Ken. I'm just sorting things out.' Colin picked up the plate of cakes that was lying on the top shelf and closed the door. They were éclairs, fresh cream chocolate éclairs, Kenny's Saturday afternoon treat, and Colin picked one up and began to suck at a stray slug of piped cream. 'Not long now, Ken. Nearly there.' The cream was gone, the traces cleaned up by a lap of his tongue. 'Hang on just another tick, Ken, I'll be right back. We can have another go on the lighter if you like. We'll jack the flame right up.'

Colin rearranged the éclairs on the plate and then walked back into the living room, holding the plate flat-handed above his shoulder, like a waiter. He sat down and held up an éclair so that Kenny could wrap his hands around it. And then he picked up the lighter again, twisting the valve between his fingers before flicking at it sharply. The flame leaped out, almost six inches tall, and Kenny leaned forward to get a closer look.

'Hold on, Kenny, not while you've got that cake in your mitts. You'll melt all your icing. Here, have a quick bite, that's it, now we'll put it back on the plate for a moment.'

Colin flicked at the lighter again, holding it aloft like an Olympic torch.

'OK, Kenny, here we go again. It's the Monsterflame again,

come out from its lair. Only keep right back, will you, otherwise Monsterflame will leap out and get you.' Colin moved the lighter in a tight circle. 'This flame's like the one that sits on top of the Unknown Soldier, only smaller. You know, the one in Paris I told you about, the one I showed you the photos of.' Colin drew the lighter back and forth, making swirls in the air. 'I've always wondered how they keep it alight. I mean, it's always pissing it down over there.' The lighter flame died. 'Just look at this little bastard. Two packets of Marlboro and it's gasping for a refill. Imagine what you'd need for an eternal flame, like the one on that grave over there. They must have a huge tank underneath, like you get in a garage. I bet they had to choose a really tiny unknown soldier, like a midget or dwarf, so they could fit him in with the gas-tank. That's it, The Grave Of The Unknown Mid . . .'

There was a scream, like that of a dog whose paw had been mashed underfoot. Kenny's head had fallen forward on to the lighter, dousing the flame but setting his own hair alight. Dark strands shrivelled, spitting acrid smoke through Colin's fingers as his hand came down on Kenny's head, hard and quick, beating at the flames.

'Bloody hell, Kenny! Sit still! I'm trying to put it out!' Colin kept slapping at Kenny's hair, only gently now, the smoke having cleared. 'There. I think that's done it.' He pushed the man's face back and examined it closely. 'Now let's have a look at you. You feeling all right?' The man's hair was burned right across the fringe, brown-tufted and frizzy, his forehead lightly dusted with ash. But his skin underneath seemed untouched, the wildness in the man's eyes more bewilderment than pain. Colin pulled his head to his chest, rubbing at the back of it softly and murmuring. Kenny sobbed a little, snuffling against Colin's chest, and then sighed and was still.

'OK, Kenny, just lean back now,' said Colin, gently easing the man's head back into the chair. 'I'm going to get some scissors, to cut off the burnt hair. You're OK otherwise, there's no harm done. Just permed your hair, that's all. Your mother pays good money to have that done.'

Colin found a pair of scissors in a drawer in the kitchen. He snatched them up and was already walking back into the living room when his stride suddenly faltered. From where he was standing he could see Kenny sitting twisted and mute in his armchair, a hang-dog expression on his face, his hand cuffing awkwardly at the burnt locks on his forehead. Poor old Ken, came the thought, and then he chased it away again.

'Kenny, my old bastard amigo!' Colin marched forward smartly into the room, snapping at the air with the scissors. Kenny looked up, his face brightening, then began to wriggle anxiously as the glinting, chomping blades came near.

'It's all right, Ken, your styliste knows just what he's about. Hold still, will you.' He draped a teacloth across the man's lap and brushed at the man's fringe with the flat of his palm. 'Flat top, you said?' And he began to hack at Kenny's hair, talking as he did it, a polysyllabic stream that gushed and gurgled around Kenny's head, the way the old barbers had done when he'd been a boy and he'd anxiously peered out from the top of a pyramid of goose-pimpling nylon. As Colin chopped he noticed how the hair was coarse and thick, like his father's, falling from Kenny's head in heavy clumps, like offcuts of scorched bristle.

'There now, I think that about does it.' Colin flicked at Kenny's fringe one last time, then carefully lifted the teatowel by its corners. 'Now you sit here while I just flush this lot.'

Colin went away again. Kenny could hear him moving around in another part of the house, making washing and shaking sounds. Then he heard him running, running towards him, and Colin burst into the room, racing round the carpet, spraying at the furniture. There was a metal tube in his hand, shiny, like the lighter, but bigger, and as Colin dived inwards, he strafed the chairs with a sustained burst of scent, landing heavily at the foot of Kenny's chair.

'Here. You have a go.' Colin put the can in front of Kenny's hand and showed him how to press the nozzle. 'That's it. Freshen things up. Make this room like a Gold Spot factory.' The can went phhtt again.

'I've been thinking, Kenny,' said Colin, putting the can behind his back. 'Today's Saturday, isn't it? Well, what do friends, what do best mates do on a Saturday? Eh? Well, for a start they don't sit around indoors eating fresh cream éclairs and setting their hair on fire. No, there's a big world outside those curtains, just begging for us to get stuck in. What do you say we go out, have some real fun, something to remember when I'm in Norwich and you're here? What do you think? Eh? Eh?'

Kenny was gazing at him, his eyes wide.

'That's it. You want to go too, don't you? Come on, let's get your coat on. I'll leave a little note for your Mum.'

They went to the park, because when Colin suggested it, Kenny had smiled, opening his mouth wide and baring his gums. They passed through the sunken rose garden, the wheels of the chair kicking up gravel, the fading wisteria trailing down from the wooden lattice-work above their heads. And emerging by the children's playground, Colin pushed the wheelchair right under the shelter, its undulating roof dripping rainwater.

'There you are, Kenny. Just as I said it would be. You're the King of the Park today, it's all yours to dispose of.' Colin put his hand on the wheelchair, rocking it softly.

'Hey. Remember this?' Colin jumped up and ran over to the row of empty swings just past the sandpit. He gave the first one a shove, then the next one, then the one after that, setting them all swinging and timing his efforts so that when the first one came back, the second one would go out and so on. But he'd pushed them too roughly, so they went sideways as well as back and forth, knocking against each other and becoming entangled. But the second time round his rhythm was perfect, the wooden seats moving in harmony, like swingboats.

'And what about this one?' Colin dashed over to the roundabout and began charging around it in a tight circle, his hands pushing at the bar until it had picked up speed, then jumping aboard.

'Now watch this, Kenny. Watch my feet for the sparks.' Colin sat down on the edge of the running board so that his feet stuck out over the end of it and above the concrete apron. Slowly his feet came down until they made contact with the ground and the roundabout ground to an abrupt and sparkless halt.

'Well, that wasn't much good, was it?' Together they looked at the heels of the offending shoes.

'Excuse me?' A little girl, about ten years old, with an even younger boy in tow, had appeared in front of the roundabout.

'Yes?'

'Can I give him a push?' She glanced over at Kenny.

'Well, I don't know about that. What do you think, Ken? You're the King round here.' Colin turned back to the little girl. 'You won't push him off the concrete and on to the grass, will you? We'd never get him out again in this damp.'

The girl shook her head, the even smaller boy retreating behind her as if to make himself invisible.

'Well, go on then. But don't jolt him too much, if you can help it.'

The little girl ran forward and took hold of the handles of the wheelchair. Kenny turned his head back to look at her, then forward again, as if to say let's go. With the little boy's help, press-ganged into service with an imperious flick of her head, the girl managed to get the wheelchair moving. And off they went, the little boy's hands shrugged off just as soon as they'd picked up speed, so that he fell in behind them, one pace back, to the left of the little girl's shoulder.

Colin watched them as they zigzagged across to the far end of the playground, the wheelchair accelerating as it escaped the gravitational pull of the shelter. When they got to the fence at the other end, they stopped and Colin looked away, out across the grass to the railings at the far side of the river. The perspective he'd been grasping for during these last few days at home now seemed close at hand, the jumbled shapes of childhood falling into a loose but comprehensible order. Yet still there was Kenny, the eternal enigma. Colin looked over again at the head of the man sitting in the wheelchair by the wire fence. The head was huge, much too big for the emaciated body that was twisted into the chair beneath it, like a watermelon, a boy at school had said, a watermelon jammed on to the top of a twisted branch. That's how Colin had seen him at first, this watermelon head and trembling body, this face and voice with its scale of discordant notes.

Then one day in the park, Colin had caught a stone loach with his net on a bamboo pole, a long thin, cream-coloured fish that had buried itself in amongst the sediment at the bottom of Colin's jamjar. He'd sprinted over to the shelter, splashing from the jamjar as he went and had held it up for all to see, an eel, or so he had thought. There'd been blank faces from the adults there, a polite 'yes?' or two perhaps, but no enthusiasm, no interest. It was then that Colin had seen Kenny's face, looking across from the wheelchair parked a little to one side. Kenny had seen it, Kenny had understood the magnitude of it all. Kenny had known, no one else, just Kenny.

'Here you are.' The little girl was standing in front of him, beaming away, evidently pleased with herself for bringing Kenny back unscathed.

'Who's your fancy man?' asked Colin, nodding in the direction of the little boy who was again shuffling sideways to stand behind the girl.

'That's Darren,' answered the girl, as if that were explanation enough. And then the two of them walked away as far as the swings, where they started running, the little girl's companion still a pace behind, to her left.

A green double-decker bus was coming up the road as Colin and Kenny came through the gates of the park. It slowed down and pulled in at the stop just beyond and Kenny, hunched forward in his wheelchair, called out to it, rocking back with his arms.

'Hang on, Ken, let's see how much cash I've got.' An elderly couple who'd been waiting at the stop climbed on to the bus.

'All right then,' said Colin, putting the loose change back in his pocket. 'But we won't be going far on this.'

Kenny chose a seat near the back of the bus, rocking forward until he got to it. Meanwhile the bus driver had got out of his seat, folding the wheelchair up while Colin was helping Kenny to his seat.

'Where does this bus go to?' Colin came back to the front of the bus again with his handful of coins.

'Corby.'

'Oh. Right. How much is that?'

'One fifty. Three quid return, that's six quid the pair of you.'

'How far would a quid take us?'

'A few miles, I suppose. As far as Rothwell.'

'That'll do.' Colin put two pound coins into the driver's plastic tray.

As the bus moved off, Kenny's eyes began to squint, the buildings were flashing by too quickly. Colin pulled him away from the window and put his arm around his shoulders, propping the man's head up against his own. The afternoon was turning now, with less than an hour to go before dusk and the shop-fronts were already lighting up, some of the streetlamps as well.

'This is all right, isn't it?'

Kenny was quiet. It was.

It wasn't long before the houses started to dwindle away and the bus began to climb. As they reached the crest of the hill, Colin tapped on the window with his fingernail, pointing out the bright windows sprinkled across the valley below. Kenny's head kept squirting free of Colin's grasp each time they jolted over a bump or corner in the road, and after a while Colin let his own join in, laughing loudly as their heads were sucked through the curves in the road. Soon, they came to a village, old red-brick houses well back with a small-spired church on a gentle rise.

'It's things like this I'm going to miss. The hills, the villages, the little red cottages with the smoke rising up from the chimneys. Oh, I know they have such things in Norfolk. But those won't have the associations these all do, the same barbs that have caught in my memory and are holding on. I'm going to be a different person soon in lots of ways. I know that. I want that. But there are still some thoughts, some images, I want to take along, and carry over, for the rest of my life even, like rings in a tree, or the letters in seaside rock. That's what I've been doing the last few weeks, just sifting things through, trying to tell which things could be basic and eternal and which things won't. Seeing which letters are going to go right through to the other end of the rock.'

It was as if he had lost his place for a moment. And then

he added quickly, 'It's the basics that count, you see. You've shown me that, you show me every time I'm with you. I'm just not sure how clearly I'll see that, when you're not around.'

The bus went over a sharp dip in the road and the two of them lurched sideways. A girl in a red jacket appeared by the side of the road, standing in a gateway, and Colin peered over at her as the bus went past.

'That's another thing. They say that a man reaches his physical peak at around eighteen. Well, here I am, eighteen and a bit, and I seem to have been given the sex drive of a giant panda. A girl has to do just one slightly wonky thing and that's it, I'm put right off them.' He felt Kenny's hand come to rest on his shoulder, only for the bus to jolt it away again. 'Yeah, next thing I know I'll be nibbling bamboo shoots and they'll be trying to ship me off to some zoo in Mexico.'

The bus was coming down off the ridge now, winding down a lane tightly bound in by tall hedgerows, the driver sounding his horn at every bend. Colin hugged Kenny closer to him, his other hand stretching out indolently to catch the wheelchair as it started to slide down the aisle. At the foot of the hill, as the bus driver crashed the gears in anticipation of the next slope, the houses began again, council houses at first and then a factory, portents of Rothwell. The driver looked back at Colin in his mirror and shouted 'Rothwell' as they passed what looked like a village hall, the bus already slowing down.

Colin jumped up and carried the folded wheelchair down to the front of the bus.

'Next stop will do.'

'OK,' said the driver. 'Need a hand to get him off?'

'Thanks, mate. We'll be all right.'

Colin felt the wheelchair sink into the soft earth of the verge as Kenny was helped down into it. They waited until the bus pulled off, Kenny twisting away from the cloud of exhaust fumes, and then they set off, joining the path at the side of the road, heading away from Rothwell and out into the country. The road rose up to the crest of the ridge once more, lush grazing land falling away on either side, and so they followed the contour, tracing it with the wheelchair instead of the finger that Colin had run across the survey maps at school.

The encroaching dusk had laid a cold hand on the afternoon breeze and soon Colin stopped to fasten Kenny's coat. The entrance to a field was just ahead and Colin pushed the chair across the ridges of mud churned up by a tractor and stopped by a wooden five-bar gate. He fastened the toggles on Kenny's duffle-coat and pulled the man's hood up over his head but Kenny's hand came up and brushed it down again.

'OK, suit yourself. But it's going to get cold.' Colin rubbed his hands together and went over to the gate, the wood of the bars green-soft and spongy, like moss. He touched it and it swung open.

'Fancy a breath of fresh cowshit then?' he said, turning to Kenny, and he wheeled him through, bumping the chair over the cattle grid.

The sun was setting behind the distant hills, a pink-red gash opening up in the darkening sky. Kenny's mouth fell open, his chin buried deep in his heavy woollen coat.

'You sure you don't want your hood up?' Colin took the man's hand between his own. 'Here, put your tinglies in your pockets.' And as he helped push the man's hands down, Colin breathed out through his mouth, a saturated cloud, like cow's breath on a winter's eve.

The field before them was pastureland, too steep for harvesting, with grey-brown cow pats, malodorous and muddily volcanic, spotting the bare earth in front of the grid. The herd itself was far away, the cows huddled together under the branches of the copse at the bottom of the field.

'This is it, Kenny. Just what we've been looking for. There's nothing here for your thoughts to bump into. No people, no towns, no obstacles at all.' He paused for a moment and looked over at Kenny. 'It's funny, Ken, what comes into your head. I was thinking then, when we were on the bus, if you'll miss me too.' He rubbed at Kenny's sleeves, more out of feeling than to warm them. 'I look to you, Ken, you know I do. But do you look to me?' He looked down at the man in the wheelchair and saw his head had fallen forward in the first moments of sleep. Colin took hold of Kenny's hood and gently slipped it on to the back of his head. 'I just need to know, the way I've always sensed things about you, that all this won't change, that you won't forget. That you'll still be here, if I come back, and it'll be cake time and Marlboros and daft things in the park, just like it's always been.'

His voice had faded to a whisper. Night was falling, the bloodied scar of the sunset disappearing rapidly under the healing touch of darkness. Colin shivered, hugging himself, then reached out for the handles of the wheelchair.

FRENCH KISSES

Alan Dunn

Over the years, Alan Dunn's work as a hospital administrator, insurance agent and now a company director has always given him the opportunity to enjoy himself as a folk singer, dancer and musician. More recently he has channelled his energy into creative writing, songs and poems, short stories and three half-finished novels. Alan lives in Penrith and enjoys reading and music and relaxes by running half-marathons.

FRENCH KISSES

Each truck spat hot air at me, hit me with dust and diesel fumes, whipped my hair into my eyes, sandpapered my skin. It was useless hitching. I wouldn't have stopped to give myself a lift. That bastard Jatte! I was angry with him, with me, with the guy in the blue Citroën who put his hand on my knee. I wouldn't have minded if he'd let it rest there, given me a few miles before his fingers started sliming their way up my thigh, but no, he was into fifth and doing one-sixty down the outside lane, fast as they come. There was one of those child seats in the back, and a doll lying on the floor.

'You've got good legs,' he said. His hand seemed intent on exploring territory beyond what would normally be defined as leg.

I told him quietly, politely, that he'd made a mistake.

'Me? Oh no, cherie, you dressed like that and I'm the one who's made a mistake? I'm not that naïve! Don't get me wrong, please, I don't mind paying, providing I get my money's worth. And I'll give you a lift as far as Arles just to show I'm a decent type. But don't play the innocent virgin with me, it doesn't turn me on and it doesn't suit you.'

He had a point. I wasn't dressed for a stroll. Short black Lycra skirt, really short, and skintight too, as if I'm offering the goods for approval before sale. No stockings (like he said, I had good legs), heels, off-the-shoulder cotton blouse, no bra (no need), plenty of eye make-up, dark red lipstick. I looked like the whore he'd taken me to be, and part of me said give in, play the part, you need the money, you need to be south, you need him. Roll with the punches, bend in the wind. Perhaps it was the fear of relying on someone that made me fight back. Perhaps it was the fact that he was reasonably young, reasonably good-looking, and it would have been easy to let go. I might even have enjoyed myself. But his index finger went too far too soon, moved from skin to cotton, knuckles grazing aside the fabric of my skirt. If he'd only waited a few more minutes he might have had me, no fee at all.

My reactions got the better of me. I wrenched his hand away and punched him in the groin (wishing I'd had the knife which must have been hundreds of kilometres ahead of me down the autoroute), reached for the door handle at the same time. It wouldn't open of course, air pressure too great, but the shock of sudden movement and pain (not too intense, I didn't make very good contact) made him pull the wheel to one side. He lurched across the lanes, missed a Mercedes in the centre, made a tanker driver realize how fragile he was, perched on a few thousand litres of instant hell fire. We spent a few seconds on the hard shoulder, a few more digging up the grass beyond, and eventually stopped. I thought he was going to chase me, he would have caught me if he'd tried, me in my heels lurching down the side of the road.

I'd gone a few hundred metres before I saw movement. Perhaps I'd hit him harder than I'd originally thought; if so he must have been a damn good driver, or very lucky. The car started slowly. I suddenly remembered that film, the first one by Spielberg or Lucas, the one where the big black truck tries to kill the hero. Dennis Hopper? I forget. Anyway, I ran up the slope so he couldn't get me. He didn't even look as he drove away.

I sat down, waited a while to calm my nerves, lay back to let the air dry the sweat under my arms. I normally let the hair grow but Jatte had said I looked better without, that men preferred naked armpits these days. He should know. He'd wanted me to shave my pubic hair as well but I said no, the regrowth is itchy as hell. There was a bird, a hawk of some type, hovering then swooping, hovering again then darting down to pick something out of the grass down below me. Twice it caught nothing, or insects too small for me to see. The third time it had a small mousey creature in its claws. It was still twitching when the bird began to eat it. I began my litany.

Screw you, Jatte.

Screw you, Jatte!

SCREW YOU, JATTE! SCREW YOU, YOU FUCKER, I'LL GET YOU! Then I started to laugh. I was shaking. I needed a drink.

My concièrge had locked me out of my apartment. Sounds good, 'apartment'. A damp room, window jammed half open, half closed. Sharing a toilet with a bunch of druggies, the smell of piss and puke and shit in the hall. Cooking on a camping stove because the gas had been cut off. It was cheap, but I couldn't even find the 300 francs a week I needed. All of my clothes, my address book, my make-up and perfumes, my glass animals, the little food I had, two bottles of damn good whisky, my stiletto, they were all inside and I was outside. 'I'm sorry, mademoiselle,' she'd said, 'I'm only carrying out my instructions. If you pay the overdue rent you'll get your things back. If not' – a Gallic shrug of the shoulders – 'well, they might fetch a little money.' I walked out. Begging wouldn't have helped. Besides, I knew her son very well. If I could find him he'd be sure to let me in when it was dark, might even let me stay one more night if I promised to be away early and offered him a little favour. But it would be another few hours before he came in, might even be after midnight. Besides, he didn't wash often enough. I went out into the street.

I had my purse with me and I opened it in vain, my fingers already too familiar with its contents. Twenty francs and some shrapnel, three condoms (one red, one black, one green; life had been quiet of late), an old photograph of a young woman holding a baby. Some receipts and fluff, the scrawled telephone number of a forgotten admirer. Two credit cards, out of date. Nothing. An old man playing boules alone in the dirt across the road whistled and leered. I whistled and leered back. 'Allo, Anglaise! Not going out tonight?' he shouted. 'I thought everyone was heading for Petitpois's party! If you're not going you can always come round to my place and keep me warm!' I declined gracefully.

I knew Petitpois. Well, I knew of him. Local hoodlum, fresh out of gaol for the sixth time, celebrating freedom. I knew where he lived. At least there'd be food there, a drink, no questions, a floor to sleep on. Perhaps a wallet to finger if I was lucky. Just enough to pay what I owed. I stopped to look at my reflection in a window. Not bad for thirty, not bad given the life I'd been leading. I patted a hair into place, smoothed down my skirt and blouse. I felt lucky.

It was easy getting in. Wait for someone looking like an American thirties spiv to drive up in a Jag, follow him and his party in, smile sweetly at the fists on the door. There was food and there was booze and from the smell in the air I knew that someone was passing joints around. I poured a triple Glenmorangie (someone knew their whiskies), then another, and didn't get as far as the food. There was no one I recognized. One spotty youth, drunk, no more than fifteen I swear, came up to me with the usual chat-up lines and seemed genuinely offended when I told him to stop stroking my backside. 'Don't you know who I am?' he slurred. Before I could think of some sarcastic reply (whisky affects me like that) he provided his own answer.

'Jean is my brother. He's very fond of me. He likes to make sure that I get everything I want. I want you.'

I could see the family resemblance but I'd been wrong about his age, he was sixteen. Where his brother was doltish but friendly and therefore well liked, this one was cold and bad. He specialized in carving his initials on his women.

I panted out the old lines, how I'd love him to screw me, I was getting hot and wet at the thought. But I couldn't, hadn't got the all-clear yet, still taking the antibiotics, hence the booze making me hazy, some reaction, sorry and all that.

'Doesn't worry me,' he replied. 'What I want from you only involves your mouth and your hands.'

I considered fainting; the alcohol or the prospect of sex with him, either could have made the pretence realistic. I swear I was on the verge of collapsing when Jatte appeared at his side and whispered in his ear. The boy blanched and left.

'I told him,' Jatte said, 'that you were a friend of a friend of mine, that you were a transvestite, homosexual, that you had open sores on your gums, and that your doctor hadn't yet told you that you were HIV positive.' His grin was disarming. 'May I get you something to eat?'

We left early with a bag full of food and two bottles, me leaning on Jatte's arm. I'd met him before, he informed me, when I'd auditioned in a club four or five years ago.

'The Blue Parrot I recall, alas no more. You didn't get the job. Good mover, no doubt about that, but it was the time breasts were in fashion. And I seem to remember you wouldn't help the punters in any way other than taking your clothes off for them. Look but don't touch. Still the same?'

I nodded. It wasn't, of course. I'd turned a few tricks since then, but I didn't see any reason to tell him. And I could remember him now. Jatte had been a pimp. Girls, boys, men, women, queers, dykes, AC/DC, twosomes, threesomes, s/m, you name it he'd supply it. So I was wary, despite being drunk. I knew I was safe, short-term; Jatte didn't go with women. But I owed him, and I wasn't sure how or when he might want paying.

His apartment wasn't much bigger than mine, but it had class. Its own shower and toilet and bidet; a balcony with a view over a small but green garden; separate kitchen; cupboards to hang clothes in. It was clean and smelled of honeysuckle and expensive soap. I grabbed one of the whisky bottles and flopped on to the bed, a huge bed, kingsize and soft and sweet. He pulled off my shoes as I lay and took the bottle from me. He was strong, in his mid-forties perhaps, possibly older, his hair white and long at the back. It was beginning to get dark so he pulled the shutters closed and switched on two or three table lights.

'I am a reformed character,' he said, smiled when I began to giggle.

'I am no longer a pimp. I no longer trifle with the bodies and souls of innocents. I prefer to steal from those whose morals prevent them from seeking assistance from upholders of the law. I am, I suppose, a gentleman blackmailer. A swindler of the unprincipled classes. An unarmed Robin Hood. I earn a living from the indiscretions of others. I am, however, suffering from a severe cash-flow problem, as, I suspect, are you. We may be able to help each other. Allow me to explain.'

And so he told me, at great length. He was fond of his own voice was Jatte, almost put me to sleep. Turns out he'd found it easier to make money from blackmailing his whores' clients than from acting as their agent. He'd stung two or three of the rich ones and they'd provided a steady income. This allowed him to live well and indulge in his other vice, poker. Just recently he'd had a bad streak. Two of his bankers had died, the third was in gaol. He'd lost steadily at cards. And Petitpois, newly released, had asked, in return for a long forgotten favour, for a 'loan'. Requests such as that could not be refused; Jatte's protestations of poverty had brought only smiles and a demand for further funds.

'I can raise money easily, but not quickly. I need a million francs before the weekend.' It was Tuesday. I giggled again, reached for the whisky in his hand but missed.

'There's a poker game in Nice on Friday, a high-stakes game, and my luck's changing. But I need the entry. I need, oh, at least fifty thousand before then. And you can help me get it, and there'll be the same amount in it for you. No risk. No trouble. All you have to do is listen. Are you interested? Or perhaps you'd like to spend some time with Petitpois junior?'

'Tell me more, tell me more,' I sang at him. For a brief moment a look of disgust plucked at his face, a look which killed my humour immediately.

'Stand up,' he ordered. I did so.

'Take off your clothes.' I did so, unquestioningly.

'You stink of sweat. Take a shower. And while you're in there tidy yourself up, you'll find a razor in the second drawer down in the cabinet. I'll find some clothes for you.'

The sweat and worry of the day were easily cleaned from my body. I found time to ask what I was doing, but no answer was forthcoming. The prospect of money, fifty thousand at that, was far more tantalizing than giving the concièrge's son a blow job. I was halfway sober by the time I stepped out of the shower, wrapped in a huge warm towel. Jatte was arranging some clothes on a chair, feeling each garment, nodding his approval. Without looking up he reached to one side and threw a nightdress at me. It was long, cotton with a floral print. I started to tell him that I slept naked but he wouldn't allow me to finish.

'You and I are sleeping in that bed tonight, together. We both need to sleep, and you will wear that nightdress. I shall explain the plan. Come here.'

He sat down, sat me down on the floor in front of him, dried my hair with a towel as he spoke. It was quite straightforward. I was to dress up as a hooker. I was to take my john to a hotel room. We would undress. Then in would come Jatte the high-ranking police officer. He would explain that the hotel was shortly to be raided, that my john, because of his position in society, would suffer more than was fair; his family would suffer, he would lose everything. In return for a large sum of money, however, he could be spirited away before the raid took place. What if he doesn't have enough money? I asked. We pick someone who does. What if it's someone who isn't married, doesn't have kids? We pick someone who does. What if the someone turns rough? We pick someone who won't. Jatte seemed very certain. I elected to follow. What did I have to lose? My virginity?

He finished my hair and I watched him undress. He took off his clothes carefully, explaining that they were all handmade and expensive. The cut was certainly flattering; naked he was far less impressive than dressed. He seemed shorter and fatter than a few hours before, his body wrinkled, his flesh pale like that of a plucked chicken. He came to bed wearing silk pyjamas. He breathed heavily in his sleep but didn't snore.

The sun was hot and I could feel my skin reacting. If I stayed on the verge much longer I'd begin to burn. Ahead of me was a bridge and slip road, as good a place as any to consider my options. After only ten metres sweat began to pool again in my armpits, trickle down my chest. My feet and legs were clouded with dust. The need for a drink was overwhelming. The bridge approached slowly, the road leading to it a slab of shivering, molten tar. I reached the crest and saw on the downward slope a bright red rucksack, a Union Jack fluttering from a thin wooden stake pushed into its frame. Shit! Competition! Above the traffic's growl I could hear music, a recorder or flute playing a tune familiar to that part of my memory which still belonged to Engand. Then the music stopped. A young man (I nearly said a boy, he was fresh-faced with blond hair and an innocent air about him) stood up. He wore a white shirt. That much at least was normal. His trousers were black and stopped just above the knee. He had on one knee-length blue sock and one green one. Around his waist was a red sash. A blue ribbon, about seven centimetres across, was looped from one shoulder to his waist; a similar ribbon in green traversed the other shoulder. On his head sat a straw hat laced with plastic flowers and badges. In his hand was a battered tin whistle – my uncle used to play one at New Year just before singing the Internationale, molesting Aunt Maisie, and falling down drunk.

'*Bonjour, Mademoiselle, j'espère que . . .*'

I pointed out with my usual impeccable manners that there was no need to embarrass himself with his bad French, that I was, for all my sins, as English as he was.

'Oh! I'm sorry, it's just that you don't look, well, you don't look very English.'

I merely glanced at his costume.

'Oh. Yes. I see what you mean. It's a traditional English dancing costume you see, and it certainly helps . . .'

. . . when it comes to hitching lifts. Yes, I knew. That's how I explained my outfit. Except some bastard stole my case with all the rest of my clothes. I glossed over the details, asked if he happened to have a drink in his bag.

The Coke was warm but wet, helped the burning in my throat but not in my head. The situation seemed to demand a different approach, so I switched into please help me mode, heard words falling ever so sweetly from my honeyed lips. Look, I know you were here before me but I'm desperate to get a lift down to Nice, I've got some rather pressing business, so would you mind if . . . ?

'Nice? Me too, there's a folk festival on, I'm meeting some

friends of mine, we're part of a dance-team, sword-dancing, clog, morris, you know the sort of thing.' I couldn't hide my look of frustration. He hummed to himself, cleared his throat. 'But you look as though your need's greater than mine. Yeah, go on then, if someone stops you've got first claim.'

No one stopped. My new friend started talking. He told me his name was Malcolm, that he was a civil engineering student in Leeds, third year, that he was engaged to a Melanie and that this trip was his final solo fling. That I could stand. It was his questions that annoyed me. A name, yes, I could make that up. Michelle I chose. Background, I told him I was a dancer. In the past I've often tended to mix lies with facts, then usually forget what I've said and give the game away. I thought I'd be rid of him quickly, so this time I decided to tell the truth. Mostly. How seven years ago I'd seen my husband off to work, dropped my kid round at my mother's, taken nearly two thousand pounds out of the bank (we'd been saving for a house) and left. No note. No message. Since then I'd been living in Paris, making a living most of the time. Dance to start with. Then topless. Then stripping. Sleeping around. Lucky to get away with a dose of clap. Beaten up once. Almost on to prostitution. I'm not sure if he believed me or not, it was a fragmented story anyway, what with one or both of us hurtling towards the road every time a car or truck went by. Eventually he interrupted me.

'Look, I hope you won't be offended. I think you look great, but that outfit might be a bit offputting to lots of people. Someone might even call the police. I've got some spare clothes in my bag, you could borrow them if you want.' He had a point. I messed around in the bag, pulled out a baggy T-shirt and some Bermuda shorts. He went a touch red when I wriggled out of my skirt, licked his lips when I pulled my top over my head. I had to laugh, there I was standing by the side of the autoroute dressed in nothing but a G-string, being ogled by a bumpkin, with murder on my mind. The T-shirt was nice though, cool. I knotted a red handkerchief round my neck, struck a pose. He actually applauded. A car stopped.

It was an Espace, seven seats and only one occupant, German. Where were we going? Well, what a coincidence, he too was heading for Nice. He could take us all the way. Promenade des Anglais good enough, ha ha? His French was poor, his English worse, which left Malcolm and me to converse. He didn't say much about himself, his life had been so commonplace in comparison to mine. I suppose I was flattered. At the first stop he disappeared for a while, came back with a half bottle of vodka. I sipped it gratefully, kept on passing it back to him; he held it to his mouth but didn't drink any. It began to get dark. I confided in him. I told him about Jatte.

We'd got up early. It was the first time I'd slept with a queer, about the only time I'd slept with a man and had an uninterrupted night's sleep. He told me in the morning that I'd been curled up around him, but that doesn't sound like the type of thing I'd do. I had croissants and black coffee for breakfast; he chose Weetabix and milk, then toast and tea. He watched me dress, gave me instructions in how to apply make-up (which I ignored), then wrapped me in a huge gabardine. We walked to the nearest Metro. His car had packed in. I thought we'd head for Montmartre but he said that was too poor these days, for tourists only. Instead he took me centre-ville. Business areas, he said, full of out-of-town executives. The hotel he chose was above a bar but had a separate entrance. Once we had the keys we could come and go without being observed. The room itself was clean, sparsely furnished, a bed, drawers and desk combined, seat, wardrobe. Jatte fussed about, turned back the sheets, closed the curtains. He switched the bedside light on, stepped back to look at it, switched it off again. He was making me nervous, I threatened to leave unless I got my first fix of the day. We went back downstairs and sat in the bar and he bought me a double. It steadied my nerves, the second relaxed me even more. I began to look forward to the adventure. I was swathed in grey cotton, but inside the skirt was riding up my thighs, the G-string was beginning to feel like a knot between my legs, the cotton blouse was arcing electricity across my nipples. Jatte nudged me. I looked up. Number one.

He was in his mid-fifties I'd say, balding, fat, heading for a heart-attack in a year or two. He was standing outside the bar, briefcase in one hand, jacket draped over his arm, other hand mopping at his shiny forehead with a handkerchief. It was hot outside, but not that hot. He could have been a salesman, but Jatte had noticed his alligator shoes, the cut of his suit, the Patek Phillipe watch, the gold bracelet and cufflinks and tie-pin. I didn't need any prompting, I felt like a bitch on heat. By the time I'd reached him the buttons of my coat were undone. With my heels on I could look down on the top of his head. His eyes couldn't decide where to rest their gaze, oscillated from breasts to stomach to groin to legs and back up again. He was hooked.

I can't remember the exact lines I used, something about me feeling as hot as he looked but the thirst I had wouldn't be cured by a pernod with ice. I wiggled my arse as he followed me up the stairs, took it very slowly to give Jatte time to catch up. I was also worried that my new friend might collapse before we got to the room. I made sure the door wasn't locked, took his briefcase and jacket from him, began to undress him. First his tie, then, oh so slowly, the buttons of his shirt. He was wearing a vest! Next his belt, his zip, his trousers lowered gently to the floor. I left him like that – Jatte told me that a man is never as weak as when he's caught with his trousers round his ankles and his socks and shoes still on. To fill in time (come on, Jatte, where the hell are you?) I started my own strip, top first, then skirt, much playing with nipples and grabbing of crotch, gyrating hips, little pants and groans. If I'd been allowed to keep going I might have begun to enjoy myself, but Jatte made his entry on cue, identification card in hand, uniform (where did he get it? I swear he was in civvies only a moment before!) pressed and neat and smart. He had his lines off pat. Mr short and fat was leaned against the wall and frisked, his wallet examined and lightened, his jewellery lifted, a credit card or two fingered. He was crying when Jatte gave him the get-out, searched through his trouser pockets for more money to hand over. We accepted, bundled him downstairs into a pre-paid taxi whose driver had had instructions to lose him in the suburbs.

We played variations on the same theme for the rest of the

day. Lunchtime was best, from midday to three, then it went quiet but picked up again about six. By ten I was exhausted, by midnight and fourteen punters even Jatte had had enough. We stayed in the hotel room counting, it came to just over forty thousand. Jatte then gathered up the other items we'd collected, let me sit the cash while he went to find a fence he knew. He tossed me a present, something he found in the pocket of number ten, I think, a flick-knife. He said it was to replace the one I'd had locked in my flat. I somehow felt reassured by this, as though he was trusting me with something which could be potentially harmful to him. I played with it for a few minutes then put it in my handbag.

It was after four when he got back with another twenty-five thousand. Five thousand for expenses he said, leaves sixty, thirty each. It wasn't enough, really, but it would have to do. He gave me my share. Thirty thousand francs! In cash! It was more money than I'd ever had in my life! But it wasn't enough for Jatte. I thought he'd want to stay on, try for some more the next day. I even suggested to him that we could do that, but he said it was too dangerous, we were operating on someone else's territory, and he or the police might object. It was then he suggested I come away with him to Nice, just to stay safe, lie low for a while. We could even try the same trick again down there, take our time coming back, work Marseilles as well. We were a good team.

We taxied to Charles de Gaulle, hired a car (I think he used one of the cards he'd kept back) then headed south. We pulled off the autoroute for a few hours' sleep in a service area. When we woke up we had something to eat and he bought two of those little instant cameras in the shop, one each. We were in the car, about to leave, when he suggested we take photographs of each other. He took one of me first, lounging over the bonnet flashing my tits and looking sexy. Then he asked me to take one of him at the wheel. It seemed a natural request so I backed away, further and further, he said he wanted the car and the background. When I was ten metres from the car he let out the clutch and roared away. I threw the camera but it missed. He didn't even look back.

*

My right hand was still holding the vodka bottle; I lifted it to my lips and drained it; Malcolm was half leaning, half lying across me, sound asleep. So much for a thrilling story.

It was well past midnight when we were woken by our driver. Nice. The cool breeze coming in from the Med was a relief after the gluey air of Paris. I'd been able to think a little during the journey; the stereo had been loaded with unrecognizable classical tapes which did little to tax the mind. I had no money; no clothes; I knew no one in Nice. It made sense that I stay, until I could hustle some cash with or from him, with Malcolm. I'd just have to make sure he conformed to my plan. After thank yous, mercis and dankes we found ourselves alone on the Promenade des Anglais, palms dancing to muted soft jazz, cliffs of brightly lit hotels our backdrop. Malcolm, bless his heart, rose to the occasion like the gentleman he was.

'I don't want to be presumptive,' he said in a professorial voice, 'but you appear to have little chance of finding somewhere to stay tonight. You're very welcome to come with me to the hotel where my friends are staying, there'll be a bed there which you're welcome to use, no strings attached, I'll sleep on the sofa or on the floor. You can stay until the end of the week or till you get yourself sorted out, it's not a problem at all. In fact,' he blushed, 'I'd consider it something of an honour.' I didn't need to reply. I just linked my arm in his and said a small prayer of thanks to whoever was looking after me.

The hotel wasn't too far away. It was smart without being stylish, a couple of marbled colonnades, rotating doors, comfortable sofas on view in the foyer. Malcolm took off his rucksack, put it down on the ground, reached inside for his wallet.

'Nice place, eh? All paid for by the organizers of the festival! In return for a dance or two they feed you and keep you for five days. Now all I have to do is find out which rooms they've allocated to us and . . . I think it might be best if you waited outside, you know, they're expecting one person, not a couple, and they might get the wrong idea, if you see what I mean. You don't mind, do you?'

I did, but had to acknowledge that he was probably right. So I watched the bag and peeped round the corner as he spoke earnestly to the man behind the desk. I ignored two men who passed by and, noticing the Union Jack in the rucksack and thinking I wouldn't understand their guttural French, suggested loudly to each other what they'd like to do to me. Then Malcolm reappeared. He was wearing that resigned 'I'm sorry' look, the one you use at funerals where you don't know the corpse very well.

'They aren't there. None of them. Just a message saying that Jack and Mojo had an accident, broke a leg each. Nothing serious, but there was no point in coming when two-fifths of the team was out of action. They couldn't get hold of me to tell me. I've come all this way for nothing. Shit! And the organizers have cancelled the rooms.' If he was pissed off, I was devastated! My mind had been in that soft hotel bed, my body had already succumbed to that hot shower, my tired legs were being soothed by that warm, mellow feeling three or four whiskies bring. He'd asked about renting a room, but he didn't have enough money.

'What do we do now?' We? I was already thinking back to the two men who would be only a block away, in fact I think I'd already taken a step or two in that direction. But there was something helpless in his voice, something sad. I don't think it was being without a place to sleep, and it wasn't that his friends weren't there. I think it was more that he'd promised to help me and had, through no fault of his own, broken that promise. What could I do?

It was uncomfortable on the beach, cold even though I was wrapped up in his tracksuit and anorak. We ended up cuddling each other and dozing fitfully, ignoring interruptions from dealers and drunks, the pervert who thought he'd caught us screwing and wanted in on the action, even, towards dawn, a gendarme who seemed as tired as we did. Searching for sleep we talked, worked out what we would do next day. Apparently this folk festival was one of the biggest in Europe, dance-teams from nearly forty countries. Malcolm had his whistle, I could dance; he said he'd teach me one or two of the easier solo dances and we could busk, see what we could collect. I agreed, more to please him than for anything else. So far as money-making went it wasn't on the Jatte scale of things, but it was legitimate and harmless. Give it half a day, I thought, you can always sneak off to find a strip-joint somewhere. And the idea of dancing in front of people interested in what you're doing rather than what you're not wearing was refreshing. That's why 8 a.m. found us outside the nearest toilets, washed and groomed and ready to go. The problem of suitable shoes was easy to overcome. I told Malcolm my size, he put on his tracksuit and jogged into the foyer of the nearest large hotel, looking suitably sweaty. Smile at the girl on the desk then straight up the stairs, along the corridors, find a pair of shoes my size, newly polished. Then back out of the service exit with shoes and, bless his cotton socks, a breakfast tray with croissants, jam, orange juice. When I told him he'd make a good con-man he laughed.

After half an hour I had two routines off pat, a step-dance from Cumbria and some sort of freeform American stuff that was as much my invention as his instruction. With a couple of tunes from him we had a fifteen-minute programme that we repeated all morning. At first he did the introductions, but once I realized how bad his French was and took over, the people couldn't keep away. We drew crowds along the promenade, sure, but the best were in the shopping centre and down by the harbour. I was really enjoying myself! I was enjoying myself enjoying myself! We broke just before noon, collapsed into a café and had coffee and cakes and watched the world go by. I didn't even feel the temptation to ask for a whisky. The barman agreed to swap our loose change for notes and watched as we counted up the piles of coins. A thousand francs for a morning's work. I felt good. Malcolm said as much. 'You look new, rejuvenated, as if all your worries have disappeared.' They had, for the moment. I leaned over and kissed him on the cheek. He blushed.

We applied a little logic to our afternoon. Those with the most money gave most money; where in Nice were those with most money? The casino! Where should we go? That's right. But first we thought ahead to tonight. We needed somewhere to stay, nothing more than a room with a bed. Or two. I hadn't quite decided what my relationship with Malcolm would be, and he wasn't forcing himself on me, so I preferred to take things as they came. We wandered into the narrow streets and alleys well away from the tourist areas, found a hotel which was cheap enough. I did all of the negotiating this time; I felt a strange mastery at asking Malcolm to wait outside while I spoke to the proprietor and inspected the room. It was first-floor, small with two beds, a double and a single, a washbasin and chest of drawers; toilet and bathroom were just down the hall. I paid for two nights and took Malcolm's bag in with me, left it there while we continued our attempts to make an honest living. We bought quiches and baguettes, some salade Niçoise, two or three different types of cheese, some pâté, a bottle of cheap wine. A skirt and blouse and underwear for me, a proper pair of comfortable shoes, a toothbrush; and still money left for the evening meal even if we didn't collect any more all day. But we did. The casino was a good hunting ground, twice as much in two hours there as we'd collected in the whole of the morning!

We decided to take the rest of the afternoon off, busk again in the evening. More essential purchases. A bikini and sun-tan oil, some mats and towels. Malcolm said he'd sunbathe in his underpants but I sneaked into a shop and bought him some trunks, nothing more than a thong really. At first he was too embarrassed to put them on, but when he saw that there were others dressed exactly the same he gave in. He looked quite nice really, sun-tanned, thin but muscled. A pity he was so young. I went topless of course. We swam and then sunbathed, he rubbed oil on my back and arms and legs, humming one of his little tunes. It felt so good, being looked after like that, being with someone who was content to be with me, to do things for me rather than have me do things for him. Life seemed worth living.

At about six we ceased our lives of inactivity to freshen up for our evening performance. On the way back to our room we passed a shop selling fishing rods and lures, guns and green knitted sweaters, all horrendously expensive. Malcolm seemed attracted by something in the corner of one of the windows, he called me back to look.

'Why not get one?' he asked. 'Replace the one you had stolen.' He'd seen a display of knives and remembered my saying that Jatte had taken the one he'd given me.

'It can be a present from me. Go on, go and pick one. I'll wait out here. Here's some money.' He pushed some notes into my hand and I found myself inside the shop, pointing at a small stiletto with a pearl handle. My frequent mention of knives was bravado; I'd never actually used one for anything other than peeling potatoes, but to tell him that would have been wrong. He'd wanted me to have something I'd said I needed, not a present which reflected his view of me. I came out of the shop to see him smiling and could only smile weakly back. I said thank you, realized I'd nowhere to put the knife, gave it to him to keep in his bag.

He sang us back to our room, and I made him sneak in without being noticed by the clerk. It wasn't difficult, the youth was engrossed in a Metal Hurlant, eyes wide open at a Bilial nude. We showered (separately). I felt ill at ease, unused to the way he treated me, unsure of the way he saw me. He started a playful argument about who was sleeping where. We both claimed the double bed, and what started as a pillow fight ended up with him astride my stomach, holding me down, holding my arms down, pushing me down into the mattress, both of us breathing heavily in the sudden surprise at our efforts. I went limp, submitted, looked him in the eyes. He returned the gaze. If he'd kissed me – dammit he should have reached down to kiss me, it's in the rules, I've seen it happen in so many films – I wouldn't have objected, wouldn't have fought back. I wanted him, then and there, wanted him to make love to me. It's not a term I use very often. Fuck, yes, screw, hump, fornicate even. I do all of those, perhaps too often. But not making love. Not love. Love.

But he didn't kiss me. He wanted to, I could feel that much, feel it in his eyes, feel it in the pressure of his body against mine. Instead he rolled off me, left me lying there, wanting him.

'Come on,' he'd said, 'we've got the whole evening ahead

of us.' He looked at me, over his shoulder, as he gathered his stuff together. He seemed sad.

It was not too far to the casino. Malcolm played his whistle as he walked. I lost myself in thoughts about him. What must his thoughts be of me? That I was an easy lay? Good God, from what I'd said he could easily see that I was the whore I denied being even to myself! A thief? A blackmailer? Certainly both of those. And I was surprised he didn't kiss me? He was probably worried that he might catch something. And he'd wanted me to buy a knife. Not kinky underwear, or a box of chocolates, or a vibrator even, not perfume or jewellery. A knife. Jesus Christ!

The crowds at the casino were good, and generous, even if my dancing was, to begin with, rather more wooden than earlier on that day, and my patter uninspiring. A constant stream of visitors passed by, some serious gamblers, others sightseers, some leaving happy (one old dear gave us a 500-franc note), others with heads bent in anger or despair. My feet looked after themselves as I watched my audience come and go: the man with the blue fedora, the woman with the gold inlaid walking stick, the little boys with ice-creams, the young couple holding hands, the older couple kissing, tongues searching each other's mouths. Money fell from heaven that evening, from the tall blond Swedish man who stared at me then left abruptly with his boyfriend, from the young girl who couldn't take her eyes off my feet, from the drunks who began to mimic me then applauded as my steps grew more and more complex. I was unstoppable, I could hear Malcolm's breathing grow hoarse, could feel him labouring for each high note and trill, yet could only move on, faster and harder and with more control, full of the selfishness which comes from doing something well and knowing it. I was leaving him behind, he wasn't necessary, I was becoming the dance.

I stopped. Sweat was running down my back and I could barely see through clouded eyes. My chest was rising and falling, I felt in danger of collapsing. Malcolm was by my side, supporting me as the crowd cheered and clapped and threw money.

'You were going some there, love,' he whispered. 'You want to watch out, you're not used to these temperatures.'

It wasn't that. I'd just seen Jatte.

He had been climbing the steps to the casino, slowly, elegantly, as befits a man who has no worries. He even glanced in my direction to see what the crowd was doing, to find out what the noise was about. He'd seen a mad woman dancing. It was of no interest to him. He continued his pilgrimage into the cool of the temple.

'OK, OK, keep calm.' It was Malcolm speaking, bringing me back.

'What do you want to do?' I must have looked puzzled; he repeated himself.

'What do you want to do? He's stolen your money. You can try to get it back if you want. Or you can forget him and we can go on as we've been doing, for the rest of the week. It's up to you.' I still didn't say anything. My brain was in neutral.

'If you want the money back, if you want to take him, I'll help you. I swear I'll do everything I can to help you.' I nodded.

It was still early evening, the tuxedos and haute couture gowns weren't yet on display. Jatte was easy enough to find; he'd always said that cards were his love, and if poker wasn't available then *vingt-et-un* certainly was. I pointed him out to Malcolm who pulled me to one side.

'Right then. If he sees you he'll run. He doesn't know me. So you go back to the hotel room and wait for me, I'll follow him and find out where he's staying. Then I'll come and tell you and we can figure out what to do next.' It was then I remembered what day it was. I counted back the nights, Tuesday at Jatte's, Wednesday the sting and Jatte's car, Thursday on the beach. It was Friday, the day of Jatte's poker game!

'That really doesn't change things, unless he manages to lose all of his money. Look at him, he's just killing time. When he leaves he'll either go straight to his game or back to his hotel room. I'd bet on the latter, but we'd better cover everything. Look, when he leaves, have a word with the dealer on the table he's playing. Ask if Jatte mentioned anything, just in case I lose him. Here, take some money, you might have to offer him a bribe. He's off now! Don't forget, stay put in the room and wait for me to come back. See you later!' He blew me a kiss as he left.

The dealer was a sweet little man. He said he knew nothing of what the man was intending to do and, when I offered him some money, still said he knew nothing and gave me the money back. I asked him about poker games in town; he still knew nothing. I believed him. I went back to our room, stopped on the way to buy two bottles of whisky. I felt in need. The clock on the entrance lobby wall whispered 8.30 as I walked in. The desk clerk winked at me and I could feel his eyes on me as I trod each laborious stair.

Just after ten-thirty, when I was two-thirds of a bottle down, there was a light knock on the door.

'*Mademoiselle? Mademoiselle?*' I opened the door a fraction to meet the leering face of the clerk.

'*Ah, mademoiselle, tu ne dors pas.*' I took an immediate dislike to his use of the personal.

'*Le téléphone', c'est pour toi. C'est un homme, je ne sais pas le nom.*'

I ran past him down the stairs to the booth in the hall. It smelt of tobacco and disinfectant.

'Listen, I don't have much change, so do exactly as I say.' It was Malcolm.

'I followed Jatte to his hotel, it's not far from you, it's called the Hôtel de la Reine and it's in the Place Victor Hugo. Have you got that?' I repeated the name and address.

'OK, get all of our stuff together, pay the bill, then get yourself round there. I've already booked a room for us in the name "Michelle Dubois". I reckon it's going to be easier to get your money back if we're in the same building as him. He's playing cards now in the backroom of a jazz club. I'll wait till he comes out. Now tell me again what you have to do.' I whispered back the name of the hotel, the name in which the booking was made. 'Have you been drinking?' came the voice from the mouthpiece, then 'Damn, my money's running out, be careful, I . . .' Love you? I added.

The desk clerk wasn't pleased that I was leaving, even if I didn't demand a refund. I didn't tip him; he didn't offer to carry my bag, Malcolm's rucksack, out into the street. I soon found the Hôtel de la Reine, and the giggle I felt as I walked up the stairs to my, Michelle Dubois's room, was due both to the alcohol in my stomach and to the appropriateness of the hotel's name to Jatte's nature. The room was hot, I opened the windows wide but closed the shutters, listened to the noise from the street. Somewhere, not too far away, a band was playing something German or Scandinavian, lots of violins and close harmonies. I raided the fridge (it was a good hotel, drinks, coffee and tea, television set, the works) for some ice and a glass, poured in the last of the first whisky bottle and felt better after two mouthfuls. The nervous, almost painful apprehension, the ache in the pit of the stomach which forces you to clench your fists and think of punching the wall, was replaced with a calmness, a willingness to accept what would happen in the knowledge that Malcolm would win through wherever he was and whatever he was doing. I took my drink into the bathroom and we had a cool shower together. We danced round the room naked to dry off, the radio playing Gershwin and Porter and Carmichael.

I can remember waking up to see Malcolm standing at the end of the bed, looking at me. I hadn't bothered dressing before lying down. Only the light at the side of the bed was on, so his face was half in silhouette, but there was a gleam in his eyes. I reached up to him and he came to me, lay beside me on one elbow, his hand smoothing my hair then diving to run fingernails harsh down my back. He smelled of smoke and sweat and beer and he kissed me, his tongue tracing the shape of my lips in hot acid, forcing my teeth apart to hunt me down in the dark, sweet warmth beyond. I pushed myself at him, I wanted to feel him against me down the whole length of our bodies. He pulled away.

'Listen, listen! Good God, I'll do this more often if I get a welcome like that every time. Are you listening?'

I purred a yes and reached for his shirt, began to undo the

buttons. Did I mention that he had no hairs on his chest?

'For Christ's sake, woman!' he said, almost angry. 'Stop behaving like a bitch on heat and listen.' That hurt, and we both knew it.

'Look, I'm sorry, but this is important. It's three in the morning. Jatte's back in his room, happy and smiling. I think he had a good game, one of the bouncers escorted him back to the hotel! Then he tipped the night porter with a 500-franc note. I managed to hear why as well, he was asking if he knew where he might find a boy to come to his room, give him a massage. I followed Jatte up and listened outside his door, he'd left it open. The porter tried but couldn't get anyone for another hour, so Jatte said to ring him when the boy arrived, he was going to have a sleep. At least I think that's what he said, you know what my French is like. After he spoke on the phone he shut the door but he didn't lock it, I waited a couple of minutes and tried turning the handle. It's still open. All I need do is go back now, sneak in, find the money, and come back. Nothing to it. I'll be back soon, don't worry. Now where's my rucksack? There was a torch in it, I might just need it.' He was a little boy playing a new game. He found his bag, rummaged around inside it and left. He'd called me bitch. Sometime in the night I'd opened the second bottle and I reached to it again now in desperate consolation.

I don't think he'd been away too long, but I'm a fast drinker. He held open a handbag, my handbag, the one Jatte had stolen. It was full of money! I raised myself up on to my elbows, blinking, trying to hold on as the room turned Picasso and melted on me.

'Go on then,' he said, 'count it.' So I did, very roughly, watching him at the same time. By the time I got to a hundred thousand he was undressed and heading for the shower. Four hundred thousand and he was back out again (I'd had to stop and start again round about two-seventy, I dropped a bundle on the floor), towelling himself and dripping all over the carpet. He came over to the bed and sat down beside me. I knew I was drunk, I knew that I'd missed some notes and counted others twice and even misread the denomination, but my final count was still just under eight hundred thousand.

'When I was putting that stuff into your bag I noticed this,' said Malcolm, pushing fingers into the side pocket and bringing out a condom, the green one, green for go. 'I thought it would be a pity to waste it. But I'm not quite sure how to use one.' His smile told the lie. 'Perhaps you'd give me a hand?'

I don't normally like making love when I'm drunk, although there've been times in the past when I've been forced to combine the two just to survive. But this time, this time the alcohol seemed to rid me of the few repressions I still had, to make each nerve-ending fire at the touch of a finger or brush of tongue or lips, my head turning from side to side in the agony of pleasure. I wanted to sing, to write poetry, to become the song itself. I reached for him but was pushed back on to the bed.

'No, this one's for you, I want you to remember this for the rest of your life.' And so I lay while he made love to me, his hands and lips moving over me and inside me, spiralling me into orgasm again and again. His shadow was leaning over me, hands on my arms, eyes closed and mouth clenched, moving into and against me, holding me, rising and falling, loving me, loving me. I think I screamed as I came for the last time.

I was almost asleep.

'Your skin is dry, so dry. You've been lying in the sun for too long. Let me help you.'

He helped me over, laid me on my back. I didn't feel dry, my skin felt slick and moist.

'This is all I have to give you,' he said. The condom was flaccid, red, a deflated balloon. I giggled at the thought, how clever, I knew they came in different flavours but I'd never seen one before that changed colour. Red for stop. He pulled at the rubber, ripped it, allowed the semen to drip on to my stomach and up on to my breasts. It smelt of newly-mown lawns. It was cool. Or perhaps I was very hot. He began to rub, slowly and lightly, then more firmly, up to my breasts then down over my stomach, up then down, up, down, down,

down. I think I love you, I slurred. I swear I heard him say the same thing.

First they questioned me, wouldn't even let me get dressed. Then a doctor inspected me, internally and externally. Then they charged me with Jatte's murder.

The evidence was all against me. The knife in the stomach had my fingerprints on it. The man in the shop remembered me buying it.

They found Jatte's camera. The only photograph on the film was of me at the service area in Paris.

From their examination they determined that I'd had sexual intercourse no more than a few hours before my arrest. They found traces of Jatte's semen on my body.

My room had been booked by phone by Mr Jatte himself, according to the hotel receptionist. He'd asked specifically that it be close to his own.

They checked my story, of course. I told them everything.

There was no English dance-team at the festival that year, no rooms booked for them at any hotel. There were lots of buskers in town; no one seemed to remember me in particular, and Malcolm had always stayed in the background. At our first room, the one I'd booked, the desk-clerk had seen no one but me. He could, however, remember the telephone call just before I left; yes, it had been a man; and he had spoken impeccable French with a Parisian accent. It sounded more like Jatte than Malcolm.

At first I thought that Malcolm and Jatte might have been in league, but that didn't last long. Then I tried to persuade myself that Malcolm had been attacked by Jatte and had killed him in self-defence. Then I considered the evidence and figured out that Malcolm knew all along what he was doing. Me.

They found no trace of anyone else having been in the room. I don't think they searched very hard, after all, they had me, the perfect suspect. I'm accepting things as they are, they say I'll get a short sentence if I plead guilty and claim it was a crime of passion. The more I think of that last night the more I'm sure he said he loved me.

I'm sorry Jatte's dead, he didn't deserve it, he was only being greedy. And I suppose we had something in common which even his death couldn't take away.

Malcolm had fucked both of us.

ME AND RENATE

Stephanie Ellyne

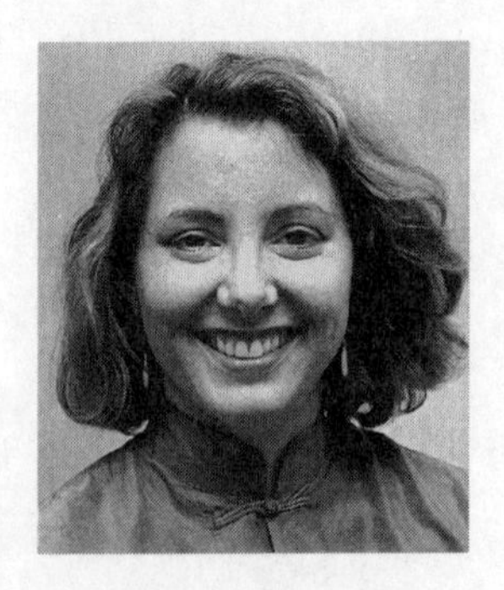

Stephanie Ellyne was born in New Orleans and raised in California and Oregon. She began acting as a child and appeared in commercials, plays and films in Oregon and Washington. After leaving acting school, she travelled around the world and stayed in London where she has lived for the past few years. Her story *Rival* was a winner in the London Writers competition. Stephanie is the lead singer of the London band 'Your Native Land'.

ME AND RENATE

Me and Renate are waiting by the side of the road. She sticks out her thumb every so often, never when we're in danger of getting picked up, just so as to let me know she's trying. I kick up some dust, shift my chew to the other side of my cheek, spit a while before I give her the eye. She knows not to go on aggravating me too long. I trained her real good.

'Honey,' she says. She got one of those butter-slick voices, soft and yellow and none too good for you if you swallow too much of it. I squint at her, push my hat back, raise my forehead to the sun. 'Something I can do for you, sweetheart?' I ask her after a while. If I respond too quick she might get cocky. She gives me one of them slow smiles her mammy taught her. It don't work as well as it use to, maybe on account of the fact she lost her knapsack in Santa Fe and ain't had the use of a toothbrush regular. 'Why don't we skip El Paso and just go straight on to New Orleans?'

I trained her good, my baby. I can see that. She almost got me saying yeah before I saw what she was up to.

'You know what's in El Paso,' I say to her, low but making sure there's enough iron in the voice to make it weigh on her. 'Yeah but,' she says, almost a whine but a bit too sure of herself for that, 'there's no need to go there for it. We can get the same thing most any place.'

This gets me interested. Maybe she's learned a thing or two on these rides while I caught myself a nap. Before I can question her any closer an old Pontiac screeches up, driver looking us over real good. Renate pouts a bit but does her stuff, eyelashes whipping back and forth like a crow caught on barbed wire while I yank off my hat and flash my poor half-bald head, more GI than prison issue to soothe the heart of preachers and patriots everywhere.

'Why hello, sir,' little Rennie breathes out. 'My mama told me to say my prayers regular and they'd be answered and I guess she was right 'cause we need a ride more'n a baby needs a tit.'

This stops me in my tracks, but she read him right, Renate, 'cause he lets out a scream of laughter that fairly rocks his rusty heap. 'Git in, git in,' he calls out, one of them high, cracked voices like a hog caller at the county fair. 'I got a ways to go and I need some company.'

Rennie flounces into the front seat, hiking up her skirt over her pretty legs and I ease myself into the back where I can keep an eye on him. He catches my eye in the mirror, gives me a wink through his little round glasses. 'Bo's the name,' he says to me and pulls away before I can get the door shut. My head cracks back against the window but I come up smiling. I like to know what I'm dealing with right from the off.

'This here's Rennie and I'm known as Link,' I say, grinning like a yokel.

'Link short for Lincoln, boy? – 'cause I'll let you know for free I don't hold with niggers taking over,' he sings out, taking a swig from his flask, whisky by the smell of him.

'Naw, Link is on account of he's always missing,' Rennie says, taking a pull from his bottle. This is a bit high-toned for old Bo, 'cause he shuts his mouth for a good five minutes and concentrates on trying to get the car up to 80.

Bo commences humming to himself. I'm expecting some Jesus wept kind of thing by the look of him, but sounds more like one of them corny songs city kids learn at tennis camp – Froggy Went A Courting, If I Had a Hammer. 'I'm heading to Memphis,' he announces presently. 'Can I drop you two anywheres in particular?'

'Well, we was in mind of New Orleans, but most anywhere that would be convenient for you would be fine with us –'

'El Paso,' I break in, closing my hand affectionate-like on Rennie's shoulder. 'Any chance you might be dropping by there?'

Bo makes a show of sucking in his breath, confused and dismayed. 'Sounds to me like you children don't know exactly where you headed! If you don't mind me saying so' – he cuts his eyes at me in the mirror – 'you look like you got some dirt under your nails, son, but this little girl ain't hardly more than a child. How old are you, darlin?'

Rennie giggles and squirms in her seat. 'I ain't no baby! Link's always bossing me around but I reckon that's what big brothers are for.'

Bo seems mighty touched by this revelation. 'Brother and sister! I should have guessed it. I thought he was a mite old for you.' He gives Rennie a paternal pat on the head that slides like a sick eel down her neck on to her shoulder.

She beams up at him. 'How old d'you think I am, mister?'

They love this part.

'We-ell.' Bo gives her a good old eyeballing, lingering so long round about the chest area I expect he's calculating inches instead of years. 'You're certainly a woman now, ain't you, sweetheart? Though I don't suppose' – he checks in his mirror to see me staring bored out the window, lowers his voice anyhow – 'no one's been *at* you yet, have they, honey? So in most ways' – a shift in his seat – 'you're still an innocent young girl.'

Renate gazes demurely into her lap. 'I'm not so innocent,' she murmurs.

A speculative silence.

'Oh, I don't know,' drawls Bo, kind of serious for him. 'I 'spect there's a thing or two you could be taught.'

High time I hit the road.

'Sir –' I venture.

'Bo, son!'

'Uh, Bo – I was wondering if it might be possible to ask you a favour?'

He purses his lips, gives a flick of his little piss-brown eyes towards his wallet pocket.

'Such as?' His voice goes all sour.

'I promised my Daddy I'd see Rennie safe to New Orleans. She's starting a new school there, staying with my Daddy's sister to make sure she stays out of mischief and goes to church regular – but it's taking a lot longer than I thought it would. We ain't getting the kinds of rides I expected. That is, we get offered lots of rides on account of Rennie here, but them boys expect something for their trouble.' I lean forward and whisper into his fleshy ear. 'It would most likely shock an upstanding citizen like yourself, sir, to hear some of the notions they got about what they can get up to, and with her very own brother in the same car.'

'I got an imagination,' Bo grunts, with a sidelong look at Renate.

'Well, sir, let me lay my cards on the table. It's getting time I was in El Paso and we ain't much closer to New Orleans than when we started.'

'What's waiting for you in El Paso, boy?'

I smile, gone all bashful. 'I thought you would have guessed 'cause of my hair, sir. I'm due back at the base in two days' time.'

He regards me suspiciously. 'Now *I* know – and if you love this fine country then I would hope that *you* know – there's no army base in El Paso.'

I guffaw at this. ''Course there ain't, sir. Just not many old officers like yourself pick us up, and that's the nearest town a civilian is likely to know.'

He likes this. 'Hell, I was a private for the duration and proud of it. Hard work's sweeter than glory to a man, son!'

Things are almost getting tearful for a minute, till thought steps in to cloud his brow.

'Let's see if I can second-guess you, boy. You want me to escort little Rennie here to New Orleans?'

'Link!' squeals Renate, fairly writhing in her seat. 'You can't expect poor Bo to go out of his way and drive me halfway cross the country like some kind of movie star! What would Daddy say?'

'It would be an honour, little lady,' intones Bo, a respectful look trying to make itself felt on his ratlike features. 'And I feel like I can speak for your Daddy as well as your brother here in saying a well-brought-up girl needs a man to protect her from the filth that stalks these roads. Just the other day there was a crime that turned my stomach. It seems a feller was driving –'

'No, please, we heard about it,' gasps Renate, clutching

her little handbag to her heart. Then she smiles and gives him a playful punch on the shoulder, sweet face all flushed. 'I guess I'll let the two of you boys convince me.'

'Why, this is fine!' I say. The three of us commence to grinning at each other, a right picture of the happy family old Bo'd like to think he had. 'This means I can get the next bus to Fort Bliss. Sir, I'm eternally grateful to you. I don't know what I would have done if –'

'Now, now, son, any red-blooded man would have done the same! That is, anyone who calls himself a gentleman.' The Pontiac jerks to a halt and the back door's yanked open. I find myself in the dirt and right happy to be there.

'I want you to know, boy, that I mean to take care of your baby sister like she was my very own,' vows Bo.

'I knew I could depend on you, sir.' I shake his hand, one gent to another. 'It's a funny thing,' I confide. 'I probably shouldn't worry about this little girl here. She looks so delicate but she can take real good care of herself.'

And anyone who gets in her way.

'Well, Renate.' I clear my throat manfully. 'Be a good girl now, you hear? Make your family proud of you.'

'You be good, big brother, and make them sergeants proud of you!' she calls out in her clear little voice. 'Remember, Jesus loves you!' They rattle away in his sorry contraption, Rennie taking turns sticking her tongue out and blowing me kisses till I can't see them no more.

I decide to stretch my legs a bit. It'll be a good hour 'fore I see my baby again and I might as well use the time for some exercise. It takes some doing to keep up with Renate and I don't aim to disappoint her.

Trouble is there ain't enough energy in this tired old world. I don't need no book to convince me there's nothing that's pure good and nothing that's pure bad. I've had my fill of preachers, and when it comes right down to it I don't care what made us or created us. Got no time for that talk. All I know's what is, what you see when you open your eyes and look around you. It's hot or it's cold, sometimes so dry all the crops shrivel up, others when it's so wet everything just slides off into ruination. But weather ain't bad or good, it's just there and that's what's real about it. A cat ain't evil for ripping a mouse apart. It's just obeying its nature.

Most people got no idea of who they are. They crawl out of bed into a car, go hunch over a desk all day taking crap from someone maybe half as alive as them, then crawl on home and goggle at a box just waiting to die. They got no suspicion of their true nature.

Now me and Renate are trying to discover what we can do, just exactly what we are and aren't capable of. We got ourselves a game plan and that plan's this. Once we've tested all the possibilities, experimented with just about everything we can think of, then we'll decide what it is we got a hankering for without too much worrying we might have left something out. One thing's for certain. We'll try anything more than once.

I reckon one of these days our true nature is going to shout out and reveal itself.

I set myself down after a spell. Don't want to go so far she can't find me again. I scoot back well off the road and sit up against a fence post, tilt my hat over my eyes. I must have fell asleep, 'cause before I know it, here she comes straight at me. She pulls up with an almighty screech, dirt and pebbles flying up in my face like bees.

'Hop in, soldier boy,' coos Renate. She peers at me over Bo's little spectacles, perched crookedly on her pretty nose. One of the lenses is cracked.

'Why, little lady, you sure you're old enough to be driving that thing?' I yodel and climb on in. His corduroy shirt is draped round her thin shoulders. Underneath all she's got on is her panties. As usual they're black with blood.

'Damn it, Renate, you're getting the seat all filthy! Lift up.' She sighs and raises her bottom while I scrub at the imitation white leather upholstery with what must be Bo's hanky, hoping I have a nice day in red, white and blue embroidery.

'How'd it go?'

'Pretty much the same.' She yawns, squinting half-hopefully out the back for a cop car. Rennie'll do anything for a little excitement.

'He put up a struggle?'

'Honey, he didn't get time,' she drawls, then busts out laughing. 'That old boy was so quick he almost went off before Pearl did.'

She calls her gun Pearl 'cause of what the handle's supposed to be made of. Like so many things these days, it's imitation. I been telling her once we hit El Paso I can afford to buy her the real thing but she keeps dragging her feet.

'That's just fine, Renate,' I say, real sarcastic. 'All we need is an itty-bitty version of Bo running around to make our lives pure perfection.'

'Bodine, if you please,' she snaps. 'I already got me a little boy, if you care to recall. Matter of fact, seems I got two.' She glares at me, steering the car with one hand and helping herself to one of my cigarettes with the other.

'You want to light this for me or do I got to do everything for myself?'

I light her up and shut my trap. It's best to give her some time to settle down after her bit of excitement.

Every so often Rennie gets worried about her baby. It's staying with her sister in Crockett, been there for over a year now and I personally feel that it would confuse the kid if some pretty piece comes tripping in and makes him call her mama. The only ma that kid knows is sturdy and solid in puke-stained polyester and it might as well stay that way. She has a court order keeping Rennie away, and if I got to go back inside it'll be for something more drastic than swiping a snot-nosed kid and its diaper collection. When she gets tearful about it I give her a slap or two, wake her up and give her something real to cry about. I'm glad to say I ain't had to do that for awhile though. Fact is it don't seem to trouble her so much no more. She hardly never mentions him.

It ain't mine, of course. My kid would be with me all day and night and first SOB tried to take him off to school would have buckshot for breakfast.

Rennie swerves to avoid a gopher and does some cussing. I give her a good hard look. She seems awful wound up for this time of morning. 'What's the matter, cupcake?'

'Lincoln, we got ourself a problem,' says Rennie.

'Didn't he have nothing?'

She tosses his wallet down on the seat. I'm amazed to find it stuffed full of hundred-dollar bills.

'Lord have mercy! Why didn't he buy a better car?'

'He couldn't exactly get rid of this one yet.' She jerks her head towards the back. 'Take a guess what's in the trunk.'

'Drugs?' I say doubtfully. It don't seem likely but it's one of the few things gets Rennie real upset, her preferring other kinds of stimulation.

'Let's just say I ain't the first sweet thing he been messing with.' Her lips twist and all of a sudden she's crying. 'There's a little girl in the trunk, maybe eight years old.'

'Damn it, Rennie, stop the car!' I make sure no one's in sight, then hurry round the back to check it's shut up tight with nothing leaking. This ain't exactly the place to take a look. I push her aside and take the wheel, starting up nice and slow. She's still snivelling to herself.

'What's got into you, Renate?' I ask, soon as she quiets down enough to hear me. 'Why didn't you leave her with him?'

'She's just a baby, Link, and he done ripped her apart! I couldn't just dump her by the road like trash.' She brightens up a touch. 'I'll tell you something, sugar, I'm right proud to have blown him away.' She chews thoughtfully on her gum. 'I feel something like the Lone Ranger.'

I don't say nothing, keep cruising down the road easy while I try to think. At least now I'm driving. To say it ain't wise to have a body in the back won't mean much to you unless you've had a taste of Rennie at the wheel. If driving was ice-cream speed would be her favourite flavour. She flashes by and the cops are on our tail like dogs on a bitch in heat. She always outdrives them, but then we always been in a newer car. This thing couldn't outrace a go-kart.

We got to be practical right now, a word that don't mean much to Renate. It was me taught her to shoot and to give her credit, she's had so much practice she's got to be a damn sight better than me. But you can love a thing too much. She gets so carried away she uses all her bullets when with her aim one would do. You could say it's a fault in her.

It weren't like this when we started. We'd set 'em up the

same but never go the whole hog. Didn't seem no point in it. We knew they wouldn't risk reporting us on account of what they'd got up to with a minor. Far as we know no one ever did. We'd relieve them of their wallets and their wheels and leave them near the road, boiling mad but breathing. The gun was just for show. Lord, Rennie loved waving that thing around! She kept hold of it in case things got out of hand.

And then she did.

The first time she emptied her pistol it surprised me. Way after he stopped twitching she kept plugging. I hollered at her to let go, finally had to knock the gun from her hand once the chamber was empty. She just kept firing like she was mesmerized. Hell, she'd be there now if I hadn't stepped in.

I take full responsibility if she goes astray. It's only right. I taught her everything she knows.

I ain't told her this 'cause some things should stay private. But I never feel so excited as when I see that little girl getting her own back. I usually arrive round about the time one of these old boys crush her to the ground, her pinned and wriggling beneath his flabby body like a bug. Then wham-bam, before you know it they're jerked backwards by the shot and she's the one on top doing the pumping.

Ain't no need to talk about it. She ought to know. Seems any more that's the only time I get romantic, and she's so fired up she's ready for anything. I can't remember the last time we done it regular.

Once you got a taste for danger, normal things go stale.

These last few rides she's had a hankering to do the whole thing herself. She's still a kid most ways, and you know how they love to feel independent. She pestered and pestered me till finally I indulged her. And look where it's got us.

I've come to know her real good and I understand the problem. My baby's a born enthusiast. Once she starts a thing seems she gets so caught up she don't know how to stop. I scold her about it. There's no sense in wasting ammunition. Plus it's so damn sloppy when they splatter. Seems I got to buy her a new dress most every day. Come to think of it, that could be why she does it. Like your average woman, she loves keeping fresh and pretty.

I can't complain about her feminine side. It's her good looks that keeps us in rides and her charm that cons the good old boys out of their cars and into their graves. But that same female part of her's got us crawling down the road with a Girl Scout in the trunk. Trust a woman to be too sentimental to dump a stiff 'cause they ain't had their grown-up teeth.

Lucky for us I ain't afflicted by such squeamishness.

As we creep along I'm scrutinizing the surroundings for camouflage. You got to have the eyes of a tracker for this type of work, everything's up to the territory and the weather. Rain's good on account of the mud. Usually we cover them with mesquite or brush, maybe some leaves if he's took her into the woods and the time of year's right. Once we come across a ditch chock-full of baling wire and that worked out fine. Most anything will do if you use your imagination. You'd be surprised the things that work.

Unless you're driving down a road like this. Smooth, flat and level, us gliding across like syrup on a pancake. On this kind of terrain you can bet any little bump sure shows.

'Teenage avenger,' says Renate.

'You mind keeping quiet, Rennie? I got to concentrate.'

'We're teenage avengers, Lincoln. This time the thing we done is pure good and no one could blame us for it. We was simply being good citizens and disposing of filth!' She blows a bubble and pops it, real excited. 'We can't just go off and bury her. Think how her mama and daddy'll feel never knowing what become of her. Why don't we leave the car somewheres the cops can find it? Even a cop hates a baby-raper. They'll be mighty grateful we took him off their hands.'

'And just how are they going to know anything about *him*, Miss Teenager? The smell of asphalt done gone and fried your brain.'

There's a short silence.

'Link, there just weren't no place to hide him . . .'

'For Christ's sweet sake, Renate! You don't mean there's two of them back there!'

She knows me well enough to duck.

'Honey, what else could I do? I knew it weren't right keeping them together after what he done but I could hardly put him in the back seat, now could I? The trunk was all there was.'

She waits a couple minutes for me to cool down, then starts stroking my arm. Backwards the way I like it, so all the little hairs go the wrong way and give you the shivers.

'It ain't no catastrophe, is it, punkin?' she asks real soft. 'No one's gonna stop us in this car 'cept an out-of-stock junk dealer. I went all peculiar when I found that child. I was running out of time and I got so scared I just couldn't figure what to do!' She gives me a little kiss side of the head. 'I knew *you'd* be able to think of something.'

She ain't going to get off that easy.

'You been on the road too long, Rennie. We ain't Bonnie and Clyde.'

She jerks her hand off my arm and sits up all stiff.

'Hell,' she spits out, 'if you was a hunk like Warren you wouldn't need me for bait.'

'There ain't a thing coming out of that head of yours but that pretty blonde hair and that ain't real. Don't you realize what they'll do to us if they catch us? They ain't going to believe you were defending your honour and then decided to take them for a Sunday drive! I'll be lucky to get out in time for my own funeral. And just 'cause you're not legal age don't think you'd get off so light.'

This don't faze her at all.

'Don't be too sure. I can tell a story about how you corrupted me so pitiful I could make *them* two cry.' She takes a long pull from Bo's bottle. 'Don't you know me by now, Lincoln? There ain't no judge drawing breath I can't sweet talk. He's a man, ain't he? Who'd ever take your word over mine? Not only are you big, mean-looking and almost twenty-one, you done time.'

'Could be the judge is a woman!'

'That'd suit me fine! A lady judge could appreciate how easy a girl goes astray without the ever-loving arms of her mama to steer her straight.' She winks. 'And I wouldn't have to spend time with her later.'

I got to admit she's got me licked. Before I know it she's caught me grinning. She starts in giggling and wraps her arms round my neck so tight I got to push her off to breathe. She's strong for a little one.

'Ain't this something, sugar? Seems lately we got so good at what we're doing all the fun's gone out of it. Like soda pop when you want a big, juicy steak. Sweet and easy but nothing to chew on.' She bounces up and down on the seat. 'But driving along knowing any moment they could get us and something bad might happen – why, it makes electricity shoot up my spine right through the sky!' Her voice goes all husky. 'Baby, I'm excited.'

I steer one-handed and give her a big sloppy kiss. Suddenly I'm feeling fine myself. Rennie makes every day a picnic. Times like this I feel so good I think about us settling down, having our own kid and raising it right. But you take two folks like us, accustomed to the smell of excitement. How long could we stay in one place before Rennie's trigger finger starts itching?

No, chances are we'll always be ramblers. Leastways till Rennie hits eighteen.

'What do you say, sweet thing?' she croons. 'We ain't done it in the car for a while.'

'Soon as we get these two in the ground I'm all yours, baby. Damned if I can see any place to turn off.'

She scowls, all sulky. 'But I like having them back there, Lincoln, I just told you! It's more spicy.' She lowers her voice. 'If I asked you for something extra, extra special, would you do it just for me?'

'What's that, precious?'

'Let's at least keep 'em till we get to New Orleans.'

I keep my temper on account of her asking so nice. 'That ain't exactly possible, Rennie. First thing is we got to ditch this car 'cause there ain't enough room for what we're carrying once we hit El Paso. And even if it was big enough, which it ain't, it's full up with grandpop and his little sweetie. That answer your question?'

Of course she decides to sass me.

'Lincoln, I been studying on this and it plain don't seem fair how you always get your own way.'

I glare at her. 'I don't see no other man in this car, do you?'

'Oh I'm not denying that, honey. You're the natural-born master round here, of course! But it's important to me to think I got some say. I mean, we don't get rides 'cause of what you got on offer. Seems only natural since it's my talents being noticed that I should decide where them rides are going to take us.'

'Rennie, once we hit El Paso, you can set your sights on the moon and I'll be right beside you.'

'We ain't going to El Paso.' She sticks her chin out like a mule. 'If you're so set on going you can go by your own self.'

I pound the steering wheel. 'And just what is it you got against El Paso all of a sudden?'

She takes a deep breath and screams at me. 'I ain't living off your drug money, Lincoln! You done that before you met me and I don't hold it against you. But we're a team now and if you can't survive on what we do together and like it you go back to prowling playgrounds! But do it on your own.'

No wonder they don't want too many women in the army. A lick or two of shooting and they think they rule the roost.

'Where do you get off telling me what to do?' I holler back. 'And since when are you such a do-gooder? Don't act all pure and holy with me, Renate, we been travelling together too long. I seen some things in my time but I have never seen anyone enjoy a thing as much as you love watching 'em breathe their last.'

'Damn right!' she says. 'I got every reason to be proud of what I do, and it ain't hooking innocent babies for profit. Every last man I wasted was begging for it. How dare they think they can stick their thing in some girl young enough to be their daughter, grandkid even! They should have found their own sweetness instead of trying to drink mine dry. Don't aim to make me feel bad, Lincoln. They was just dirty old men that paid the price for their filthy stinking lust.'

She stops for breath. 'They had plenty of time to repent what they were doing. But did they see the error of their ways? The hell they did! They went on sinning and sinning till I come along like the Lord's own angel to strike them down.'

I had no idea she held such strong opinions.

'And just what in hell are you going to do if I go to El Paso? Go back to high school? Start knocking off football players?'

Rennie just grins. 'I'll do what I'm doing now only a damn sight better. I'd get a lot more rides without you tagging along to cramp my style.' She muses on this. 'Maybe I should get my baby back. It would be impossible to drive past a helpless young mother and her innocent child.' She giggles. 'I can train J.T. to use a pistol. Lord, just think of their faces!'

It's time to knock her down a peg or two. 'Just 'cause you got familiar with Pearl don't mean you're dangerous, darling. Not to me you ain't. Before you met me you couldn't load a BB gun.'

'That's a fact, Lincoln, and I thank you kindly. You're one fine teacher.' She shrugs. 'I do believe it's time to graduate.'

I try reasoning with her. 'So you don't want no part of drug-dealing. You're plain not interested in having a big new car all our own, lots of pretty clothes, plus any little thing you set your heart on in the store windows? There's big money to be had, baby, and it's all ours if we want it.'

'What do I need with fancy clothes? Mostly someone's taking them off me. And I like different cars all the time.' She tosses Bo's bulging wallet into my lap. 'Besides, we ain't doing bad for cash right now.'

'What about a real nice place to live, with a pool table and a barbecue and our very own swimming pool?'

She snorts at this. 'A wall-to-wall grave called home sweet home! At least in motels you don't have to clean up. I'm sorry, sugar, but I can't live like that. I got to keep moving.'

The car goes quiet while I think things through. My heart's been set on going back to El Paso and picking up the pieces of my old life. But I got to admit half the fun was going to be showing Rennie off to my buddies. They never seen anything like her and that's before she opens her mouth. Without her there, don't seem much point.

I sneak a look at Renate. She's staring out the window and humming to herself, acting real unconcerned. I clear my throat. 'Rennie, I'll make a deal with you. I'm not saying this'll be for ever, mind. But if you want to skip El Paso for the time being that's OK by me.' She whoops but I put my hand up before she can start in hugging and kissing. 'On one condition. That we dump these stiffs before we go to New Orleans.'

'It's a deal, cowboy!' she squeals, flinging her arms around me. 'You won't be sorry, Link. I'll make it up to you.'

'Just let me know one thing. Why is it you're so all-fired anxious to get to New Orleans?'

She rubs her cheek against mine. 'Don't you know nothing, silly? It's almost Mardi Gras!' Her voice gets dreamy. 'My mama said it's the biggest party in the US of A, even more spectacular than the 4th of July! I aim to see it before I'm too old to enjoy it. People don't do enough celebrating.'

The Lord himself must be riding with us because just then I spot a little turn-off, a bumpy tractor trail heading off towards what looks like, in the distance, a stand of big, leafy trees. The kind that grow out of wet, rich earth.

We turn off down the track and, sure enough, after fifteen minutes of rattling along come to the perfect place. The trees are growed in so thick it's dark as a chapel inside. Ain't no one around, but even if they was they couldn't see what we're about to do.

'He's got a shovel in the trunk,' says Renate. She's real cheerful now she's made up her mind to be. 'I reckon he was planning to use it himself.'

I strip off my shirt and get to it. Each time I stop to rest Rennie grabs the shovel and works on a little hole some ways from mine. She feels quite strong about keeping them apart. With both of us working, seems like we're through in no time.

I drag him by the ankles and drop him in. Renate leans over and spits, then starts kicking dirt and sticks down on him like a wild thing. I pull her away when her breathing gets ragged.

'Let me do this, honey. Why don't you take care of the kid?'

The little girl is a sight. I got to admit it ain't pleasant to look at her. Rennie lifts her out real gentle, smoothing her little pink dress together where it's been torn. 'It's a shame to lay her to rest with her dress all nasty. I wish we got something else to put her in.'

'Well, we ain't.' I'm itching to get out of here. I ain't had a thing to eat since breakfast.

Renate carries her over and lowers her in as smooth as though she was tucking her in for the night. I get the shovel but she grabs my arm before I can use it.

'Just one more second, Lincoln.' She opens her handbag and takes out her beat-up rubber doll. Petunia, she calls it. Rennie stands looking into the grave for a minute. Then she drops it in.

I'm real surprised. 'Are you sure you want to do that, sweetheart?' I know that doll means a lot to her. It's one of the few things her mammy ever give her.

''Course I'm sure.' She smiles kind of shaky and for a minute I think she's going to cry again. She don't. 'It's high time I gave up baby stuff.'

I go to put my arms around her. She lays herself down on the moist earth and smiles at me, lifting up Bo's shirt. 'Tell the truth now, Lincoln. Wouldn't you say I'm pretty near a woman?'

I pull her apart and in I go. I'm the only man still living that's felt this heat in her, and I like keeping that thought inside as I feel my way through. No matter how deep I go I never feel more'n halfway there.

I use her eyes as beacons. I press her forehead to mine and try to tunnel through her but sooner or later I got to give up and still her life's a secret to me. She lends out her control, never loses it, spins it out in a thread too even and tight to be more than plucked.

I'd consider it an honour to have someone kill me if I was so occupied. That's why I get a sweet warm feeling in my heart when I think of the men we've done. We're the best friends those mothers ever had.

ADIDAS

Sarah Gracie

Sarah Gracie was born in Bahrain and grew up in Aberdeenshire. After obtaining a First in English Language and Literature at Oxford, she travelled around Europe and on her return to Britain became a teacher in psychiatric hospitals and prisons.

Currently Sarah is working on a collection of short stories and a film script for an independent production company. In October she will begin studying for her MA in Creative Writing at the University of East Anglia and start work on her first novel.

ADIDAS

All the time that Little Eddie was in prison they told Little Eddie's son, Mikey, that his father was in hospital. The hospital was a large, far-distant place, difficult to get to and unwelcoming to visitors. There Little Eddie, over the next two years, was to undergo a series of complex heart operations, which would be performed by some of the country's leading and most formidable heart surgeons. He could be visited only once a month by Mikey's mother, Kath, dressed in a special sky-blue suit, and carrying baskets of shopping; but due to the risk of contagion, was not to be visited at all by the under-fives, of whom Mikey, at the time, was one.

'Are you better now, Dad?' asked Mikey watchfully, when his father finally came home.

'Much better, son, ta very much. Much better. No more trouble in the heart department.' And Little Eddie knocked his heart, the receptacle of so much top-level care, and gave an embarrassed laugh.

Mikey did not look quite satisfied, and a frown passed across his pale five-year-old face. But just then he said nothing.

Over the following weeks father and son attempted to get to know each other again. But two years at that age seemed a long time, and Little Eddie found the pale-faced solemn fellow who greeted him, with the air of being his mother's protector and his father's adjudicator, rather unnerving, and not at all recognizable as the chubby laughing infant he had left behind, and for whom he had been colouring in Bambi cartoons so lovingly on prison notepaper for the last two years.

'I think he hates me,' he said to Kath one night, finally acknowledging the truth of his fears.

But Kath dismissed it. 'No,' she said. 'It's not that. It's just that we've been very cosy, him and me, for the last two years . . . And you're a bit of a shock. It'll take time.'

And when Little Eddie considered this, he thought it was true. After all, he could not expect to walk back into his old position as father and husband as if nothing had happened. He had been away almost half his son's young life: he must now *earn* his position, *earn* his trust, as he had resolved to do in prison.

In prison Little Eddie had had plenty of time to reflect upon his life. Prison 'empties you out' as the saying goes, and there is not much that you have been or done that does not come back to you, while you stare at the bricks on the wall of a cell. Little Eddie knew that if he didn't break the pattern of petty thefts and incarceration which had dominated so far, he would spend most of the rest of his life in gaol, stack up to nothing, and lose his family as well.

Certain characters hardened his resolve. These were the 'gaolbirds', whom he saw ahead of him, haunting the warrens of the big city prisons. They were thin, sketchy men with fading gestures and chalk-white skins. It was impossible to tell their age – somewhere between thirty and sixty – because prison seemed to have a strangely preserving effect. And though their skins, due to bad food and a lack of sunlight, would age badly, their eyes, staring out of shadowy sockets, seemed to retain a permanent guileless gleam, a sort of candid thirteen-year-old wistful hopefulness; which reminded Little Eddie of the thoroughly defeated yet gallant roguery with which the slumboys of Victorian photographs looked out from their slums.

As far as Little Eddie could tell, the 'gaolbirds' spent most of their lives in prison. They would have periods on the out, before which they would boast a lot about women, 'big jobs' and 'living off interest'. But the minute they were on the streets again, they became so terrified by the pace and ruthlessness of a city which had long moved on from them, that they would rush to do some petty crime – a crime distinguished for the smallness of its rewards and the certainty of being caught – and would find themselves back in gaol again.

There they would take up their little jobs in the laundry, or canteen. And, bristling with self-importance, they would flourish mops and fold up shirts, fawn flirtatiously on the prison officers with cups of tea and whispered gossip. The certainties of locked doors and subservience were by now a secret relief to them; and – despite the pornography dutifully displayed on every cell wall – they succumbed steadily to homosexuality, of a threadbare ducking type, which Little Eddie could not stand.

Little Eddie did not want to be one of these men. They frightened him. He hated their weakness and their pallor and their lostness. He hated their subservience and their hopelessness. He saw them as some strange subterranean form of life, which had retreated to a dark place, as on an ocean bed, never to see sunlight or blue skies again. And he wanted nothing to do with them, their reconciledness and the little frameworks of affection and resentment they built up. He wanted nothing to do with the self-deceit and fantasies which protected them from the knowledge of what they had become. And he kept clear of them. For prison was a place he was only moving through.

So when he got out, he faced reality and got a job. It was not a great job, but the best he could do with no references and a record. He was to work a fishstall in the East Street market, long hours and low wages . . . But it was steady, and it symbolized his accession to adulthood and responsibility. He bought home eighty pounds a week, significantly more than the social security Kath and Mikey had been living on, and his presence, in that respect at least, was a bonus to the family.

Now he could enjoy the little services that Kath would do for him, the cup of tea in the morning or the evening meal when he came home. He could enjoy the fresh sheets, and the shirts, and all the little rituals which made up family life. He began to unwind slightly, to relax the paranoia and the deep sense of unworthiness that was buried deep in his heart, and in the heart of almost every convicted man he had ever known. Once again, he found himself able to touch Kath;

and when he asked his son about his homework, he could look him in the eye.

It was in this new period of security that Mikey – who seemed to have responded to Little Eddie's confidence – reopened the subject of the latter's illness.

He picked as his time a Sunday afternoon – the only day of the week Little Eddie now had off – and as his scene the concrete terrace just outside the front door of their seventh-floor council flat, where Little Eddie was bevelling planks to make a small bookcase for his son's bedroom.

It was a cold wintry afternoon, with a flat yellow sun going down behind the skyscrapers of the Elephant and Castle. You couldn't see much of the council estates of South London – their little graffitied balconies and choked-up lifts, the dank little yards and fire-gutted floors – because the sun did not reach down that far. At ground level things were filling with dusk. Only in the distance, gleaming by the river, was a vision of St Paul's, with lucid shining dome and flanking columns.

Mikey stood watching his father intently as he worked. On his face was an expression of great concentration and respect. Now and again he would stoop to sweep away the wood-shavings as they fell beneath the bench, or hurry to pass his father plane or bevel when he needed them.

After a while he stopped doing this and focused more purely on his father's face. A new quality of curiosity and calculation came into his expression.

'Dad?' he said tentatively, after a long pause. 'Dad?'

'Yes, son?'

Little Eddie did not immediately look up. He was very absorbed in his work, with his lower lip jutting out in concentration. He was bevelling with a good steady rhythm now, the bevel held at just the right angle to the plank, and the shavings flying off smooth and clean, with a good sharp scent of pine. He was enjoying the feel of the tools beneath his hands, the heavy cool weight of them; and also the feel of the wood, whose exact knot and grain he seemed to sense with the heat of his fingertips, in some intuitive pre-conscious way, as if through the memory of another life. If he had it all again, he would do something with his hands. Be a carpenter. Even work in a sawmill. That would be the life.

'Dad?'

Finally Little Eddie looked up. He did not immediately take in his son, however, but allowed his gaze to drift through the sooty tunnel of South London council flats to the distant river, where he saw the pewterish glints of the water, and, like a far-off dream or a half-heard piece of music, the palely gleaming dome.

'What is it, Mikey?' he said gently, and smiled when his gaze dropped and took in his son. For the boy was so solemn and grave before him, so like a little man, with his little bomber jacket and trainers, his stiff masculine posture, legs apart and hands shoved in his pockets. It seemed to Little Eddie that Mikey had an air of manliness, a kind of embryonic machismo, which was already far bolder and more successful than anything he himself had ever pulled off. And not for the first time, he found himself slightly in awe of his son. 'What is it son?' he said now, with the same gentleness, but a slight sense of foreboding. 'What is it that's bothering you? You can tell your old Dad . . . '

When Mikey finally responded, after much shifting of the feet and staring out at the emptiness around, Little Eddie's first thought was that he must go inside and fetch Kath. After all, the whole thing had been none of his doing. If it had been left to him Mikey would have been turning up with his mother at the visitors' area once a month for the last two years, like all the rest of the kids. Crawling around the dusty visitors' cubicle; sitting on his father's convict canvas leg; and learning not to bawl when the alarm bell went off and a dozen big POs in uniforms and closed-off faces started manhandling someone who couldn't bear to say goodbye to his wife.

But Kath hadn't wanted it. She hadn't wanted Mikey to see his father in gaol, a convict, and subjugated. She hadn't wanted him to see his father locked up, like an animal, by men in uniform no better than himself. She had said that all this might damage him; that it might sow a seed of self-defeat in him, a feeling of worthlessness and self-doubt; or that it might make him bitter on behalf of his father, alienated and hostile to society. And she wanted Mikey to have all the chances that other children had: to go to school and work hard, to have ambitions, a sense of self-worth, and to get on.

Although at first Little Eddie had taken it hard when his fellow inmates had visits from their kids, while he had only a few photographs on his cell wall to remind him of Mikey, in time he had come to be grateful to Kath. He saw how those same children became acclimatized to the nick; how they imbibed its atmosphere, its distorted human relationships, and even the strange fantasy life it seemed to breed. And he saw that by adolescence they had learnt the pattern, and were fixed for a life of crime. For the realities of punishment did not seem to check habits or alter them, but rather to generate the fiercer fantasy life. The fantasy of bigger and better crime, crime for which you would not be caught, and which would cancel all the previous degradations.

So all in all, though it came at a price, Little Eddie was glad that Mikey had been kept clear of it. But now he had a problem on his hands, a problem he felt very uncomfortable with, since it presented him with the messy alternatives of admitting a lie, or elaborating it.

'What is it you want to know, son?' he said now cautiously, reaching for the tobacco tin in his pocket, and rejecting the notion of running for Kath as too weak. 'What is it you want to know about the hospital?'

Mikey wanted to know all sorts of things. He wanted to know what the hospital looked like, how big it was, how many patients it had in it and what diseases they suffered from. He wanted to know what the doctors and nurses were like, and whether they had TV. He wanted to know what time they had to put the lights out, and whether they had to take a lot of medicine. And most of all (and here his voice quavered fractionally with the frustration of two years of vagueness from his mother), he wanted to know about the operations. Who did them, where, with what implements, and how.

All this was accompanied by a rising sense of indignation

that he should even have to ask, and a sense of almost tearful grievance that he should feel uncomfortable – as he evidently did – about doing so.

There was a long pause while Little Eddie rolled himself a cigarette. He took out several strands of damp tobacco, and laid them out carefully along the Rizla paper on his bench. Then he began to roll. He rolled long and thoroughly, until he had a thin fine tube, slim and white, and in every way like a normal cigarette except that it was a quarter of the width. Then he took out his matches and lit up. The raw bluish flame flickered momentarily between his cupped hands. He took a deep puff, inhaled, and threw the match over the terrace. As it dropped through the blue dusk, inspiration came to him.

The hospital, he began slowly and hesitantly, was a very unpleasant place. It was huge and old and ugly; built some time in the last century, and never updated. It was full to the brim of sick people, languishing in various stages of a wide variety of diseases. They lay in their beds all day and never went anywhere or did anything. Sometimes the sickest of them even lost track of day and night. Their skins got paler and paler, because there was not enough sunlight for them to manufacture the right vitamins, and they often lost the use of their muscles, because the hospital didn't have enough yards for them to take proper exercise.

Unfortunately, there was such a shortage of people with the relevant surgical skills that they had to wait a great amount of time for their operations. But every now and again a vacancy would come up on the waiting list, and then they would be plucked out of their beds suddenly by two hospital porters in uniform, rushed along endless corridors to a white van waiting in the yard outside, and then rushed very fast through the city to the big hall where the operations took place. (It must all happen very fast in case the patients escaped and their germs got loose in the city.)

Once in the big hall of operations, they were laid out on a table in the middle of a great many doctors and nurses, who carried all sorts of special surgical equipment – needles and knives, drills and scalpels – and gathered round to investigate.

Up above them, on a small platform, sat the chief surgeon, a very grim-faced man, who superintended proceedings and wore a special headdress to mark his importance.

The doctors and nurses would then begin poking and prodding, peering and testing, in pursuit of a diagnosis. If the patient was 'resistant' to diagnosis, they would cut him wide open with their knives and fold back the flesh until they could get a really good look down inside him.

There they would usually find an enormous black lump, a hideous sort of tumour or something like that, growing on his heart.

They would gasp with horror and turn to their chief. 'Excision?' they would ask.

Then the chief surgeon would get up slightly out of his chair, and stare down into the patient's innards with an expression of fascination and disgust. 'I have never in my life seen such a revolting, filthy, evil, stinking black tumour!' he would burst out with a voice of great authority. 'Excision! Immediately!'

Here Little Eddie paused, pushed his thinning hair back over his forehead, and took several quick puffs of his cigarette. Then, after a reflective glance round the crumbling dusky skyline, he began again.

After this, he said, all the doctors and nurses would gather round, really close up to the patient. They would murmur to themselves, 'Excision! excision! Immediate excision!'; and then, after taking an enormously deep breath, they would all lean over the patient, and of one accord, land an almighty spit down into his gaping black heart.

'A spit?' Mikey interrupted at this point, his mouth falling open and his face expressing a powerful surprise.

'A spit.' Little Eddie insisted. 'A spit. But not an ordinary spit,' he added. 'Not a common kind of spit. A spit with very special, extraordinary sort of properties.'

And he explained that the spit in question contained a special kind of vitriol, of such a powerful concentrated kind, that just a few drops of it landing on the black tumour were enough to burn and corrode it like acid. This vitriol could burn right through all the evil cells of the tumour, to the very core, and then the tumour was supposed to just shrivel up and fall off.

There was a long silence while Mikey digested this. His face struggled for a while between surprise and disappointment. There were no surgical strikes, no knives and lasers, pumps and stitches. But in the end he seemed to accept the explanation, and even began to find it quite satisfying. For experience had taught him that the ways of adults were mysterious and profound. And in the interim, before a full comprehension, he just absorbed the rituals, which came to him with the force of magic incantations, their authority perhaps even enhanced by their qualities of the surreal and irrational.

Meantime Little Eddie smoked his cigarette and wondered if his ordeal was over. He was suffering the nervous tension of the unaccustomed raconteur: his mouth was dry and his pulse racing. Led astray by his involvement in his own story, he wasn't even sure whether his son was still listening.

'Are you OK, Mikey?' he said, by way of getting a response. 'Do you want to go in now, son?' For it had become very cold on the balcony, and the sun had gone down.

But Mikey, it seemed, wasn't finished. And by his next question, it was evident that he had in no way switched off during his father's story, but had grasped the whole thing clearly, and already moved on to implications.

'Where do you get it?' was the question, in a sharp voice that brooked no opposition.

'Get it, son?' Little Eddie was confused.

'The disease,' he said impatiently. 'The black thing on the heart. Where does it come from?'

Little Eddie had just enough detachment to give a muffled bark of laughter. Then he sighed heavily. 'Goodness, Mikey, you don't half ask them,' he said, reaching again for his cigarettes.

He couldn't fail at this point, or the whole pack of cards would come tumbling down. And if that happened, he wouldn't be able to look Mikey straight in the eye again. So, buoying himself up with the success of his previous effort, and even beginning to find a certain intellectual interest in the question, he resumed his story.

'It's like this, son,' he said, rolling the tobacco between his fingers. 'It's like this . . .'

The gist of Eddie's next story was a comparison between the growth of the black tumour, and the growth of envy in the human heart. 'You see, the world is full of two types of people,' he said slowly. 'Rich men and poor men – or so it seems to the poor man. Now the rich man seems to the poor man to be a very fortunate sort of person; he seems to have everything in the world that would make the poor man happy. He has a big house and beautiful furniture; he has lovely food and clothes and women and wine. Everyone treats him with great respect, opening doors for him, and listening to everything he says. And when he dies, he is buried in a nice plot of land, with a great big gravestone, and lots of people come and sing songs at his funeral . . .

'Now the poor man, on the other hand, sees none of this. He lives in a small dingy house, with bad food, bad clothes, bad air, and boring work. No one ever opens doors for him, or listens to a word he says – even though what he says might be just as intelligent and worth hearing as what the rich man says – but he isn't rich you see, so people reckon there's no point listening to him. And when he dies, he gets a little bit of scraggy grass and a little stone above his head; and his name is forgotten by everyone, for ever and ever.

'Now when the poor man gets to thinking about the difference between him and the rich man, he gets very bitter. A sort of envy begins to grow in his heart. And this envy begins to take over everything. He envies the rich man all his possessions and the respect they get him. And he begins to look down on everything in his own life by comparison. And every time he has one of these thoughts – how small he is by comparison with the rich man, how little people think of him – a little drop of blackness seems to enter into his heart. And the little spots of blackness grow and grow and grow, until finally they take over the whole heart, and then he gets very sick . . .'

'And then he has to go and have an operation!' Mikey exclaimed with satisfaction.

'And then he has to go and have an operation.'

'And they spit on him.'
'And they spit on him.'
'And it shrivels up.'
'And – *most* of the time,' Little Eddie added carefully, 'it shrivels up.'
Now there was awe in Mikey's voice, awe at the dimensions of this new type of fairytale, which had a structure so unlike that of any he had heard before. But there was also satisfaction in his voice, the satisfaction of one who has clearly grasped the point of a story, and with it a new way of apprehending the world.
He fell silent in thought.
'Well, son, if you've no more questions, I think we'll go –'
But Mikey did have another question. And he looked up sharply now, with an anxious expression in his face. 'Is yours gone, Dad? Is yours gone? Will it ever grow back again?'
Little Eddie was now liberated. With a sudden spurt of fierce exhilaration, and more physical freedom than he had shown with Mikey since he was a baby, he lifted him on to his shoulders.
'Totally gone, Mikey! Totally gone! It got one look at that vitriol, and it just shrivelled right up. For ever and ever.'
And he began to gallop clumsily up and down the terrace with Mikey on his shoulders, puffing from unaccustomed exercise, and scattering the woodshavings as he went. They flew up over the edge, paused stationary in the blue air, and then began to fall soundlessly, like so many winged seeds, through the softly freezing dusk.

After this conversation Little Eddie entered a period of genuine confidence and relief with his son. He hoped now that the matter of the hospital was settled between them; and would not be opened again until some date far in the future (adolescence perhaps). And he also had the feeling that some important transaction had taken place between them out on the terrace, and that although he had lied, he had somehow 'levelled with' or been 'straight' with Mikey at the same time, and that this should earn him a new and better relationship.
For some time, his hope seemed justified. After their con-

versation Mikey relaxed with him. He took to searching out his father's company more, and volunteering all sorts of information about himself, his teachers, friends, football games, career plans, favourite foods and dinosaurs. He seemed to find it quite exciting to have a man in the house, and wanted to copy the things that his father did. They developed hobbies together: knocking a ball about the park on a Sunday afternoon, building a bookcase together or going to the cinema. Mikey would even trail his father to the doorway of the bathroom, and watch with fascination as he shaved. 'What is that stuff, Dad? Your beard?'

'Stubble, Mikey, it's called stubble. You'll have some one day. And then you'll have to shave.'

'YUK! Never! Disgusting!' he said.

But for several days afterwards, Little Eddie noticed him putting up a careful hand to his chin, testing cautiously, in almost hopeful anticipation of a few stray hairs.

The conversation between them seemed to have so calmed Mikey on the question of his father that he felt liberated into becoming a child again. It was as if Little Eddie had passed a test, and was permitted to take on the role of the responsible male adult of the house. And now Mikey could become a boy again. He laughed and ran and squalled and stamped. He threw tantrums and became capricious and crazily fun-loving. He lost his pale watchful look, that look of a little oriental gentleman too old for his years, and became more youthful. His face filled out, and he got quite chubby.

Little Eddie had never been happier. For the first time in his life, he felt as if he was in control of himself, with a set of aims and objectives which it was realistically possible for him to satisfy. He was a husband, a father, and a bread-winner. All right, so he wasn't making a packet – and certainly, they couldn't afford any of the things that many of the people around them had, like a decent car, or furniture or holidays – but he was employed. He could pay all the basic bills, and get food on the table. He was stacking up to something.

He now avoided the old haunts where he might meet up with former friends who would be talking about jobs and casinos and nightclubs and cars. He didn't need any of that. They would all mock him, his seedy jeans and plastic watch, his little job at the market, and his two-pint limit. 'Come on!' they would say to him. 'You're suckering yourself. Drudging away for eighty pounds a week, when there's boys in the city making thousands every week. Don't do it – don't treat yourself like that.' And they would offer him a part in some 'job' or other, just out of pity.

But Little Eddie didn't need all that. He would just ignore them. He didn't need the fear and the thrills; the hole-in-the-corner lifestyle, and the knock at the door. He didn't need the break-up of his family, and thousands more nights staring at the sick brown paint on a cell wall, and spilling his seed into a prison-issue blanket. He was through with it. (Because, of course, they were all losers in the end. Losers, and self-destroyers. In all his life of petty crime, Little Eddie had met only a handful of people who had the real self-respect, the real hard-headedness, to try and succeed with their crime. Most of the people he knew were just joy-riding, financing some addiction or other, till they crashed and got a bed in casualty, which is what he sometimes thought they were all secretly looking for.)

So Little Eddie kept clear of this world, and instead he concentrated on his family, and in particular Mikey. And Mikey amply repaid the care. He was such a bright child, happy and hard-working and successful. Already, he knew far more than his father had ever known in his life. He knew that the plates on the Stegosaurus were there to cool down its overheating blood, that Saturn was the planet with many rings, and that eight times eight make sixty-four, something Little Eddie still had to think about carefully before answering.

It seemed to him extraordinary that he should have such a son. He, such a dunce at school, should have such a smart son, going off to school each morning with his satchel bobbing on his back and regularly scoring ten out of ten in the tests.

He was bursting with pride of him; and just as he reached the point of accepting the limitations of his own life – he was a barrow-boy basically, in the low-income bracket, and not the tycoon he had once dreamed – he determined that the life of his son should have none. No constraint of time, education, or money would hamper Mikey. He would have all the things that Little Eddie never had; the best of everything. He would have all the books, the ties and blazers, the footballs and cars, and visits to museums or zoos, that his young life seemed to need. And if he and Kath had to do without themselves, then so be it. He was going to bring his son up properly. Make a good job of it, even if it did cost him. So Little Eddie did a lot of overtime to cope with the demands that were made of him – for children at school these days seemed to need a lot of very expensive things – and he and Kath ate simply, and rarely went out. But they were happy. Mikey rewarded them with his youth, his brightness, his confidence, and success. They were content.

And then one day it all changed.

Little Eddie came home that day from work, and found the flat dark and Kath in a great state of anxiety, summoning a doctor on the phone. There were none of the usual signs of order: the smell of the evening meal coming through from the kitchen, and the picture of Mikey sitting very straight at the table doing his homework.

'What is it?' he said in panic when Kath put down the phone.

'It's Mikey,' she said. 'He's sick. He's got some terrible pain, but he won't even talk about it. I'm just getting the doctor. Would you go and see him, Eddie,' she added. 'I'm really worried – and he won't even talk to me.'

Little Eddie took the stairs two at a time, and went straight into Mikey's room. The room was in semi-darkness and at first he found it a little difficult to focus. Then he began to make things out. His son was a tiny figure in bed, a little embryo curled up under the blankets. Above his head loomed a poster of Tyrannosaurus Rex, reared on its hindlegs, with its great maw gaping wide for smaller creatures; and there were cars and books scattered everywhere on the floor.

'What is it, Mikey?' said Little Eddie, sitting down beside

him on the edge of the bed. 'What's wrong with you? Please tell me.'

For a long time Mikey did not answer, and Little Eddie had to repeat his question. Mikey lay small and silent in the bed, pale and motionless. His thumb was held perilously close to his mouth; and his eyes were downcast. But Little Eddie thought that he could detect their expression: something hard and hurt and hostile. And he thought he could detect a trace of tears on his cheek.

'What is it, son? Please tell me where the pain is – I can't do anything about it unless you tell me where it is.'

And then again, when there was still nothing: 'Point it out to me, Mikey. Show me where it is. Please.'

There was such a long silence, Little Eddie was about to give up and try some new tack, when he noticed the beginning of a movement. A small fist appeared out of the top of the bedcovers and travelled slowly to a spot on the left of his chest, just above the heart. There it came to rest.

'Near your heart?' Little Eddie asked.

There was a nod, listless and self-pitying.

'A sort of burning pain, just above your heart?'

Mikey nodded again, more strongly this time.

Eddie thought for a moment, then sighed and leaned back.

Mikey began to snuffle, soggy, hopeless infantile tears.

'Son,' Little Eddie said gently. 'When did this come on, this pain?'

There was another silence.

'Eh, Mikey? When did it begin?'

Again Little Eddie had to wait. But this time, he didn't have to wait so long. Mikey's face began to move; every little muscle in it seemed to gather and ripple, in preparation for an explosion. Little Eddie leaned forward to hear better, but needn't have bothered, as what followed was very audible, emerging in a long impassioned rush.

'Bill Brewer and Andy Manser and Dicky Boyd and Joe Mullins have all got Adidas Flash trainers and I ain't they says I've only got scummy second-hand Reboks 'cos my Dad's a gaolbird and he can't afford no Adidas, only Rebok and that's what they wear in prison, I beat up Dicky Boyd and took his trainers they all beat me up and says my Dad's a filthy con and I want Adidas Flash and I don't want no scummy Rebok –'

This was followed by a burst of louder snuffles, fluent and indignant, and full of self-pity and indignation.

Little Eddie flinched, and took a long breath. The question of the trainers again . . .

Now, with a sense of drowning, he groped for words, while Mikey's snuffles got less, and he looked at his father with an increasingly sharp and demanding curiosity.

'And that's when the pain started in yer chest, eh? . . .' said Little Eddie finally, his hands fluttering nervously over his pockets, and his eyes unable to meet those of his son.

An expression of profound amazement now entered into the boy's face. His mouth fell open and the snuffling was arrested in an instant. The silence in the darkened room now became tangible, and passed back and forth between them like some current of immense voltage.

'I . . . I . . . it's just . . . we can't afford –' began Little Eddie, but the sight of his son's expression made him stop dead, and he drifted off aimlessly, still unable to meet his eye.

After a few more seconds' silence staring at his father, Mikey suddenly burst into howls. And this time his howls were for real; not weak and manipulative and infantile, but the tears of someone suffering a real grief, who knows that he is alone in it, and that no one can comfort him.

'ARRY 'AD AN 'ORSE

Louise Lear

Louise Lear is a fire breather and juggler who (according to her last employer) is used to not getting paid. In the past she has worked in the film industry, spent five years as an artist's model and currently is apprenticed to a cabinet-maker.

Louise says that most of the material for her stories comes from the somewhat accident-prone lives of those around her but confesses that she has been known to draw on personal experience as well.

'ARRY 'AD AN 'ORSE

Actually, it wasn't the horse that Old Harry had, but the box the beast came in that we needed. You know – one of those big trailer affairs with a ramp, and doors, and a roof on – so's we could move a piano.

Except that it wasn't a piano, as such, but a huge pianola. A great black ugly thing it was, and Our Nan hated it, with a passion. She mainly hated it because it were in her house, and Our Dad treated her house (and ours, and her shed, and her outhouse) like an extension of his pockets. All full of bits-o'-string-and-sealing-wax, not to mention his rubber-band collection, and the twelve old alarm clocks . . .

You see, Our Dad can't abide to throw anything out. He feels sorry for it, and he keeps it.

Anyway, one day, the factory where he works decided to get rid of their pianola. They'd got a good piano for the works choir, and they didn't want the pianola anymore. Of course, nobody actually wanted to *buy* it, and it got wheeled out into the yard to be broken up before they carted it off to the tip.

Da-deedle-da-dee-DAAH! (That's a fanfare, you have to sing it.) Out rushed Father, the Overalled Crusader, the one-and-only Captain Crud, threw himself upon the ill-starred instrument and volunteered to take it home.

Fourteen blokes, forty Players Weights and a block-and-tackle later, and there he was leaping from a flat-bed truck with arms full of paper-rolls-with-'oles-in, and a daft great grin fit to bust his face.

Having informed us all that we were now the proud possessors of a rare and wondrous thing, Our Dad, his Mates, The Bear, Big Ted, Mrs Braithwaite's Lodger and a few besides ran about with ramps, bricks, planks, wedges, two bell-ropes and a blanket, and eventually, with a little help from the natural gravitational pull, the thing was on the ground.

Well, the blokes were all cheering and hooting, and Our Nan was going crackers saying where was it to go, and what did it have to come here for, and they were all pushing it and shoving it up the front path and up the ramp they'd made for the front steps – and they stopped. 'She inner goin' in thur, Mon,' said Mrs Braithwaite's Lodger. 'Nope. Dunner fit, that 'un,' said another, 'it's a big bugger, that.' They all nodded, scratched under their caps, and smoked some more while Our Dad fetched a tape-measure.

Our Nan ran out with ashtrays to save the flower borders.

Dad came back with the measure.

The suspense while he measured first the door, and then the pianola was amazing! We all held us breath. You could've heard a pin drop!

Our Nan diagnosed the problem instantly. 'It's half an inch wider than the door,' she snapped, and slammed it, as if that might be that.

'Right!' the men chorused, and promptly took the door out, and the frame, and then did the same to the front room!

Nan took it really well. She rolled her eyes up, and went 'Tut', just like that, and slammed the back-room door too.

'Ar!' said Our Dad, with a grin, 'thee knowst what 'er is,' and stuffed the pianola in the front room.

There was never any beer at our house, and so all the men went home then, as I think they might have had an idea that Our Nan (and Our Ma too when she came in), might not have been too chuffed with things. I was a bit disappointed, because they were all good fun, and took us rides in lorries and that, and you never got a wallop when they were round.

Nan boiled some milk over and we all had half a cup of coffee.

Ma came home and did a lot of 'What's *that*'-ing before she flew completely off the handle and called Our Dad a silly old sod.

Our Dad was saying nowt. He just sat there with 'is eyes on full beam, fingering the rolls of paper. Our Ma slammed the back-room door too, seeing as how it were the only one left, and went to join our Nan.

'Pearls before swine, me Titchums, pearls before swine . . .' said Our Dad, putting his arms around me and my horrible little brother, Robert.

'I heard that,' said Ma, materializing from nowhere, and quick as you like she'd run upstairs, fetched a pillow and Dad's pyjamas and threw them at him. 'If you're *that* taken with the thing you can bloody well kip with it!' she snapped, and then looked all confused because there was no door to slam.

Our Dad put the doors back, with a bit of struggling and swearing, because they seemed to have got bigger since they were taken out, and then showed us how to work the pianola. It was really hard! There were little doors in the front where the paper rolls went, and Our Dad explained that the holes in the paper told the pianola which notes to play. There was a flap in the front of the keyboard, and one at the bottom too. That was where two enormous pedals came out, and we all took turns at pedalling to make it play. Me and Our Robert weren't big enough but Our Dad made it play song after song, and we laughed to see all the keys going up and down by themselves.

Of course, this charming family fireside scene didn't last. It wasn't long before Ma decided that me and Our Robert were taking sides with Our Dad, and she found me three pounds of mucky carrots to scrape for tea. It's not fair!! I *always* get the kitchen jobs, and Our Robert never has to do anything like that, just for being a boy! But for an accident of birth, I could've stayed with me Dad while Our Robert stood in the cold, stripping his nails along with the vegetables. He's a spoilt little prawn is Our Robert.

Anyway, we weren't allowed to stay up much after we'd had tea. I got to help with the dishes, naturally, while the Prawn had an early bath. Normally I'm allowed to watch a bit of telly after tea, but this particular night Ma suddenly announced that I had black eyes and had better go to bed!

I think she had a cheek, myself, but I went anyway and lay listening to Our Dad pedalling away with the pianola wheezing in time (because it had a hole in one of its bellows) and he was playing and singing lots of really old songs I didn't know. They were still going around in my head when I woke up next morning and I was full of it!

'*We've* got a pianola,' I said, on the way into school.

'*We* know,' said Paula Braithwaite. 'Mummy's guest helped your Dad unload it.'

''E's yer lodger!' yelled Our Robert, and smacked her! Nobody knew properly what to do then. She couldn't hit him back, because he was still only in the babies' class, and everyone knew you couldn't hit the little 'uns. I was really chuffed with him, for the first time ever, and it must've showed because she pinched me really hard and said she wasn't going to mix with my sort anymore. Then she came back and said, 'At least *we* have our own house', all sneery and horrid, and flounced off again.

Well, I didn't care. Anyone could see she were only jealous, and besides, she'd flounced around so much that her starched frock was all up on itself at the back and we could all see this funny little birthmark she's got and never wanted anyone to look at. So I nudged Jenny Bullen and Kate Price, and we all chanted, 'We can see yer birthmark! We can see yer birthmark!' until she found out why and ran into the girls' toilets, screeching like Old Nick himself was after her . . . and that's where she really got some come-uppance!

P'raps I'd do better to tell you about our school toilets just now. They were dead old, like the school, and in a little brick outhouse round the back. There was a boys' half, and a girls' half (of course), and cubicles in each half. The seats were wide wooden planks with smooth holes in them, and they didn't flush. The reason they didn't flush was because the water just kept running through a gully in the whole lot, and so they lent themselves very well to some pretty horrible tricks.

I suppose you can guess the next bit, but I'll tell it anyway. It was Jenny's big brother who did the deed. Jimmy was a junior, not a middle infant like us, and didn't normally walk with us lot. We looked into his face, and just *knew* we were witnessing the birth of a notion. All of a sudden he legged it into the dunnies, brandishing their dad's Zippo lighter. Two minutes later there was a lot more screeching and Paula Braithwaite erupted into the yard not caring anymore who saw what!

'Wodja do, Our Jimmy?'

Jimmy zipped the Zippo. 'Two yards o' bog roll,' he said, and scarpered quick.

In class we all had to tell our news. Paula was drivelling on with some slop about their cat's latest batch of kittens.

'Eeooh!' she smarmed, 'they're *minute*!'

'Hush everyone,' said Miss with her hand to her ear and her head on one side. 'Did you all hear that?' Anybody'd think she'd heard the first cuckoo; but no, she was just being impressed by Paula saying 'minute'. Wow. I were so taken aback I forgot to gasp.

I said, '*We've* got a pianola, Miss,' but Miss just looked a look and I think I might as well have said, 'We've all got rickets-nits-and-lice' for all the interest she took.

Still, the news got round, and pretty soon *everyone* was round our house to see the pianola. 'Ooh, it's criminal what some people will just throw away' they all took turns at saying, and I giggled at the idea of 'just throwing' that great thing anywhere. 'Oh yes,' said Mrs Parslow, 'that does bring back some memories.' Of course, Our Ma had to pretend to be pleased with it now the neighbours were in, and I suppose it had pretty much earned its space in the front room.

Soon enough, funny Miss Evason was round. 'Can I see it?' she asked, all round-eyed and craning, so we let her in.

She ran her hands all over the pianola, but never actually touched it and said something about feeling strong vibrations. I was just putting that down to the railway line that ran up the backs when she opened her bag and took out the black velvet bag she kept her cards in. They were odd for playing-cards, but I thought they were lovely although I was never allowed to look at them properly. Our Nan said I mustn't, and that they were made of tallow, or something like that, but I think she must've been wrong.

Miss Evason was talking. 'I can feel it speaking to me,' she said, and her voice was all husky and quiet (Woodbines, Our Dad said). She had a way of looking at you that made you go all squirmy, and she did it then. 'I feel many things here, many emotions . . .' She tapped the pianola. 'There are discordant beginnings, but its intention is only to please.'

By this time Our Robert's chin was on the mat, and I was ever so glad when Our Nan came in and gave Miss Evason a rickets-nits-and-lice look. Miss Evason worked her mouth round into a smile, said, 'There won't be any charge for this reading,' picked up her cards and gloves, and left.

Reading? I call it stating the obvious! What's a pianola for, if not to please people? As for the discordant bit, well, with all that pushing and shoving and clattering about on a lorry, it were bound to need tuning, wasn't it? Our Nan said she didn't mean that, and it was just her way of saying that she knew everyone'd rowed about it. (Honestly, why can't Miss Evason just be snide like all the other neighbours?)

Some time after all this, Our Ma and Dad started having a lot of 'money' conversations, and one day they said they'd saved enough for us to have a house of our own.

Our Robert said what did we need another house for, and what was wrong with where we lived? I agreed with him, but the grown-ups all knew best (as usual) and we started going out in the car a lot after tea, to look at other people's houses. (You can be really nosey in other people's houses when you want to buy one of your own! They let you look in their bedrooms and outhouses, and just anywhere at all you might feel like looking, and nobody seems to think it's rude! I can just imagine what Our Nan would have had to say if strangers had just walked in and had a look to see how big her airing cupboard was!)

Ma and Our Dad had a lot of arguments too, mostly about which way to go, and whose fault it was that we were lost. I said, what was the point in buying a house if you couldn't find your way home again once you lived in it, and Our Ma told me to keep me nose out. Our Robert just sat quiet and picked his. (I wish he wouldn't do that; it'll go all baggy one day, doing that with it.)

Anyway, they must've thought I had a point, because when they did buy a house it were only two streets away from Our Nan's, so we could just sort of flit between the two.

Dad started to have all his mates around again, and they talked about moving furniture and scratched their heads a lot. I thought, 'Why? We haven't got any furniture, except the pianola,' but we had you know, and it were all hidden away!

Out of other people's lofts and cellars it came, *and* out of garages, outhouses and sheds! For years it seemed, Our Dad had been collecting furniture against the day when he'd have a house to put it in.

Our Nan kept dropping hints when the men were round, like, 'I expect you'll be wanting these doors out soon,' and 'I hope the weather keeps fine if you're going to be taking these doors out again,' but what she didn't know was that they weren't taking the doors out. They weren't moving the pianola at all! You see, the factory choir had bought a new, modern piano; one that wasn't so tall so that the lady who played for them could look over the top at the men, and Our Dad, true to form, had bought the old one for a fiver and stuck it in the shed!

Well! There were ructions in our house when he told us! Our Nan went up the wall, and Our Ma followed not far behind. I thought it was a nice piano. It had roses on it, in a different wood, and little swivelly brass candlesticks. It was every so pretty, really, and I felt sorry for it, being unwanted and unloved an' all. I bet funny Miss Evason would have had something to say!

'You're not your father's daughter for nowt,' said Our Nan, when she found me sitting under it, crying into me frock. 'Well, never mind – the pianola can stop where it is. With you lot gone there'll be plenty of room for it as well as me, and you'll have the piano at your house.'

The piano looked very fine in our front room, all polished with the china dogs on top. It also had two gruesome pictures of me and Our Robert when we were babies, which I felt it would have been better without. Still, there's no accounting for taste, is there?

We also had *two* grandfather clocks (one in the hall and one in the front room), three wall clocks, five mantelpiece clocks, two carriage clocks and one of those pretty ones with the spinning balls in a glass dome. Most of these were in the front room, and we weren't allowed in there much, except on Sundays. We got a lodger of our own too.

Next day, I caught up with Paula Braithwaite on the way to school. 'You can talk to me now,' I said. 'We've got our own house now, and a piano, and our own lodger.'

I must've looked daft standing there smiling at her, because she just looked disgusted and skipped off.

In class, when Miss asked for our news, I said, 'We've got our own house now, Miss!' and saw her eyes roll up so I added, '*And* it's got a bathroom!' because I knew her house still didn't have one. She made me take the bins out.

Well, we all jogged along, living our lives and wishing for summat else for a year or two, until Our Nan started to get restless over the pianola again.

'Ar, arr,' said Our Dad, 'Arr', and then, 'Arr, I'll make some enquiries', but you could tell he didn't mean to. There was no room for it at our house, and he didn't want to sell it.

'But Mum,' he said one day, 'this room's crammed full of things we've all found and brought home.'

'Exactly,' said Our Nan. 'It's crammed full o' things.'

'From travels abroad,' said Our Dad. He was right too. There were pictures of Egypt, India, China, and Brazil. There was a piece of rock from the Pyramids, a Dragon Lamp, a set of Japanese tables, a French clock and a German nut-cracker. Nan gestured round the room. 'From your Father's travels abroad,' she said, and pointed at the pianola. 'They built that in Birmingham.'

'I had to go out and get it though, didn't I?'

'Only from your works yard! You've never been further than Nottingham, and I was pregnant with you then!'

'Well, that's abroad.'

'How?'

'Well, what about Hallowe'en?'

'What about it?'

'If we said the "night when spirits walk abroad" and meant they were taking a stroll in St Tropez the kids'd have nowt t'be making anything of!'

And they say my arguments are daft! Well, it were the reasoning of a desperate man, wasn't it? 'It *must* have a good 'ome,' he kept saying, and I cried for it, because I didn't want it to go anywhere either. I asked if they couldn't wait for me to grow up and then the minute I was old enough I'd get a job and a house big enough for me *and* the pianola, but they all said, 'Oh, you don't want that old thing,' and told me not to be so soft and to get off to Sunday School else I'd be late.

In Sunday School, the Vicar talked about the power of prayer. He said the War was won with prayers, and that a man in South Wales had got loads of people to ask God to turn the Germans back, and when they got to Russia he made it snow (I expect it was easier to do it there) and they did. The Vicar said you could ask God for anything you wanted, and if you wanted it enough, he'd answer you.

So I prayed very hard to God, not to let Our Dad sell the pianola, but the answer must've been 'No' because one day he said, 'I think I've found a good 'ome for that old joanna round me Mum's,' and I crossed all my fingers, and then myself, and thought, 'Oh *please* God, don't let him do it!', but he did.

Dad put on his long mac, and his best cap. 'You'd best come with me,' he said, 'and make sure you approve of this new home it's getting.' Then he took his cap off again and said, 'Seeing as how it's just you and me, how about we go on the bike?'

Well, why ask? I'd go anywhere for a ride on Our Dad's old motor-bike, wouldn't I? So I ran upstairs and changed into warm clothes and was back in our yard quicker than anything. The bike was a big old BSA, and he swung me up on to the back, kicked it over a few times, and then we were off, thumping out into the countryside with me hanging on to his belt.

We came to a town, built up both sides of a deep gorge, with a river running at the bottom. The sides of the gorge were so steep that the houses looked as if they were all piled up on top of one another. The road zigzagged up, and when you stood in front of one of the houses in the back streets, you were looking straight across at the roofs of the houses in front. In some places there were steps up between the houses to the next bit of road, and in some places there was no road at all – only steps! We found the house where the pianola was going without having to try to get the bike up any steps, but the road was so narrow, I thought, 'We'll never get a lorry up here.'

I said, 'Dad, we'll never get a lorry up here.'

'Arr, well,' he said, 'perhaps we shan't have to use anything quite so big,' and knocked on the door.

A young man opened it, and seemed pleased to see us. I liked his house. It was a bit dark inside, and cram-packed full of things he'd collected off the railway, like a huge sign that said 'Whistle' and some old signals. He had lanterns too, and on the kitchen door a brown and cream sign that said 'Buffet Car'. He and Our Dad talked about railways, and how it wasn't the same now they only had diesel locomotives. The young man said I could look around the house if I liked, and told me where to find some good books. When I knew it was going to get a bit boring (when I heard Our Dad say, 'I've always been a GWR man myself . . .'), I did.

Like I said, I liked his house, and felt better about the pianola going there as he obviously felt the same way about throwing stuff out as Our Dad – but I still couldn't quite see how we might get it there.

It was nearly dark when we left, and we were hungry, so Dad bought some chips. We found a bench by the river and ate them there. 'What do you reckon?' he asked, and I told him that I didn't mind the young man having our pianola, now that I knew it really was a good home, but how was it to get there?

'Oh I shouldn't worry about that,' said Our Dad. 'We'll cross that bridge when we come to it.' He sounded so cheerful, but I couldn't help thinking that if there really was a bridge, we might not have to worry at all.

A few days later, all Our Dad's mates were filling the house again, discussing the best way to move the pianola. Our Nan popped in and called them all 'a bunch of bloody-minded optimists', then went to get her hair done.

'Well, we canner fit a truck up thur,' said Mrs Braithwaite's Lodger, 'but 'asn't 'Owd 'Arry got that 'orse box?'

'Arr, that might do it,' said someone else, and they all took turns agreeing with him, and then went round to Harry's house, saying, 'We mun go'n ask 'im,' and 'Arr, we atter ask 'im soon.'

The posse must've been successful, because the next weekend everyone was round Our Nan's house. The horse-box was out in the road, and they'd borrowed a car modern enough to tow it. Nan kept smiling, and Our Robert got in everyone's way, and the men set to and took the doors out. Very carefully, they eased the pianola out on to the path, and, with the usual collection of levers, ropes and blankets, loaded it into the horse-box. I cried. The men put Our Nan's doors back.

Harry and Mrs Braithwaite's Lodger were just about to shut the horse-box when Our Dad shouted to them not to.

I said a quick prayer. 'Oh *please*, God! Make him change his mind!', but Our Dad only said, 'I think I'll just have one last little play . . .' and climbed in the horse-box with it. He pedalled out a few old dance tunes, but I didn't much feel like dancing any more.

'Right!' said Our Dad, emerging from the box a while later, 'let's get a move on, shall we?' and plonked me on the bike like *we'd* been the ones who were holding up the big move!

Harry, Mrs Braithwaite's Lodger and three others got into the car. Our Dad followed with me, on the bike, and behind us were two more cars, full of Our Dad's mates, including The Bear in his big old Rover. The horse-box didn't go very fast, and it felt like we were all going to a funeral.

Ages later, much longer than it had taken us before, we arrived at the town where the young man lived. Everyone stopped in the main street and got out.

'Where to now?' said Harry. Dad pointed. 'Bloody 'ell! 'Ow's 'e go on then? 'E'm livin' on a shelf!' Our Dad never turned a hair. 'There's a road up,' he said, 'it inner bad, but you might 'ave to back 'er up.'

They examined the turning and reached a verdict. 'Atter back 'er,' they said, and Mrs Braithwaite's Lodger, with much shouting-of-encouragement and waving from the others, turned the car and horse-box around.

It was the first time I'd got a good look at the car they were using. It was a huge *purple* Vauxhall Cresta, with flames and chains painted over the bonnet and wings, and a great, bleeding, broken heart in the middle, with a dagger. It looked as if it might have once belonged to a crazed tattoo artist, and Harry got ribbed about it something chronic from everybody except The Bear, who took his shirt off to show us the same pictures on his back. He called it 'corporeal artistry'. I didn't say anything. I was just too gobsmacked. Miss has a word for things like that. 'Ignominious', I think she calls it.

Eventually, when they'd all stopped carrying on and taking the rise out of each other, Harry got back into the car and began to back the trailer very carefully up the hill. The first couple of bends weren't too bad, but at the third we were glad of The Bear's extra muscle to help bounce the horse-box round a bit. A little way further and the thing wouldn't fit.

'Mind my bloody box!' yelled Old Harry, even though he was driving, and stopped. The road was so narrow he had to walk along the top of somebody's back-yard wall to get past the horse-box. 'Another foot an' I'da bin stuck thur,' he said, like it were our fault.

'Arr, dunna worry, Mon – get the brake on,' said Our Dad. 'We can wheel 'er from 'ere.' Mrs Braithwaite's Lodger produced a trolley from the back (or was it the front?) of the horse-box. 'Emergency measure,' he said.

So out came the ropes and the blankets, and the pianola was hauled out on to the trolley, and up they went. Some pulled, with ropes over their shoulders, and some pushed from behind. Harry said he was too old for all that, and stayed with the horse-box, and smoked. I didn't blame him. It was hard enough work getting myself up the hill, but the men were all sweating cobs. The Bear and Big Ted started to sing the 'Hovis' advert, and I wished we *were* going home, and had a quick nag to God about it.

God mustn't have been too busy just then, because the pianola got stuck! The road got narrower and narrower, until it just wouldn't fit any more. Out came the Players as the men stopped for a breather. Everyone at the back clambered across the back-yard walls to get to the front, except for me because Big Ted swung me up on to the pianola (and frit me half to death doing it, I don't mind saying) for The Bear to swing me down again.

Well, when a thing's too big for the doorway, you can always take the frame out, but when it's too big for the street, you can't go taking people's back-yard walls down, can you?

Mrs Braithwaite's Lodger walked up the street a little way. 'It widens out a bit up here,' he said. Someone produced a tape measure, and measured the street. Then they measured the pianola, and then they measured the street again. 'It's wider up here,' they all agreed.

''Ow about . . .' began The Bear, who wasn't given to talking much. ''Ow about, if we could get some wood, and a bit o' summat to 'old 'er, and if we could lever 'er up a bit, 'ow about if we lift 'er up ower this bit?' Then he added, 'An' put 'er down again. Ower thur. In the wide bit.' I think that was just about the most that The Bear had ever said! The men were all nodding slowly, trying to pull the words out of him. When they were all absolutely sure that no more were coming, some of them said 'Arr' a bit, all thoughtful, and Our Dad went all round-eyed and looked over the little wall into the cavernous drop to someone's back-yard.

Big Ted clapped him between the shoulder-blades, nearly sending him down! 'Arr! Dunner worry, Mon! We wunner drop yer pianola for yer!', but Our Dad just looked down at the dustbins and had another smoke.

Mrs Braithwaite's Lodger joined him. 'It's a steep 'un, this gorge. Look at the cracks in that wall – this whole town's sliding into the river, slowly!'

'So long as I'm at 'ome when it goes,' said Our Dad, and turned his back on the drop.

'So, about this instrument o' yourn,' said one of the men, to bring his attention back to where it was needed.

'It's iron-framed!'

'Well arr, but we got 'er on a lorry once, didn't we?' said Big Ted, clapping an arm around Our Dad's shoulders. Our Dad suddenly looked much smaller than I'd remembered him.

The men turned their attention to devising a way to lift the pianola up and over the narrowest part of the road, without actually paying any attention to the pianola, if you see what I mean. Which is when I noticed that it wasn't stuck quite so fast as anyone thought.

'Er, Dad . . .' I said.

' 'Ush a minute, Titch.'

'But Dad!'

' 'Ush up a minute!'

'Dad!! She ain't stuck!!'

I was too late. The pianola took this as its cue to work free of the walls and to make off home by itself.

'Bugger!' said one of the men, and a great shout went up as they all took off down the road after it, nearly shoving me off my perch on the wall as they went. I ran too, as fast as I could, but I didn't really want to know!

The pianola was still flapping bits of blanket and its ropes of course, and the men were all after grabbing these. The Bear, whose weight and size must've been pretty close to the pianola, was elbowing his way through *everybody*, and, with a final body-blow to Mrs Braithwaite's Lodger, he threw himself at it in the best flying tackle I think I've ever seen!

Big Ted followed suit and caught hold of The Bear, and then just about all of them were leaping into the fray. One or two fell off on the way, but The Bear had the pianola by a leg, and slowly, very slowly, it began to waltz about in the road.

'We'm got the bugger!' yelled a voice, and then everyone started shouting instructions.

'Get round the front!'

'Gerroff me face!'

'Cop 'owd o' them ropes!'

'Wedge the bugger!'

The men started to untangle themselves and get to their feet. The pianola began to slip again, but The Bear, scarlet by now, was still hugging the leg to his cheek. He gave an extra squeeze but they were coming to a bend and the pianola swung round on itself, jamming its back to a stone wall that was holding up someone's front garden. The garden's owner, shears hanging limply in his hands, surveyed the scene below. Nobody spoke.

The pianola slid a bit more, and left its blankets behind. This was followed by a horrible tearing sound, as the hessian backing began to rip.

As it happened, the stone that did the damage stopped the pianola in its flight, as it jammed against a strut which ran up the middle of the pianola's back. Carefully, the men eased it off the wall to have a look.

It wasn't too bad really. The hessian was hanging off in all directions, and the wood was scratched – well, gouged would be nearer the mark, but it was only on the back, and not beyond repair.

Our Dad started to laugh. He put his head back and roared, but I swear he'd rather have sat and cried. They were all standing like this, giggling and shaking, with their clothes and knees all in ribbons when Old Harry came trudging up the bank to see what was going on.

'Bugger it, Mon!' he grunted. 'It's a bloody 'oming device – you weren't meant t'be rid of it!'

'Arr, tek 'er 'ome,' said Mrs Braithwaite's Lodger, and with a lot more care than they'd ever taken before, they loaded the pianola back into the horse-box.

They were a sorry sight when they went up to tell the young man. All bloodied, and tattered, and dirty, they stood in the street and shuffled about.

'Errm, I dunner think you'm goin' t'git that pianola . . .' someone said. The young man looked confused. He opened the door wide, and we all piled in. The room was very dark with all of us in there, and The Bear and Big Ted had to stoop so as not to keep banging their heads on the ceiling.

When everybody had had a go at explaining, and they'd all commiserated with each other, the young man said that he made his own beer, and wouldn't everyone feel better for a jar. I thought, 'That's it! We're in here till Doomsday, now,' and went to sit on the stairs.

Ages, I waited, listening to the disaster stories being aired, trying to make the Vimto last. (That was a surprise – Vimto!

It's not a thing you'd expect as a rule, in a house with no kids. Mind you, single blokes do keep some odd things in their cupboards.)

Eventually, when they'd listed every derailment, every explosion, every landslip, crash and fire, it was time to go. I was amazed to walk out into bright sunshine – I thought it surely must've been dark by then – and stood blinking on the step, feeling as if I'd just woken up.

'Get a move on, Our Titch,' said Our Dad, and Mrs Braithwaite's Lodger said, 'Never you mind, Our Kid,' and gave me a piggyback down the hill.

Everyone piled back into the cars, and Our Dad kicked the bike over. Then they all got out again and went into a scrum. I think they were wondering what to tell Our Nan, but they couldn't have been too worried about it, because very soon we were all headed back home, this time with The Bear and Big Ted steaming on ahead.

By the time we arrived, Our Nan's doors were already out on the front, and Our Nan was on the yard wall so as to be high enough to give The Bear what for! She was furious!

When she was quite finished, The Bear cleared his throat, and then, very gently, lifted her down. She straightened her pinny and came stomping down the front path. Mrs Braithwaite's Lodger looked sideways at her. 'Should'a' left 'er up there,' he muttered, and they carried on unloading the pianola just the same.

Our Nan stood and eyed Our Dad up and down, taking in his ragged knees and elbows, and a bruise on his cheek.

'I like to think,' she began, 'that I am a patient, and reasonable woman, *BUT*,' she pointed at the pianola, 'it would make me very happy to see the back of *that*!'

Everyone was very quiet. Our Dad cleared his throat. 'Well, er . . .' He grinned. 'Well, you'd best come and stand round 'ere a minute!' Nan grunted and walked round the pianola to join him. Dad whipped the blanket off and gestured in grand music-hall style at the torn hessian. 'There y'are, Mother! Rejoice!'

With a swift kick he got the trolley moving, and the sniggering mob started heaving and shoving it towards the house.

Laughing out loud now, Our Dad turned to face Our Nan, who was still standing, ramrod-stiff, on the pavement. He flung both arms wide, to the whole world. 'Rejoice!' he cried, and ran back to the horse-box for the paper-rolls.

'Ta very much, God,' I said.

SHREDS

Marion Mathieu

Marion Mathieu is a painter and was born in New York but has lived in Ireland since 1979. Her poetry has been published in *Women's Work*, *From the Harbour Mouth* and *Women's Work is Never Done*. In 1990 she won first prize in the Book Stop New Writers Awards and was runner-up in the IMAGE short story competition. Her paintings have been shown in many exhibitions and she has formed a group called 'Come Together' with three other women artists.

SHREDS

Struggling writers have a high mortality rate and 1979 had been a lousy year. Instead of committing suicide, I decided to get out of New York.

I moved to Dublin. In mid-December.

It had been raining all week and the bed and breakfast was costing a fortune. The sign in the window of Deegan's Newsagents said, 'Flat, Suit One Lady'.

The shadow of a man behind the counter did not look up.

'Brian. The flat.'

A younger man with a face like a weasel appeared from the back of the shop, gave me an appraising glance, and threw me a set of keys.

They were all marked: 'Front Door No. 38', 'Flat 4', 'Back Door'.

'Should I just let myself in?'

'No doormen here, love.'

I went back out on to the street and found a numberless door with several colours of paint peeling off it. The first key worked.

Three flights of sagging stairs led me to a dusty landing and Flat 4.

It was horrible.

I took it.

Horrible meant orange and yellow flowered wallpaper and a red paisley rug infested with silverfish.

I could deal with horrible.

Disgusting meant a communal toilet that didn't flush and a sink piled high with empty beer cans and the remains of a Chinese takeaway.

I had reservations about disgusting.

Unsafe meant a two-hundred-year-old building with floors that tilted so badly all the furniture had to be propped up on wooden blocks.

I tried not to think about unsafe.

The rent was ten pounds a week and the Deegans didn't ask me for a security deposit. I would find a job and get something better soon.

I moved in the next day. It wasn't much of a move. A portable typewriter, a few clothes, and several hundred letters were all that I had salvaged from a five-year relationship. Peter had been so fastidious. I wondered what he would think of this place.

I cleared the beer cans and takeaway boxes out of the sink and scoured it. The toilet was unspeakable and someone had recently thrown up in and around it. I poured boiling water down the loo until it approximated a flush and found an ancient mop in the hall closet. Everything still stank but it was marginally less repulsive than before. I put an 'Out of Order, Please Go Downstairs' sign on the toilet door.

Flat 3 was my neighbour on the landing and, I suspected, Grand Prize Winner of the Slob Sweepstakes.

Might as well start off friendly. I knocked on the door. No answer.

I was hoping to find an off-beat café or arty restaurant where I could wait on tables and meet intense young Dubliners.

Avant-garde employment was in short supply that winter.

I was down to three pounds and sixty pence the day I saw the ad. The Classifieds hadn't exactly been a goldmine, but I was desperate. Poseidon Freight was looking for 'an energetic young person' for 'general office duties, temporary position'. I was at least two stone overweight and twenty-nine years old. A man with a Northern accent answered the phone. He didn't ask my age and I didn't tell him my weight. When I asked what sort of qualifications the job required, he laughed.

'A trained monkey could do this job. The only thing is that

it's hard to get down here and we're not paying anything worth mentioning. Are you a Yank?'

'My mother is from Wexford. I'm an Irish citizen.'

'Relax, love. It's off the books.'

'When can I start?'

'Yesterday.'

I dug out my 'interview' outfit – a white blouse with a lace collar and a little red bow at the neck, a navy-blue woollen suit, and red pumps with medium-height heels. I stuffed my passport, a mouldy lipstick, a plastic hairbrush, a packet of tissues and what remained of my money into a shiny red handbag. I tied my hair back neatly with a navy and red polka-dot ribbon. A façade guaranteed to reassure the potential employer.

The flat was ice-cold. I was afraid to leave on the electric heater all night, so I took a hot bath and went to bed wearing a flannel nightgown, a sweatshirt, legwarmers, and woollen socks. Freezing to death in a garret was a romantic notion, but I still missed central heating.

The cold shook me awake at three a.m. I stared at the clock in disbelief, and wrapped the duvet around me. My teeth were chattering.

Tea. A cup of hot tea would help.

I leaned over, retrieved my bathrobe from the floor and pulled it over my shoulders. When I finally stopped shivering, I slipped on my shoes, grabbed the kettle, and stumbled out on to the landing. I collided with Annie Oakley.

'Jesus fucking Christ! You nearly knocked me down.'

'Sorry, sorry! I'm really out of it.'

'Yeah. You don't look so good.'

I blinked my eyes, but the image of a freckle-faced young woman wearing a cowgirl hat, boots, circle skirt, and western-style shirt, complete with tassels, did not go away. All she needed was a six-shooter, and she probably had one of those tucked away somewhere.

'I'm OK. It's just so cold.'

The apparition grabbed my hand and held it to her cheek.

'What do you mean, cold? You're a fucking corpse! Right. You're coming upstairs with me for a hot cup of tea. I'm Maureen but they all call me Mad Mo.'

'I'm Alice. Frozen Alice. Tea sounds good.'

She took the kettle from me, set it on the sink and put her arm around my shoulders. I broke away, grabbed the kettle, put it back in my room, locked the door, and rejoined her at the foot of the stairs.

'Careful, aren't you?'

'I'm very security conscious.'

'What the fuck are you doing here, then?'

I hadn't realized that I'd been living downstairs from Disneyland.

'Flat 5' didn't begin to describe Mo's fantasy world. Fairy-lights twinkled. Gold and silver garlands shimmered. Plush toys ran rampant. I spotted a plastic shrine to Bernadette of Lourdes and a Holy Water font. A tapestry of Pope John Paul II was overshadowed by a black velvet painting of Elvis Presley. Hideous dolls in satin dresses with matching hats and parasols had taken over the chairs. Through some oversight, a corner of a couch was clear. I sat down.

'I see you've already got your Christmas decorations up.'

Mo plugged in the 'coal effect' electric heater, filled up the kettle, switched on the television and tuned in the radio.

'Nope. Haven't had a chance, yet.'

I silently resolved to pay Mo a Christmas visit. My frozen limbs started to thaw out. Mo slipped a tape into the cassette player. It sounded like country and western music but it was hard to tell in the general din.

'That's the new one from Big Sky and the Ghost Riders.'

'Are they a band?'

Mo dropped a spoon.

'You've never heard of them? Didn't you ever hear "Roscommon Roads" or "Baby, I'm Your Daddy but Your Mammy's Heart is Cold?"'

'Nope.'

'No wonder you're so miserable-looking! Big Sky would warm you up in a hurry.'

'I'll stick to tea, thanks.'

'The ballroom's just around the corner. You should come with me some night.'

'Is that where you were tonight?'

'Yeah. But it was only the Connemara Cowboys.'

I tried not to laugh.

'I'm not really into that sort of thing.'

'Suit yourself. But you don't know what you're missing.'

Mo was eager to impart information. I found out that the inhabitant of Flat 3 was 'on the game', Mr Deegan was an old stiff, and his son Brian would rape you with his eyeballs. By the time I got back to my own flat, early light was seeping into the room. I lay down on the bed.

The alarm jangled me awake much too soon. Thursday morning. First day on the new job.

The 53A was a grimy single-decker. I gave a careful description of my intended destination to the driver. 'I'll let you know, love,' he grinned, handing me a ticket. 'You can't miss it.'

I sat next to a dirt-streaked window. We passed through a security gate and bounced over railway tracks. A sign welcomed us to Dublin Port and Docks.

The bus stopped and a group of weatherbeaten men wearing heavy coats with reflective strips got off. The only passengers left were myself and two teenaged girls in denim mini-skirts and high heels.

I ran up the aisle towards the driver.

'Have I missed it?'

'Didn't I tell you I'd let you know?'

We passed endless rows of warehouses before the bus finally jerked to a stop.

'There you go, love.'

'Thank you.'

I could hear the girls giggling as I stepped out of the bus and into a field of mud.

This couldn't be it. A few cars and trucks. Not a soul in sight. A ramshackle prefab and a rusting caravan.

A crudely painted sign was lying flat on the ground. My heart sank when I saw the words 'Poseidon Freight'.

I stood outside the door marked 'Office', searching for a tissue. My skirt and tights were splattered with mud and the heel of my shoe was coming off.

A barrel-shaped man wrenched the door open. His grey hair was parted in the middle and slicked back. The services of both braces and a cracked leather belt were required to hold up his baggy striped trousers. The pattern on his wide tie reminded me of cabbage leaves.

'How do you do, I'm Alice Sullivan, your temporary employee.'

'I'm James McManus, your temporary employer, and it's about fucking time.'

A Northern accent. The man on the phone.

'I'm terribly sorry. I thought I was supposed to start at 9 a.m.'

'I mean it's about fucking time they got somebody down here to clear all that shite out of the caravan.'

'I beg your pardon?'

'Didn't I tell you what you're going to be doing? No, I guess not, from the look of you. What are you supposed to be? A stewardess?'

He started to laugh, stepped down into the yard, and walked towards the caravan, motioning for me to follow. My loose heel disappeared into the mud. I retrieved it and hobbled after him. When he pulled open the door the entire caravan shook. Black plastic bags that appeared to be filled with refuse tumbled out on to the muddy field.

'That's it. Twelve years' worth of paperwork. It has to be shredded because it's confidential. The lads say they're too busy to do it and they'd only shove all the papers in at once and banjax the fucking machine anyway.'

'How long do you need me for?'

'As long as it takes. Ten pounds a day. Into your hand.'

'I'll get started right away, then.'

'Don't you want to meet the lads? That shite'll keep a few more minutes.'

I followed him back to the prefab, jammed my heel back on, stamped my foot to secure it, and scraped the top of my shoe on the cinderblock steps. So much for first impressions. The air was so smoky inside, they probably couldn't see me anyway. I fixed what I hoped was a bright smile on my face, blinked my eyes, and spoke towards what I dimly perceived to be desks.

'How do you do? I'm very pleased to meet you all.'

Laughter.

'Oh, the Yanks are coming, the Yanks are coming . . .'

'Put the caravans in a circle. Bleeding John Wayne's here.'

'Where's yer fuckin' manners? This is Alice Sullivan and she's going to be hauling all that shite out of the caravan. Now, Sullivan, what are you waiting for? We're not paying you to exchange pleasantries.'

I turned towards the door. An extra from 'Whatever Happened to Baby Jane?' blocked my way. My own outfit faded into the background. This no-longer-young woman was squeezed into a white brocade cocktail dress. Rhinestone jewellery glittered on her ears and wrists. Some medieval torturer had forced her orange-coloured hair into a combination of a beehive and a punk hairdo and jammed her swollen feet into silver high-heeled sandals. Her face was a blur of pancake make-up, turquoise eyelids, and scarlet lips.

She grabbed my arm with red-taloned fingers.

'Don't be afraid of the children, dear. I'll show you how to survive here.'

I could feel the gooseflesh rising.

'Thank you. I'd appreciate that.'

'Wonderful! Someone with a bit of class around here for a change! I've been starved for conversation with these ignorant brutes. We're going to be great friends, I can tell already. But then I can always sense things about people. I'm very good like that. My last husband was convinced that I was a psychic.'

As if on cue, the murky figures at the desks started heckling.

'No, Dymphna, you've got it all wrong. HE was a PSYCHO for marrying you!'

'Was that the fifth husband or the sixth husband, Dymphna?'

She threw back her head and delivered a throaty Bette Davis laugh. My arm was starting to ache.

Thank God for James McManus.

'Let the girl get by, Dymphna. We don't have time for your fucking foolishness.'

'Don't you mind, him, Alice. Since none of these clowns is going to introduce me, I'll introduce myself. I am Dymphna Highgate. I helped my late husband build this company and I know more about shipping than any man in this room. I've kept this place running for the last eighteen years. If there's anything you want to know, ask me.'

'Yeah, she'll be able to tell you all sorts of things, Alice.'

'Things they don't teach you at the American Embassy.'

'Ignore them, Alice. Well now, don't you think it's about time you started working? Bring in the first bag and I'll show you how to operate the paper shredder correctly. None of these creatures has a clue.'

I walked to the caravan, selected one of the smaller sacks, and dragged it towards the office. I swung open the door and pulled the bag through. A blast of cold air blew in after me, lifting papers off the desks and scattering them over the room.

'Fer fuck's sake, there go me fucking dockets!'

'Jaysus, Alice, would ye ever shut the fucking door.'

'Ah, now me fuckin' tea's all over the fucking dockets.'

'I'll call you back in a minute, Christy, it's bleeding Hurricane Hannah.'

I ran back, closed the door, knelt down and started picking the papers off the floor. The men sat and watched as I tried to stack the dockets neatly before handing them back.

'You missed one.'

'Ah look, it's Santy Claus!'

'What am I getting for Christmas, Santy?'

'I know what I want.'

'I know what I need.'

'I know what none of youse are fucking getting.'

The men started back to work. I dragged the sack over to the paper shredder. At least the air was a little clearer now.

I arrived home that evening in a state of shock.

Soup. A hot bath. A good night's sleep would help me face anything.

Two a.m. Noises out on the landing. A woman screamed.

'Jesus, God, no!'

A heavy weight crashed down the stairs. I heard glass breaking, then a man's voice.

'Fucking whore! Bitch! Cheat!'

Sobbing sounds.

I pounded my fists against the wall and yelled, 'Leave her alone!' Someone tore back up the steps and threw their full weight against my door. The panelling started to splinter.

'Mind your own fucking business.'

I ran to the window and screamed, 'Help! Police!'

The assault on my door ceased.

He spoke quietly in clipped tones. Almost an English accent.

'If you don't stop that right now, I'll shut you up for good. And no police will be around to help you.'

I stood with my back against the wall, trembling with cold and fear.

'That's better, love.'

Someone stumbled back up the stairs. A woman whispered through the keyhole, 'I'm OK. Please don't call the gardai. Everything's all right now.'

The man must have been standing right next to her.

'Sorry about that, love. Don't let us scare you. We're old friends. We're leaving now.'

The alarm woke me at 7 a.m. Back to work. I groaned and pulled the covers over my head. Then I remembered the previous night.

I ventured out to the sink. The window on the stairwell was broken. When I turned on the tap the door to Flat 3 opened. A puffy-faced young woman with short brown hair came out wrapped in a flannel bathrobe. There were dark rings under her eyes.

'You won't tell Mr Deegan about last night, will you?'

'What happened?'

'Ah, it was just an accident.'

'Who fell down the stairs?'

'I slipped.'

'Who broke the window?'

'Some kids must have seen the lights on and threw a rock through it.'

'Who was trying to break down my door?'

'My brother Christy thought it was the door to the loo.'

She crossed her arms, leaned against the doorframe, and stared at me defiantly. I flirted with the idea of challenging her, but her face was a mask.

'Look, I have to live here too. I won't tell Mr Deegan as long as it never happens again.'

'Christy will be around later. He'll fix the window and your door.'

'I don't want to meet him. He threatened me.'

'So go out tonight.'

'I shouldn't have to be afraid in my own home.'

'You moved into the wrong neighbourhood.'

'By the way, we've never been introduced. My name is . . .'

The door slammed shut.

It was time to go to work, anyway.

I swapped the suit for jeans, a sweatshirt, and hiking boots. Dymphna turned up her nose and sniffed. 'Oh my dear!', and there were predictable lumberjack jokes from the men but at least I was comfortable.

I made it through to the weekend, anyway.

The first thing I noticed when I got home that evening was that the window had been repaired.

The second was the new panel in my door.

How had 'Christy' managed that on his own?

*

Saturday morning. Clean-up time.

Brian Deegan spotted me coming out of the bathroom with a mop and bucket.

'Where'd you find those?'

'It's pretty obvious you don't know where they are.'

'That's women's work, love. We don't rent to girls for nothing.'

'You use that toilet. The dirt in there was petrified. What are we paying you rent for?'

'For a bed to sleep in that's convenient to city centre. At the cheapest prices in town. Don't expect room service.'

'A toilet that flushes would be nice. The one upstairs is broken.'

'Use this one.'

'For six flats? How about some repairs?'

'Your door's fixed up, isn't it?'

'I meant to ask you about that . . .'

'Hey, are you going to stand guard all day? I'm dying for a slash.'

'The floor's still wet. If the toilet upstairs was working, you could use that one.'

'The floor'll be a lot wetter if you don't let me by, Mrs Mop.'

He pushed past me and shut the door.

'No peeking, now.'

I carried the bucket back to my flat. Brian's flat Dublin accent was nothing like the ominous voice of the other night. But how had he known about my door?

It was a sunny afternoon, but I didn't have time for that. I set my typewriter up on the table. The Great American Novel would be born in this shabby flat. I started drinking coffee and reading through some of the letters I had carried with me from New York.

I was undecided about using my own name on the book. I didn't want to embarrass my family with the shocking disclosures about drugs and sex that were essential to the book's integrity. If I used a pen-name, however, Peter would probably never realize that I had torn our relationship apart in print. I wanted him to wince at my raw honesty.

By Saturday evening, I had hit my stride. I was inspired by an old letter referring to a party down in the Village. Peter had deserted me that night and I found myself in a designer loft, surrounded by complete strangers, drinking a toast to the health of a minor porn star who had received a special commendation in *Screw* magazine. I was deep in the middle of a searing social satire when someone started pounding on my door.

'Alice, Alice, open up! It's me, Mo!!'

'I'm busy right now. What is it?'

'For fuck's sake, open the door!'

I opened the door. Mo was holding something behind her back and hopping up and down with excitement.

'You'll never guess what I've got!'

'I was trying to write.'

'You had all fucking day to do that. Look at this!'

She handed me Elvis Presley.

'Isn't it brilliant? He's a fucking radio!'

Elvis was about a foot high and made of moulded plastic. He was dressed in a silver lamé jumpsuit and held a tiny microphone. His hair was sculpted into a jet-black pompadour and his perfectly proportioned features were fixed in a miniature sneer.

'Where did you find him?'

'Jupiter Discount. They're on sale for £5.99.'

I was severely tempted to run out and buy one for myself. Then I remembered my limited finances and the purity of my artistic vision.

'He's great.'

'Are you coming out tonight?'

'No, thanks. I have work to do.'

'But it's Saturday night!'

'So?'

'God, you're strange. Suit yourself. Elvis and I are going to have a fucking BLAST, aren't we, sweetie?'

She disappeared up the stairs, humming 'Saturday Night's All Right'.

I had other Saturday nights to write of.

I stayed up until 3 a.m. The flat was so cold my hands were trembling as I tried to type. I cut the fingers off an old pair of gloves and managed to keep on working.

Suffering was supposed to be good for the soul.

11 a.m. Church bells. A chilly Sunday morning. Perfect for hiding under the covers and reading Doris Lessing.

I was starting to recognize Mo's knock.

'Wakey, wakey!'

I staggered over to the door. Mo was dressed in a long navy-blue coat with a kerchief tied under her chin.

'What is it now? I was in bed.'

'You'll miss Mass.'

'I don't go to Mass.'

'You should. No wonder you're in the state you are. It's bad luck to miss Mass.'

'So say a prayer for me.'

I slammed the door.

Monday at Poseidon Freight. Dymphna decided to take a fresh interest in me.

She waddled over at mid-morning with a tray piled high with tea and biscuits.

'There you go! A *proper* tea break! Who says we girls can't look after ourselves?'

'I never did.'

'Drink up, now. Shredding's thirsty work.'

'Thanks.'

'Now. Tell me *all* about yourself.'

Shredding was mindless but exhausting work. I dragged myself up the stairs to my flat, thinking only of sleep. A tall, gangly man was waiting out on the landing. He looked uncomfortable in his suit.

'Hello there. Can I trouble you for a moment?'

A country accent.

'Yes?'

'Is that your flat there?'

'Yes.'

He lowered his voice dramatically.

'Do you know Rita Cooney?'

'No.'

He pointed to Flat 3.

'The girl in there.'

'Sorry. I've only seen her once.'

'Do you see any people . . . I mean, do you see any fellows . . . are there many men around?'

'I can't help you.'

'But if you could . . . and maybe if you heard the odd English accent . . . you'd tell me that, now wouldn't you?'

'No. I respect her privacy.'

'Ah, but if I were to drop in from time to time and have a sociable cup of tea with you . . . you'd let me know then, wouldn't you? And get something nice for yourself.'

He shook my hand. I pulled away. A twenty-pound note fell on the floor.

'I don't spy on my neighbours.'

'Shh . . . Shh . . . I didn't mean to offend. Ah, you're taking me up wrong altogether.'

'I think you should go now.'

'I'm gone, love. And don't be telling Rita that you saw me, now.'

'Goodbye.'

He crept down the stairs in an elaborate charade of stealth. I waited until I heard the front door slam before I opened my door.

I went out to the sink to fill the kettle. The door of Flat 3 opened a crack and then shut again.

I woke up on Tuesday morning with the novel sensation of having actually enjoyed a good night's sleep. When I went out to the sink, I surprised an elderly man in his shirtsleeves splashing water on his face. He turned away and disappeared into Flat 3.

I didn't care what she did as long as I could sleep through it and the sink was kept clean.

Lunch-time at Poseidon Freight. I headed towards the 'kitchen area', in reality a green-stained sink and an ancient fridge surrounded by mousetraps. Dymphna was waiting for me.

'You're coming to lunch on Thursday.'

'I am?'

'At my flat. A pre-Christmas treat.'

'You don't have to go through any bother for me.'

'Nonsense. I refuse to take "No" for an answer. It's not like you have anything better to do.'

The office air was murkier than usual and the men were lighting up fresh cigarettes as they unwrapped their sandwiches.

'OK. Thank you.'

'Dress up. Not that there's anything *wrong* with the way you look, of course. But if you feel ready for a change, stick with me. I'll show you a few tricks. I didn't get four wealthy husbands by wearing sensible shoes, did I, gentlemen?'

There was no response. Dymphna stalked over to the nearest desk and gave it a resounding kick.

'I SAID that I didn't get four rich husbands by wearing ARMY BOOTS, DID I, BOYS?'

'Ah, now Dymphna, I'm trying to drink me fucking tea.'

'We thought it was more the things you *didn't* wear, Dymphna.'

'If they were all so rich, what are you still doing here?'

'Leave Grizzly Adams alone, we love her big boots.'

'Never you mind, Alice! We're going to have a SMASHING lunch.'

What had I done?

The evenings were mine and the writing was going well. The world would soon know of the terrible night I decided to commit suicide, locked myself into my closet, pushed the key under the door, and then realized that I had forgotten to bring the pills in with me.

Someone was knocking on the door. I jerked myself back into the here and now. Mo's voice was crying out.

'Are you there, Alice, for God's sake?'

I pulled open the door. Mo came flying into the room in tears.

'There's no shagging God.'

'What?'

'Look at my jumper!'

There was a cigarette burn on the back of her jumper, a fuzzy white one decorated with glass beading.

'That's a shame, Mo. Maybe you could buy some beading and decorate over it.'

'It's fucking ruined. How can there be a God if He'd let something like this happen to my jumper?'

'The Lord works in mysterious ways.'

'Doesn't he fucking just.'

Wednesday. I began to regret my hasty decision. Dymphna beamed every time she walked past me.

At lunch-time a thin man wearing an obvious toupée appeared at Dymphna's desk.

'And what the fuck do *you* think you're doing here, John?'

'I just wanted to see you, Dymphna.'

'Bullshit! You're just another married man looking for a bit on the side. Well, you're out of luck today, darling. I have a guest for lunch.'

'Is he anybody I know?'

'Get your exceedingly limited mind out of the gutter. Alice, come here!'

I jammed a printout into the paper shredder and pretended not to hear.

'ALICE!'

'Yes, Dymphna.'

'John, this is a good friend of mine, Alice Sullivan. She has a bit of class, not that you'd recognize what that was if it hit you on the head.'

I nodded my head and continued working.

'So, you're having lunch with Dymphna today, are you, love?'

'No. It's tomorrow.'

Dymphna glared at me.

'That's what I fucking *meant*!'

'Why don't I join you two charming ladies? For old time's sake.'

'Fuck off.'

'Don't be like that, Dymphna. The more the merrier.'

'That sounds very nice.'

'Mind your own business, Alice. Oh, all right, since you're all conspiring against me.'

'See you tomorrow, darling. You too, Alice.'

'What the fuck is *wrong* with you, Alice?'

'I thought he was a friend of yours.'

I felt safer. With two of them there, Dymphna wouldn't be able to pump me for information.

Home sweet home. I cleared a pizza carton and two soft drink cans out of the sink. Nobody answered at Flat 3. I left a note: 'Please do not throw refuse in the sink.'

Somebody had been using the broken toilet. I poured boiling water and disinfectant down the loo, and taped up a bigger and better 'Out of Order' sign.

I knocked on Mo's door. A mournful voice answered, 'It's open.'

There was hardly enough room for me to open the door. Mo sat on the floor, surrounded by boxes of tinsel, a plastic Santa Claus, light-up reindeer, and a friendly snowman. The Pope had been turned to the wall, Bernadette of Lourdes was sitting in the closet and the Holy Water font was dry.

'Are you OK?'

'Yeah.'

'How's your jumper?'

'I burned it.'

'Did that make you feel any better?'

'A bit. These will, though.'

'You have a lot of Christmas decorations.'

'I love Christmas. But I'm not putting the fucking crib up this year.'

*

Thursday morning. D-Day. The stewardess outfit was out of the question. I wore trousers rather than jeans and picked out a brightly coloured jumper.

I wasn't going formal for paper shredding.

The lunch break at Poseidon Freight was from 1 to 2 p.m. A quarter past two found me sitting at Dymphna's dining-room table, picking over the remains of a steak and kidney pie. The luncheon had been a great success.

'Everything was lovely, Dymphna, but don't you think we should be getting back to the office now?'

She was swanning around the room, playing with a glass of red wine.

'Stop fucking worrying, Alice. A few minutes isn't going to kill anybody.'

John beamed at me.

'You listen to what our Dymphna says. She is wise in ways we cannot see.'

He was on his third drink.

'Oh do shut up, John. You're talking like a lush.'

'I am a lush, my one and only love.'

'I'll make some coffee.'

'The kettle's just boiled, Alice, but not for boring old coffee. It's Christmas and I'm going to make you one of my special IRISH coffees.'

'Don't you think we should . . .'

'I insist. That sleazy little office will just have to continue without us for a while longer.'

'Don't worry about me, my love. I'll just make myself another drink.'

Dymphna grabbed the bottle.

'Keep your fucking hands off my whiskey.'

She flounced into the kitchen. I started stacking the plates and tried to remember if I had seen a payphone in the hall-way. John staggered to his feet.

'Penny for your thoughts, love.'

'I was just thinking that I should call the office.'

'God, you're a real serious one, aren't you? What do you do for fun?'

'I haven't had time for fun yet.'
'There's always time for fun. And I love big girls.'
A bony arm crept around my waist. I pushed him away. He fell backwards on to the rug, spilling his drink.
I grabbed a serviette and started to mop up the stain. John crept over and tried to pull me towards him. I threw the wet rag in his face.
'What the fuck do you think you're doing?'
Dymphna had returned from the kitchen with the Irish coffees. She slammed the tray down on the table.
'The second my back is turned, you can't wait to jump on each other.'
I stood up.
'Dymphna! He fell . . .'
'Don't patronize me. I have eyes in my fucking head.'
John sat up, laughing.
'Oh, I do love it when you're jealous, Dymphna. It proves that there's life in us yet.'
'There's no life in you, you pathetic drunk. You're just preserved in alcohol.'
'I'd like to leave now.'
'After all my hard work? Now sit down and enjoy your Irish coffee before it gets cold.'
The bottle of whiskey had arrived back on the tray. John quietly refilled his glass. Dymphna wrenched the drink out of his hand and emptied it into the sugar bowl.
'Is your Irish coffee sweet enough for you, Alice?'
'It's fine, thanks.'

Half past three.
I stood out in the hallway staring at the 'Out of Order' sign on the payphone. It had started to rain.
I climbed the stairs back to the flat.
Dymphna was sitting on the floor sipping a gin and tonic. She was barefoot and her skirt was hiked up around her hips. John was curled into a foetal position and was gently snoring.
Dymphna waved at me.
'We are going to Dollymount Strand, Alice. Right now. You can come too.'

'It's pouring rain outside. How about some black coffee?'

'Fuck coffee! You only live once, Alice! I didn't get four husbands by getting back to the office in time!'

John stirred.

'This woman was a legend down in the docks!'

'What do you mean "was"? I AM a legend!'

'Of course you are, love.'

'I don't need your fucking pity!'

I picked up my jacket.

'Goodbye.'

Dymphna looked like she was going to cry.

'Oh, let's just forget about everything! We'll go back to the fucking office.'

She stood up unsteadily and pulled down her crumpled skirt.

'Look at the state of me! I stink of gin.'

'I'll help you find something else to put on.'

'Stop treating me like a child, Alice. I'm going to have a bath, change my clothes and drink that black coffee you're so intent on making. I'll explain everything to McManus.'

Dymphna staggered into the bathroom and shut the door. John rolled on to his side and fell asleep again. I threw my jacket on a chair.

A quarter past four. I sat alone in the kitchen drinking a cup of coffee. How much longer could a bath possibly take?

A voice rang out from the bathroom.

'John, bring me my drink.'

'Did you call, darling?'

'Bring me my drink. I want to talk to you.'

John had made it to his knees and was creeping towards Dymphna's drink. I knocked on the bathroom door.

'Don't you want that black coffee, Dymphna?'

'Oh my God, is the Girl Scout still here?'

'Not any more.'

I swung around and collided with John. He stumbled, spilling Dymphna's drink over the front of my jumper, and pushing me against the door. We swayed together for a moment before our combined weight pushed open the flimsy lock and sent us sailing into the bathroom.

Dymphna was sitting in the tub, her mascara-stained eyes blinking in amazement as we skidded on the wet floor, locked in an ungainly embrace. I grabbed the sink and regained my balance. John cracked his head against the side of the tub and slid face downwards on to the floor, still clutching the empty tumbler. Shards of broken glass scattered over the wet tiles.

'NOW look at what you've done! You've killed him, you stupid, bloody cow!'

She gripped the side of the bath and hauled herself out of the water, creating a minor tidal wave. Her face contorted with pain as her bare foot came down hard on a jagged piece of glass.

'Oh, my God, Dymphna. I'll call for an ambulance.'

She kept walking towards me, smearing bloody footprints on the soapy tiles.

'You fucking bitch. You murderer!'

Dymphna's pale flesh glistened with soapsuds. She tried to slap me. I held her off easily.

'Get dressed, Dymphna.'

She backed away from me and fumbled for a towel.

John was groaning. His toupée had slipped on to the back of his head, and clung there like a drowned rat.

'Do you want me to call an ambulance?'

'Fuck the ambulance. And fuck you.'

I grabbed my jacket and walked towards the door.

'Thanks for lunch.'

I could hear Dymphna shrieking all the way down the stairs.

I walked home. The rain washed away the soapsuds and the liquor.

By half past seven that evening, I was climbing the creaking stairs that led to my flat. I felt like I had been away for days.

The sink was filled with beer cans and shiny paper that smelled like kebabs.

Someone had scrawled 'Fuck Off' on my door.

*

I could have cried or I could have screamed. I made myself a cup of coffee instead.

There was a perfunctory knock on the door. Before I could react, a key was turning in the lock. Brian Deegan strolled into the room holding a bucket.

'You can't just walk in here like that.'

'I knocked!'

'Well, wait for me to answer! Don't ever do that again!'

'That sign on your door must be for me, so.'

'Did you see the sink? That Rita Cooney is making my life miserable.'

'Nag, nag, nag!'

'What do you want?'

'To empty the shagging meter, if you'll let me get on with it!'

'Go ahead.'

'I bet you didn't even *notice* that I fixed the loo!'

'Sorry, Brian. Will you sort out Flat 3?'

'She's off to London. Better business opportunities.'

'With her English pimp?'

'You're shocking, you are. A lovely fellow like that?'

'I guess you'll miss the kickbacks.'

'I just look after the flats, love.'

'I bet.'

He opened the meter. My hard-earned fifty-pence pieces clattered into the bucket.

'So tell me this, Miss America, where are you off to on Christmas Day?'

'I don't know. Why?'

'There are lots of break-ins over the holidays.'

'Aren't you insured?'

'Here's a piece of good advice, love. Don't stay here. Besides, you should be with lots of people on Christmas Day. Get into the spirit of things.'

'What people do you suggest I go and stay with?'

'Ah, there I go again, assuming you have friends.'

'I have friends. They're just not in this country.'

'Yeah. They fucking *left* it!'

Brian laughed all the way down the stairs.

I washed the writing off the door and cleaned out the sink. I put the garbage in a bag and left it outside Flat 3.

I dreaded going to work the next morning.

James McManus laughed when I apologized.

'Get back to work. Just don't go thinking you'll get fucking *paid* for that!'

Dymphna showed up at 11 o'clock wearing dark glasses, a tracksuit and runners.

She did not speak to me.

The men were all in a good mood. It was the last working day before Christmas.

'Dymphna, me love, are you running the marathon?'

'Where's yer pointy shoes? I need a hole punched.'

She slammed her desk drawers, muttered 'Shit!' under her breath, rammed a pencil into an electric sharpener and held it there firmly until only the rubber tip remained.

'You try to HELP someone and what do you fucking GET?'

I sat with my back to her, feeding documents into the shredder.

At 4 o'clock James McManus told everybody to go home. He slipped me a bottle of whiskey as I was leaving.

'There you go. Don't drink it all on the one day.'

'Thanks!'

'Don't thank me. Thank the suppliers.'

'See you next week.'

The garbage was still outside Flat 3 when I got home. I was filling the kettle at the sink when an old hippy sauntered down the stairs. He peered at me through wire-rimmed glasses held together with masking tape.

'Hey, neighbour! Do you know where Jan and Monica are?'

He was American.

'I don't even know who they are.'

'Now *there's* a voice from home! They're your Aussie neighbours from upstairs. Flat 6. Little Melbourne.'

'I can't help you.'
'Could I trouble you for a cup of something hot? I stashed my gear on the landing, but it's freezing out there.'
I assessed his greying hair tied back in a ponytail, well-worn jeans, tie-dyed T-shirt and faded denim jacket with a rainbow embroidered on the pocket. I'd have to feed him and he'd be hard to get rid of.
'I'm sorry, but I don't know you.'
'Hey, don't feel threatened. I understand. It's a crazy world out there and you can't be too careful.'
He tried to follow me into my flat, but I closed the door in his face.
'What are you so angry about?'

I tried to work on the book again but couldn't concentrate. I could hear the American moving around upstairs. He came downstairs once and used the loo. I turned my light off so he wouldn't knock at my door.
I heard footsteps on the stairs. Good. The Australians.
Wrong. A visitor for Flat 3. An angry one. Pounding on the door.
'Rita. Are you there? Goddammit, girl, answer me!'
It was the country man.
'I don't know what you're fucking playing at, Rita, but I've had enough!'
Someone came downstairs.
'Hey, man.'
I was actually glad to hear the hippy's voice.
'Why don't you cool it?'
'I'll thank you to mind your own business. This is no concern of yours.'
'Hey, if that's a friend of yours, she's obviously not home. Why don't we stroll downstairs.'
My doorknob rattled.
'She knows. In there. But she won't tell me!'
'What's to tell? People have got to be free. Take a stroll with me, my friend, and I'll tell you all about it.'
'I'm going mad not knowing. Rita's all that I have.'

They walked down the stairs together. I stood by my door, trying to hear what was going on.

Only one set of footsteps came back up.

'Are you OK in there?'

'Yeah.'

'He's gone now.'

I opened the door. The hippy smiled at me.

'Come on in. I'll make some coffee.'

His name was Jesse. He had taken a year off school in 1961 to backpack across Europe and had been travelling ever since, picking up seasonal jobs and quitting them as soon as he had enough money to move on. On his first day in Dublin he had been robbed by a gang of children on O'Connell Bridge. He had met the Australian girls in a café and they had offered to put him up.

'What are you doing in Dublin?'

'I'm writing a book.'

'Hey, that's great. What's it about?'

'It's very personal.'

'Hey, I wasn't trying to be nosy. So, you're really into the Inner Life, huh?'

The warmth of the coffee and the monotony of Jesse's unending questions soon made me drowsy. I sat back in my chair. The next thing I knew it was morning. A blanket covered me. Jesse was asleep on the bed, his knapsack on the floor beside him. I stood up stiffly and prodded him awake.

'Wake up, Jesse, it's morning.'

'Hey, another day. How are you feeling?'

'Much better. Thank you.'

'Can I have a cup of coffee?'

'Sure. But then you'll have to go.'

'I'm history. Be careful who you let in, OK? There are some *very* bad vibes here.'

Christmas Eve. Flat 3 still seemed deserted. I thought I was alone in the house until I ran into Mo on the stairs. She was carrying two massive shopping bags and singing 'Jingle Bells'.

'Well, you're really in the spirit.'

'Ah, I love fucking Christmas! Don't you?'
'I'm indifferent.'
'You sure are! Where are you going?'
'I'll probably stay right here.'
'Ah, Jesus! You can't stay here on Christmas Day!'
'Why not?'
'It'd be a fucking disgrace! Come home with me!'
'Thanks, Mo. But I'm OK.'
'Me da's picking me up early tomorrow morning. It'll only be for the day. Any longer and we're at each other's throats. They'd all love to meet a Yank! Come on!'
I hesitated. The house suddenly seemed very bleak.
'I'd love to, Mo.'

I called my mother that night to wish her a Merry Christmas. It was nice not to have to lie to her about what I was doing.

Christmas morning was cold and bright. I wrapped up the bottle of whiskey and put on my red, white and blue outfit.
If they wanted to meet a Yank, I might as well look the part.
I walked upstairs to Mo's flat. Jesse was washing dishes at the communal sink.
'Hey, what's up?'
'I'm going home with Mo.'
'Dynamite. Country music. Bright colours.'
'Yeah, she's something else.'
'You have a cool Yule, now!'
'You too.'
'I will. The girls have to work, but we're having a big party when they come in. I'm preparing a vegetarian feast for us.'
'That sounds great.'
'Hey, I'm the best.'

Mo's father nodded his head when we got into the car and remained silent all the way to Monaghan.

*

Mo helped her mother in the kitchen all day. Neither one of them seemed to eat anything. I sat with the silent father and Mo's five brothers. We were presented with steaming plates of food at regular intervals. I ate everything that was put in front of me.

Once Mo's father had fallen asleep in a chair, the brothers interrogated me about job prospects in America. They were all planning to emigrate.

Mo's father drove us back to Dublin that evening. To a house that no longer existed.

Streaks of black stained the brick front of Deegan's Newsagents. Charred curtains wafted in and out of the smashed windows. Broken glass covered the pavement. The front door was bolted shut with strips of metal.

Nobody was around. We drove back to Monaghan.

We returned the following morning. The Deegans were standing on the pavement talking to two gardai.

Brian turned to face us. His eyes looked strange.

'It's a bad business, girls.'

'Was anybody in there?'

'You were all supposed to be gone.'

'What do you mean "supposed to be", Brian?'

Mo grabbed my hand.

A garda walked over.

'May I ask you ladies a few questions?'

Jesse had died of smoke inhalation. There was no fire escape and the windows had bars on them.

The fire was suspicious in origin. It had started in my flat. Someone had poured petrol over my papers and set them alight.

The only thing I had left to wear was my interview outfit. It would look good at the inquest.

Mo and I sat in her family's kitchen drinking tea.

'You amaze me, Mo. All your precious toys and clothes burned up and you're just carrying on.'

'I don't have any fucking choice, do I?'
'But you loved all that stuff.'
'Ah, it was only a load of old shite.'

I called James McManus the next day.
'I'm staying up in Monaghan and I won't be able to come in for a while.'
'What the fuck are you doing up there?'
'My house burned down.'
'Very careless of you. Did you lose much?'
'Only some old letters. A man died.'
'That was your fucking place? It figures.'
'I have to find a new flat. Can I come back to finish the job when I'm settled?'
'Who else would do it?'
'Thanks. I'll call you soon.'
'Dymphna misses you.'
He laughed and hung up.

It was raining the next morning. I bought a newspaper and got on the bus to Dublin.

THE ADMIRAL'S DAUGHTER

Michael Morris

Michael Morris was born in Portsmouth and spent twenty years as a taxation specialist before, at the age of thirty-seven, he went to college to study for a degree in Education and Literature. Having been bitten by the academic bug he then spent the next fifteen years as a lecturer.

Michael, who now lives in Chelmsford, took early retirement in 1990 to concentrate on writing and enjoyment. He has written comedy sketches for a local drama group and is currently working on a novel.

THE ADMIRAL'S DAUGHTER

It is not far from my place in New Bond Street to the house where, according to the blue plaque high on the wall, Horatio Nelson lived in 1798. Emma Hamilton once had lodgings close by but there is no plaque to record that. Of course, it was some years later; Nelson was dead and her descent into poverty had begun. I often raise my glass (German engraved goblet, early eighteenth century, about five hundred pounds) of sherry (fine old oloroso, a gift not to be valued, I am not a wine merchant) to the memory of Horatio and Emma but principally I drink to Miss Hetherington, who changed my life.

I met her twenty-five years ago at her small cottage in a village just outside Portsmouth where I had my first antique shop. I suppose the village will be a town now with its quota of supermarkets, estate agents and ethnic takeaways, but then it was quite pretty and a likely source of good quality antiques and naive sellers. She had telephoned to ask if I would value an Italian gilt metal box, late eighteenth century she said, left to her by her father, Rear Admiral 'Swisher' Hetherington. He had gone to that great quarterdeck in the sky some years before, quickly followed by his widow who no doubt felt she had spent quite long enough waiting for him to return from foreign parts. Later, when I knew her better and the money had changed hands, Miss Hetherington confided to me that the nickname referred to her father's propensity to use the cane when disciplining young midshipmen under his command. She also believed he used it on her mother and on other ladies not connected with the family. He was, she reminisced with obvious affection, 'a bit of a blighter', but he had always treated her with kindness. After his early retirement from the navy, an event I gathered not unconnected with his nickname, she had been his constant companion. 'Daddy and I played cards together, hour after hour.' What Mummy did was not clear but it did not seem to amount to much.

Now, after she had suffered a prolonged bout of influenza, Miss Hetherington's doctor had insisted that she should take a holiday and the Italian box was the only negotiable capital she had. It was a common enough plight in that area where relicts of naval officers maintained a frugal gentility in the shadow of former glories.

I had been recommended as a fair man by her friend whose name I have forgotten. I do remember that she had brought in a small medicine chest, late eighteenth century, the type carried by naval officers to deal with minor ailments. Major ailments usually involved needle and thread, a few yards of canvas and a heavy weight, but they had a good rate of success with boils. Some contents missing but good condition; unlikely to have belonged to Nelson as the lady's late husband, a retired captain, had always insisted, but very marketable. I gave her forty-seven pounds ten shillings and sold it for one hundred and fifty. Well, it could have belonged to one of Nelson's captains, the period was right.

My speciality was naval memorabilia, anything from a lock of Emma Hamilton's hair to a wardroom table complete with the marks of musket balls. I steered clear of Nelson's hair; punters shrewdly calculated that the amount on offer indicated that on the voyage home after Trafalgar the surgeon had reverted to his traditional trade of barber to the fleet. Business was usually brisk. Punters were anxious that the minute rooms of their restored eighteenth-century houses in the Old City should be decked out with appropriate vestiges of our naval heritage and there were enough Miss Hetheringtons to ensure that the fakes and reproductions were salted with a few genuine articles.

Her cottage was small but pretty enough and furnished in an unremittingly nineteen-thirties tea-shop style. I did not see the bedrooms but I guessed about three hundred pounds for the lot on a house-clearance basis. She was a small, grey-haired woman, probably in her fifties, but she had the kind of face that does not change much between the thirties and sixties. The only remarkable thing about her was her skin. She was of a generation and type that did not pursue a suntan. Quite the contrary, they went to great lengths in those far-flung outposts of the empire to avoid anything that might identify them with the natives. But despite their hats, veils and creams, they usually ended up with skin the colour and texture of walnuts. Miss Hetherington's face was pale and unlined. I remember thinking 'peaches and cream' although the relevance of that description to a flawless complexion still escapes me. Only a light touch of lipstick embellished a face that was not beautiful but certainly interesting. She wore the home counties uniform; an open cardigan over a jumper and skirt, pale pastel shades, nothing to disturb the quiet image except, in place of the expected imitation pearls, a small sapphire set in a gold filigree mount suspended from a golden chain so fine as to be almost invisible. About £50, excellent taste. She had been writing letters when I arrived and the writing pad and fountain pen were still on the table.

'Shall I show you the box first and then we can have some tea while you decide on the value? It's the last of the Hetherington pieces, everything else has gone. My father didn't leave very much and my mother had practically nothing of her own. I've kept it because of the family connection and my father told me it was very valuable. He always referred to it as the family insurance policy.' She unlocked the cupboard and lifted out an ornately decorated metal box, placing it on the small coffee table as a priest might offer a chalice for blessing.

'Lady Hamilton gave it to my father's great grandfather's brother.' I guessed from her precise enunciation of her family tree that she had told this story many times before. 'She brought it to England when she and her husband had to leave Naples.' The tone of her voice suggested that the Hamiltons were driven from Italy by scandal rather than the imminent arrival of Napoleon's troops. 'I like to think of it being in her drawing room while she chatted to Admiral Nelson.'

I picked up the box and gave it my professional scrutiny, the one calculated to assess the object and impress the punter. The box was certainly Italian, late eighteenth or early nineteenth century. The Hamiltons left Naples about 1800 so that fitted. On one side was a painted panel depicting Actaeon spying on the naked Diana and, on the other side, he was getting his come-uppance from the hunting dogs. The story had always struck me as an early feminist tract; it was just the kind of thing to appeal to Emma Hamilton. If genuine, it could well have been present when she entertained Nelson, but chatting was not the activity that immediately sprang to mind. In good condition it would be worth about five thousand pounds, more if the Nelson connection could be established, but the years had battered it, the gilding had been restored and the lining replaced. The work had not been done very skilfully and I doubted if it would raise more than two thousand, Lady Hamilton notwithstanding. Inside the box was a small portrait of Nelson, faded and badly stained, the wooden frame disintegrating. An enthusiast might give a fiver for it. There was also a sheet of notepaper, yellow with age, on which was written in a large, confident hand, 'This box was presented to my brother, Edward Hetherington, by Lady Hamilton as a memorial to Admiral Lord Nelson with whom he served as a Midshipman at the Battle of Trafalgar.' It was signed George Hetherington and dated 25 September 1839.

'Edward Hetherington was your father's . . .'

'My father's great grandfather's brother. He died while still quite young. He never married and George, his brother, treasured the box and eventually it passed to my father. The portrait has always been there but it's in poor condition; I don't suppose it's worth much. Now, before you say anything, let me get the tea, then you can tell me what you think it's worth.'

I was going to offer her five hundred pounds, after a protracted description of all that was wrong with the box, but I decided to enjoy the tea and cakes first. My news would certainly spoil her appetite. I picked up the little portrait and turned it over, looking for a printer's name or some mark that might impress a punter and boost the price. As I lifted it, the heavy paper backing came away on two sides, revealing a folded sheet of notepaper which I assumed had been used to keep the printed portrait in position. The paper had been written on and I eased it out and spread it on the table. It was badly creased and the writing was faded but still quite legible. It was a letter and from the opening words, 'My own darling Ned', clearly a love letter. Ned was probably Edward Hetherington. I was intrigued at the prospect of eavesdropping on a long dead love affair but as I read the loving and detailed description of Ned's body interspersed with words of what I took to be Italian origin and erotic intent, it occurred to me that I had tumbled upon a hitherto unsuspected and potentially lucrative aspect of Emma Hamilton's love life. I looked at the signature for confirmation. At the same moment a floorboard creaked in the doorway. Had I been called upon to speak, I could have done no more than croak.

Instinctively I placed my hands over the paper, a totally ineffective attempt at concealment but I was not used to coping with that level of excitement. I heard the rattle of teacups from the kitchen and resumed breathing. I looked again at the signature and the final sentence. 'God forgive me but I pray that I may soon clasp your young white body to this scarred and wounded carcass in which I am imprisoned. Until then you are ever in my thoughts. My love, my life. Horatio.'

At which point I heard Miss Hetherington returning with the tea. That I did not immediately stuff the letter into my pocket I blame on my confused state of mind and barely controllable hands. I knew that she must not see the letter and I lifted it into the box with the frame and there, as though I were washing my hands in a basin, I refolded it, inserted it behind the backing paper and replaced the portrait face up on the bottom of the box just as she came into the room.

'Sorry to be so long, that kettle takes ages. Mr Young, are you all right? You're looking awfully pale.'

'No . . . no . . . I'm fine . . . fine.'

'Well, have a cup of tea and then we can discuss business. Sugar?'

Thankfully, she then launched into an account of her attempts to give up sugar which only required an occasional nod and smile from me. I was frantically trying to organize my thoughts. The signature had to be Nelson's. I had seen enough examples to recognize it but how could I be sure? How could I get the letter out of the house without disclosing what I had in mind? Should I come clean and share the find with her? I dismissed the thought so emphatically that I actually said 'No!' quite loudly but it was apparently an appropriate response to whatever she was saying. She was by now castigating the quality of shop-bought cakes. If I made her an offer for the portrait alone, she might examine it. No, the less attention drawn to it the better. I should have to buy the box with the portrait included as a makeweight; that would make me the legal owner of the letter which I would discover when repairing the frame. Some time later I was discussing the ethics of a similar transaction with a colleague but I cannot remember giving it much thought at the time.

The tea poured, the smalltalk over, Miss Hetherington was on to the matter in hand.

'Now, tell me the good news. I hope it's good news. You see, I don't own this house, father had to sell our home and buy an annuity when he left the navy. My doctor wants me to take a holiday but actually I'm trying to get enough money together to buy a little place somewhere, perhaps abroad. I'm told houses are much cheaper on the continent. I've got a little money saved but I'm pinning my hopes on the box. There was one just like it in Sotheby's catalogue last year valued at £5,600.'

God damn Sotheby's and all catalogues. They should carry a Government health warning. I would have to raise the stakes. If I underbid, I might lose the whole deal, box, portrait, letter, the lot.

'Catalogues are not a reliable guide, Miss Hetherington. You see, value depends so much on the state of the item, how rare it is, whether there's a demand for that kind of thing. This is a very pretty box but it has been greatly restored, there is very little of the original decoration left.' I closed the lid and showed her the more obvious areas where the gilding had been touched up. 'I'm afraid one of your father's forebears was unwise enough to have it regilded. That greatly reduces the value of an antique.'

'That was probably my great grandfather. He had a mania for brightening things up. But nothing else has been touched and it is very old. After all, it did belong to Lady Hamilton.'

I decided not to mention the replaced lining, that would have involved opening the box again, perhaps disturbing the portrait. Time to exhibit my impressive technical knowledge.

'You see, the Italians churned out thousands of these, there were factories in Venice, Florence, all over the place. This is certainly Italian but it's Neapolitan and Naples was regarded rather as the Birmingham of Italy. The Venetian and Florentine workmanship, as you might expect, was far superior. There is, of course, the Hamilton connection, but the note doesn't prove that it was this box that was given.'

I decided to offer one thousand pounds for the box with the portrait thrown in. If I started too low and then had to increase the offer substantially, she might suspect something. It offended my principles but the letter, properly handled, would cause a sensation. The literary rights, newspaper articles, television and finally the auction with American universities scrambling to get it. Would the Japanese be interested?

'I can give you . . .'

She interrupted me. 'I know this must sound, well, greedy, but unless I can get at least five thousand pounds, I'd rather not sell.'

'Five thousand!' The woman was mad. You could buy a small house for that in 1965. It was nearly twice my net profit for the year, three times the profit shown in the accounts. I was nearly speechless with the horror of it and could only repeat, 'Five thousand!'

She was clearly embarrassed at my reaction. 'The one in Sotheby's catalogue was valued at five thousand six hundred. It looked exactly like this one and it hadn't belonged to anyone famous.' Her words tumbled out in a rush as if they had been well rehearsed. 'I hate to part with it but I would feel it was justified if it meant I could have my own home. I did think of taking it to the Victoria and Albert Museum for their opinion. Not that I don't have confidence in you but it must be difficult to value something like this. The V & A may be more interested in the historical association.'

I was sure they would be. In fact, if they had a sight of that letter, their screams would be heard all over Kensington.

'Miss Hetherington.' It is not easy to adopt a fatherly tone to a lady who is at least ten years older than oneself, but I tried. 'Please believe that I have your best interests at heart when I tell you that five thousand pounds is not a realistic value. You see . . .' I was about to repeat my lecture on Italian gilt metal boxes in general and this one in particular when she cut in politely but firmly.

'I know I am probably being silly but I have decided that nothing less than five thousand pounds will do.'

I am not a gambling man but I occasionally indulge in a little roulette at the local sporting club. It makes a change to be manipulated by someone else, to relax and let the house calculate the odds. I stick to the even bets, red or black, odd or even, and sometimes, on the rare occasions I have accumulated a respectable pile of chips in front of me, I slide the lot on to the black, knowing there is an even chance that, when the little steel ball comes to rest, the croupier will place several more little stacks of chips in front of me and I will walk from the table, having demonstrated to the envious spectators my superior skill, knowledge and luck. I had that feeling then. The letter must be genuine, how could it not be? If only I could get to to Alan, he could spot a forgery a mile off, even without the chemical tests. But Alan was in London and I was standing at the table with the chips in front of me. A find like this was so fanciful that dealers don't even dream of it. But I did. It was more than the money. This would place me above the grubby little deals, the shady stratagems, doling out disappointments and false hopes to little people who should have stayed with chipboard and plastic veneer. I could have a proper business, deal with people who appreciate the worth of fine furniture, beautiful paintings. I slid the chips on to the black.

'It is a lot of money, Miss Hetherington.' I was examining the box again, I even raised the lid and looked inside. I could see the edge of the letter. Damn. In my hurry, I hadn't quite got it behind the backing paper. Anyone looking now could not fail to see it. The wheel was spinning, the little ball racing round the outside. 'However, it is a fine example of a gilt box, despite the restoration. The connection with Lady Hamilton can probably be confirmed through the insurance and shipping records and it will certainly add to the interest.' Steady now, don't overdo it, she might up the price. 'In the circumstances, I am prepared to offer you five thousand pounds for the box and contents. The portrait isn't worth anything but I'll take it as a makeweight. It might help with the Nelson link.' *Les jeux sont fait, rien ne va plus.* They did not actually speak French at the local casino but it fitted my mood at the time.

She clasped her hands together. 'It is a lot of money, isn't it? But I'm sure you won't regret it. When I hold it and I think that Emma Hamilton's hands rested here, where mine are, as she gave it to young Edward, I can hardly bear to part with it. Surely other people will feel the same way? It may make you a fortune. I hope it does. You have dealt very fairly with me and I am quite happy with my five thousand pounds. I didn't like to say this before, it seemed like tempting fate, but I intend to visit Naples. The Hamiltons' house is still there and who knows, I may even find a little villa that I can buy. Wouldn't that be marvellous?'

She chattered on and I made my last attempt at damage limitation. 'Of course, I'll have to give you a cheque, I don't carry that much cash with me.' I already had my chequebook out with my pen poised, ready to write.

She looked thoughtful. 'I hadn't thought of that. Yes, of course. I can give you a receipt for the cheque and then you can collect the box next week.'

'Don't you think the box would be safer with me? I can give you a receipt for it and then it becomes my responsibility.'

For a moment she hesitated. 'Yes, that sounds sensible.' The little ball was about to fall on to a black number. The criminal classes seldom accept cheques and never part with the goods before the cash changes hands. I smiled at the notion of Miss Hetherington as one of the criminal classes and she smiled back. 'I'm glad you're happy about the box.

Now I must give you a receipt. That's your proof of purchase, just in case you find something wrong with it.' She giggled and reached for the writing pad she had been using when I arrived. She wrote in a large, flowing hand and repeated as she wrote, 'I hereby acknowledge a cheque for £5,000 from Mr Young paid for an Italian decorated metal box, once the property of Lady Emma Hamilton, a certificate signed by Mr George Hetherington and a small portrait of Lord Nelson.' She signed and dated it with a flourish. 'There, that will do, won't it?'

It was better than nothing. I could hardly complain if there was anything wrong with the letter, but George Hetherington's certificate would be equally suspect and that would justify stopping the cheque.

'I think that something more than tea is called for, don't you? I have a rather good sherry that I keep for special occasions.' She looked at me, and smiled. 'And this is a very special occasion.' At that moment I may have felt a slight twinge at the thought of the money that the letter would bring me but no doubt I reminded myself that she had done very nicely out of a battered old tin box. The sherry was rather good and as we drank to our mutual success, she chatted to me about her life with Mummy and Daddy during their long years of retirement. I was anxious to get the letter to Alan and I declined a second glass.

She brought some sheets of brown paper for me to wrap round the box and as we shook hands she smiled and said, 'I'm so glad I chose you to advise me, I just knew you were the right man for the job.'

I drove straight to London. Alan's workshop was in one of those small streets off Long Acre and I arrived as he was packing up for the weekend. I convinced him that anything that would make me drive to London on a Friday afternoon must be extremely urgent. I gave him the letter and George Hetherington's certificate without explaining the circumstances. He was used to giving opinions on documents without knowing why they were important but the significance of Horatio's signature and the purple prose of the letter could not have been lost on him.

'Is it Horatio Nelson?' I tried to sound calm, even offhand, but the drive to London had stretched my nerves and I had to clasp my hands together to keep them from shaking.

Alan was not a man to be hurried. Had he been a pipe-smoker, he would have gone through the prolonged ritual of filling, tamping, lighting, drawing and finally smoking the damned thing before speaking. As it was, he merely weighed the letter in his hands, rubbed a corner between his thumb and forefinger, held it up to the light, sniffed it, examined it through a magnifying glass and then placed it on his work-bench and studied it, his chin in his hands. Eventually, he spoke. 'The paper feels right, could be late eighteenth century, the ink looks OK, but I would have to do a spectrum analysis to be sure.'

'How long will that take?'

'About thirty minutes . . . if you think I should bother.'

'What do you mean, if I think you should bother?'

He held the letter out to me like a schoolmaster rejecting an unsatisfactory essay. 'I don't know who wrote this but it wasn't Horatio Nelson.'

The steel ball fell into the red space.

'It isn't even a good try. There's a superficial likeness but it isn't consistent. I should say someone sat down with a specimen of Nelson's handwriting and copied the words that were needed. Some are quite clearly made up . . . and not very well at that. Sorry. Is it important?'

I shrugged. 'It would have been nice, a new view of a national hero, but I thought it was too good to be true. Still, worth a try. What about the certificate?' I was surprised at how steady, even matter-of-fact, my voice was. My hands had stopped shaking. I felt something like relief, perhaps because now I was dealing with certainties, walking away from the table, back to the world that I knew, that I could cope with.

Alan was speaking again. 'The paper seems OK but it's not difficult to get hold of; facing pages from contemporary books, old stocks, there's quite a lot of it about. I'd have to do an analysis of the ink. As for the signature, I've no idea who George Hetherington was, it might be his. I would need to see a reliable specimen, his will, other letters, something like that.'

I was thinking now of that five-thousand-pound cheque. If the certificate was a forgery, at least I could save that. 'Check the ink. I'd like to know if it could be genuine. I'm going to get something to eat, I'll be back in half an hour.'

The pub on the corner had just opened for the Friday evening office rush. I remember it was full of young people, talking at the tops of their voices about plans for the weekend, office scandals, the latest Beatles concert. It was just the beginning of long hair for the men and short skirts for the women. I felt about ninety years old and wondered what the drill sergeants who had made my brief army career so miserable would have said about it all. I had been called up in the last year of the war but was quickly returned to civilian life because of the asthma that had plagued me since childhood. I went straight to university and never suffered from asthma again, which was a mixed blessing because, at school and in the army, it had given me a convincing excuse for an occasional day off. Of course, that was no way to run an army. There is something about being alone in a pub that brings out the philosopher in me, probably because there is a ready supply of case studies and no one to question or correct my conclusions. I ordered a pint and a sandwich and had to stand at the bar because there were no tables free. There were a few men of my age there but we clearly had little in common. They were obviously businessmen with the world to run while I was wearing a large bow-tie and a very crumpled linen suit. I hoped I looked like a journalist. I don't recall there being any women of my generation, I suppose they had all rushed home to get the family tea. There were women like that then but they were outside my experience. My brief attempt at marriage had lasted about as long as my army career but had been more instructive. It had taught me that, unlike a good antique, it is impossible to assess the value of a woman in advance of purchase and a dissatisfied customer can neither return the goods nor be sure of passing them on at a reasonable price.

I thought about my wife in that pub and about Miss

Hetherington. Most of all I thought about myself and how I came to be in this situation. After university, I had tried various jobs, even teaching for a brief, inglorious spell. I came into the antiques game through a friend who needed a trustworthy but not very knowledgeable associate with a bit of money to put into the business. I soon discovered that I had not just a good eye for the furniture, paintings and general bric-à-brac that were our stock in trade, but an acute awareness of the skill and loving care and attention lavished on them by generations of craftsmen. I was upset by shoddy imitations and the irreparable damage caused by neglect and ignorance. I developed a passion for those inanimate objects that I had never felt for human beings and for a time was as happy as I had ever been. Gradually I realized that passion was not a good basis for making money, at least not in the antiques business, and I became more concerned with selling the illusion of quality. It was much cheaper to buy than the real thing and there was a great deal more of it about. Well, I had just bought an illusion and it was going to cost me all that I had acquired by trading on other people's passions.

Surprisingly, I did not feel very disappointed about the letter. There was the same inevitability about it as there was about not breaking the bank at roulette. But I had to stop that cheque. The loss of five thousand pounds less what I could sell the box for was a very real concept, I had no difficulty imagining the effect on my business. I quickly finished my drink and the sandwich and hurried back to the workshop. Alan was putting things away in drawers, the note was lying on the bench. It was not in his nature to speak first.

'Well?'

'As I told you, I can't comment on the signature but the paper and ink are both right for 1839. It's not uncommon for the paper to be right but it is very difficult to get the correct composition of the ink. If it is a forgery, then I'm sure it was done at the time or very soon after. Which means that it is highly unlikely that anyone today would even be aware that it is a forgery.' Bang went five thousand pounds.

'An interesting thing about the letter. I did some tests out of curiosity, the paper could be right except that it has obviously been cut out of an old book. Someone has tried to straighten the edge but not very well. And the ink is wrong. It is just modern ink diluted and coloured to make it look old. It hasn't been done recently, maybe thirty or forty years ago. I don't suppose you want to tell me about it?'

I shook my head. 'I'm not sure I understand it myself. It's just an enquiry for a client. The family want it kept quiet. Thanks for your help, Alan. Don't forget to send me your bill, or would you prefer cash?' There was no VAT in those days but cash always seemed friendlier.

'I'll send you a bill. I think it would be as well to keep this one formal.'

Driving from London early on a Friday evening requires skill, judgement, iron nerves and total concentration. Fear usually helps me summon up the last quality. I shall say nothing of the first three, but I could not get Miss Hetherington out of my mind. After the third narrow escape in fifteen minutes, I pulled into the car park of a small restaurant. I was not particularly hungry but I calculated that in two hours the traffic should have reduced to civilized proportions and I needed a chance to work out what had been done to whom, by whom and how. Clearly, it had been done to me. But by whom? If Alan was right, Miss Hetherington would have been in her teens when the letter was written. A teenage forger? Strains the credulity, M'Lud. Which brought me to the main point. I had bought the box and the certificate. They were genuine. 'You paid five thousand pounds for that . . . that . . . box? Have you been in the antique trade very long, Mr Young? I dare to suggest that, if you continue to conduct your business in that manner, you are unlikely to remain in it for much longer.' Yes, M'Lud. No, M'Lud. I was not quite the condemned man but I decided to eat a hearty meal.

'Waiter, I shall have a very large whisky while you find me a menu.'

'I'm afraid we're not licensed, sir. A soft drink? Tea? Coffee?'

The delights of travel in 1965. At least today one can get

blind drunk within easy reach of every major road. I settled for chicken and chips and coffee. This would have been a good day for a heart-attack at the breakfast table.

I lay awake for some time that night, trying to decide whose victim I was. The letter had been written forty years ago, but why? And by whom? I had been conned by it but was that an accident, a coincidence, or was Miss Hetherington really an arch criminal? I decided to call on her in the morning and tell her I had found the letter but not that I knew it was a forgery. I should at least get an interesting reaction. Perhaps I could sell it to her, get some of my five thousand back. Which hallucinatory fantasy reminded me that tomorrow I should have to give some thought to raising that amount.

At that time, I lived in a flat above the shop and the next morning I was down early to tidy up and arrange for someone to look after the place while I visited the Professor Moriarty of the South Downs. At five minutes past nine the telephone rang. It was my bank manager. Banks were open on Saturdays in those days and I calculated that he had telephoned me as soon as he had someone there to dial the number for him. The man was a cretin but next to gullible punters and at least some items of quality among the stock, an antique dealer needs an accommodating bank manager. In fact, with the right bank manager, it is possible to manage without the other two for a limited period. He had tried to contact me yesterday after his colleague in one of the small country branches had asked him, on behalf of a Miss Hetherington, whether there would be any trouble honouring a cheque for five thousand pounds. As the balance in both the business and my private accounts did not amount to five hundred pounds, he was rather surprised that I had issued a cheque for that amount without consulting him. It was a very substantial amount and, without prior agreement with the bank, the cheque was of doubtful legality. And so on and so forth until I managed to interrupt his flow to explain that it was potentially an extremely lucrative business deal and that I intended to call on him this morning to arrange for the sale of securities. He, as a man of business, would appreciate that it was occasionally necessary to strike while the iron was hot, take the tide at its flood and ride the current when it served. He was a man of literary as well as financial pretensions. I agreed to call on him at eleven o'clock, which would give me time to visit Miss Hetherington. I had decided to tell her that I had consulted an expert and he doubted the authenticity of the certificate signed by George Hetherington. It would take time to investigate further and in the meantime, I would have no option but to stop the cheque. I would make a very generous offer to buy the box without authentication at a value to be decided by an independent expert, stressing my belief in her good faith and ignorance of any attempt to defraud by using a forged certificate. The more I rehearsed my approach, the more confident I became in my ability to salvage my five thousand pounds.

I picked up the morning's letters and quickly sorted through them. It was the usual collection of bills and advertising circulars which could wait and one envelope addressed to me in a strong, vaguely familiar script and, judging by the absence of a stamp, delivered by hand. It was from Miss Hetherington.

Dear Mr Young,

I have had such an exciting day since your visit this morning and as I really owe my good fortune to you, I want to share my news with you. I have been to see my bank manager and although it will take a few days for your cheque to be officially cleared, he assured me that a businessman of your standing would hardly risk his reputation by failing to honour it! I told him that I had the utmost confidence in you and I showed him a copy of the receipt I had given you. He does tend to treat me as a rather simple, unworldly little woman, which I suppose I am, but he agreed that I had acted in a thoroughly businesslike way. Then I went to the travel agent in Portsmouth and booked a flight to Naples for tomorrow. They have also arranged an hotel for me. I don't know how long I shall stay there, I may not come back at all!

I can hardly believe it is happening. I'm sure with your knowledge and experience you will be able to sell my lovely box at a good profit and then we shall both have benefited. Thank you again for being so helpful.

Yours very sincerely,

Diana Hetherington.

P.S. If you need further proof of my ownership of the box, I have George Hetherington's original will among my papers at the bank. I have told the manager to send you a copy if you need it. D.H.

So that was that. I had not realized her name was Diana. I thought about the decoration on the box. I had been well and truly bitten and I hadn't even seen her naked. Quite the reverse. My lust for the letter and what it would bring had left me totally exposed but I was still unsure whether she had arranged it or was merely an innocent beneficiary.

I met the cheque by selling my investments and mortgaging the shop. I sold the box for eighteen hundred pounds and set about restoring my fortunes. Surprisingly, it did not take me long to make up the loss. It was the beginning of the boom in popular antiques and I worked hard to establish a reputation as a reliable expert, dealing exclusively with genuine, high-quality antique furniture and fine art. If I were given to psychoanalysis, I suppose I would say that subconsciously I was ashamed of the greed and inclination towards shady deals that had led to my downfall and needed to rebuild my self-esteem. On the other hand, I may simply have realized that I could make a great deal more money and with less risk by using my considerable skill and knowledge to operate at a higher level. Whatever the motivation, today I am a respected authority, something of a television personality, and owner of premises in New Bond Street. The Hetherington Galleries. Well, I could hardly call it Young Antiques and the name gives me the opportunity to reminisce about my early years in the business and to hint at a mysterious but honourable link with Nelson and Lady Hamilton through that fine old

English naval family, the Hetheringtons. I looked them up in the Navy Lists. Edward Hetherington was a midshipman on the *Victory* and George 'Swisher' Hetherington was a Rear Admiral until his sudden and early retirement in 1925. Diana Hetherington did not return to England, the furniture from the house was sold at auction for three hundred and fifty pounds. I did not bid and I never saw or heard from her again.

Until this morning.

I was busy working on my notes for a new television series when one of my assistants asked me if I would see an American who had something to give me. I am well protected from casual callers by my staff but he had mentioned the name Hetherington and produced a card which showed that he was on the staff of the United States Embassy. He was quite young, about thirty, and very businesslike in the manner of his countrymen. After a brief handshake, he waved away my offer of a glass of sherry almost before I had finished making it and then sat facing me across my desk, clutching his briefcase on his lap.

'Mr Young, did you own an antique shop, Maritime Memorabilia, in Portsmouth, England in 1965?' I had neither heard nor thought of that name for many years and I winced at the memory. I nodded.

'Did you know a Miss Diana Hetherington at that time?' He asked it in the manner of a young district attorney in a Hollywood courtroom drama. I paused for a moment, nodded and said, 'Yes.'

He relaxed, leaned back in his chair and smiled with the air of a man who has come to the end of a great quest. 'Mr Young, I have been looking for you for over a month. I thought the trail had gone cold and then I saw you on TV the other night talking about Nelson and I knew you were the man. I'm afraid I have bad news. Diana Hetherington is dead.' He paused, presumably to see what effect the announcement would have on me. I think he was slightly disappointed.

'I haven't seen Miss Hetherington in over twenty years,' I explained, 'and I didn't know her very well then. I'm sorry you have had trouble finding me but I can't imagine why you should want to.'

He took a small brown paper parcel from his briefcase and handed it to me. 'Diana knew she was going to die. Cancer. Terminal. She asked me to find you and give you this. She did not explain and of course I did not ask.'

His sense of the dramatic owed a lot to soap operas and it was impossible not to join in. I nodded and gave him my slow, sad smile.

He hurried to reassure me. 'She died peacefully. She's buried in the English cemetery in Naples. That was her wish. She had spent so many happy years in Italy.' He carried on reminiscing about the gatherings at her modest villa and I opened the small parcel he had given me. It was a miniature portrait on ivory of a beautiful young girl, her face framed by a mass of tumbling auburn hair, smiling at the artist, her eyes inviting and at the same time laughing at the foolish old men who would fall at her feet. It was a copy of one of Romney's early portraits of the young Emma Hamilton painted before time and the foolish old men reduced her to drunken wretchedness. The copy was signed Grimaldi, worth about five hundred pounds. There was no message.

The young man had stopped talking and was waiting for my reaction to the gift. 'How did you come to know Miss Hetherington?' I asked.

'I was stationed at our consulate in Naples. She had that lovely little villa, you know?' I nodded rather than interrupt his story.

'Did you know her father?' I nodded again. I felt that a mystery was about to be solved.

'From what she told me, he sounded something of a rogue but I gather he left her well provided for. An insurance policy I guess, although she always called it a letter of credit. She used to drink to his memory. "My father and his letter of credit" she would say and then she would laugh. Did you know she played poker?'

'No,' I said. 'But nothing Miss Hetherington did would surprise me.'

'She was the best darned poker player I ever came across,

bar none. I think it was her main source of income. Apparently she used to play with her father.'

I remembered. 'Daddy and I played cards together, hour after hour.' I had assumed it was bridge.

'You know, she could kid you that she was holding the hand to beat all hands and then, when we chickened out and she scooped the pool, it would turn out that what she had wasn't worth a damn. You know what I mean?'

'Yes,' I said, 'I know what you mean.'

MISSIONARY ENDEAVOUR

Patricia Mowbray

Patricia Mowbray's last short story won a BBC Young Writers competition. It has been a long gestation – 23 years – until her second story but in the interim she has been bringing up her six children and working as a freelance journalist, most regularly for the *Sunday Times*. She has covered a wide variety of subjects but is most interested in health and social issues.

MISSIONARY ENDEAVOUR

As she drove the children towards Somerset House a murky drizzle descended. The Toytown wipers on her Deux Chevaux batted back and forth, making little impression on the streaked and greasy windscreen.

The ageing vehicle was performing like Un Cheval as it coughed and lurched through the London traffic. It was not a well car, she reflected grimly. But it was somewhere well down the priority list and would only rise to the top on the morning when she turned the key and found life totally extinct.

He had taken the Jaguar with him when he went. Although it had been bought with money that her father left her, she was not sorry to see it go. She loathed watching the fuel gauge falling rapidly in city traffic, the flash trash feel of it, the bilious colour, a perfect match for Peaudouce when babies had been fed a surfeit of fruit.

The children, in their freshly laundered school uniforms, sat bolt upright on the rear seat of her little tin car, fidgeting nervously and staring out of the rain-speckled windows. 'Everyone all right?' she shouted over her shoulder. You had to shout in a Deux Chevaux to be heard over the racket.

'I've got a hole in my tights,' Sophie yelled back plaintively.

God, this was mad, she thought for the fiftieth time. Here she was collecting three kids from three different schools to drag them across London for a conciliation meeting with a maniac, who had beaten shit out of her and had smashed them up pretty effectively too.

Conciliation? Were they all crazy? How the hell did you conciliate with a madman? It had taken her sixteen years to summon enough strength and courage to divorce him. For most of those years she had been, what? A victim of 'domestic violence'? That sounded too cosy, like domestic appliance or domestic help. So had she been 'knocked about'? No, too slapstick, the typical tacky script of a North Country comic. There was no way to describe what she had been to anyone who had not been there.

Endlessly the media focused attention on street attacks. That women were not safe out alone was a matter of public concern. But what of women like her, who were in constant danger and forever afraid inside their own homes? Then there was nowhere to run to, no escape. Home sweet home was nightmare territory.

In her smart Victorian semi the Yale lock on the front door did not protect her, it trapped her. There were no walls that she had not bounced off, no banisters, no sharp corners in the kitchen. Even now she stepped into rooms with apprehension, expecting him to spring out from behind the door.

Yet it was not just the constant fear, the unpredictability of his crazed attacks, which froze her, it was the isolation that came with feeling ashamed. All the guilt was hers; for a long time she was convinced that she must be to blame. She had heard that people often presented themselves as mentally sick when they were, in fact, quite normal but married to partners who projected their madness on to them. She found it entirely plausible. In the crazy world she had inhabited black was white, the guilty innocent and the innocent guilty.

There was, though, a kind of lunacy attached to her behaviour. She became part of his conspiracy. While he, clever mad, lived out a Jekyll and Hyde existence, she aided and abetted it, presenting a picture of the perfect family to the outside world. 'No one would ever believe you,' he had sneered and she knew he was right. Why should they when she had worn polo-neck sweaters to hide the bruises, sunglasses to cover black eyes?

Once you had connived at your own victimization, through shame and the kind of stupor that descended, once you had tolerated the intolerable, your instinct to survive was lost somewhere along with your self-esteem. She was still infuriated by the mad media line that some wives enjoyed being victims of violence, needed it. It was not exciting, it was dehumanizing. Life became a process of surviving day by day. Each good day was a bonus so wonderful that you hung on to it, blotting out the grim reality of all the others. You were a hostage, forever intent on not offending your captor; it became a whole way of life.

When she married him she already knew that he was a flawed human being, that was probably part of his attraction. He had endured a terrible childhood, was a loner with no one to care about him. His cynicism she mistook for hurt, his coldness for need. Her parents thought him impossible, they could not understand why she should care for him, although they had brought her up to care.

Robert Graves wondered, 'Why have such scores of lovely, gifted girls married impossible men? Simple self-sacrifice may be ruled out, and missionary endeavour, nine times out of ten.' But she had believed that she could save him, love him better. It was a naivety she paid for dearly. Better to have joined the Sisters of Mercy.

Perhaps if she had not grown up in a world of good and gentle men she would have recognized the risk in marrying him. But he was the first and only cruel man she had ever met. The overpowering emotion when he first hit her was of total disbelief. Her capacity for amazement amazed her. Even now, after all these years of torment, she sometimes wondered if she had imagined the horror of it all. He had fed on that, rewriting reality, almost convincing her that what had happened had not happened at all.

The bruises, the blood, the eventual unbearable consultation with her doctor were her proof, her grip on the truth. She had sat in her GP's surgery, removed sunglasses to show the blood clot streaking her eye, peeled back her sweater, revealing the swollen collarbone, the gouged neck, and wept. 'Your husband did that to you.' It was a statement, not a question. She nodded. 'And it is not the first time.' She nodded again.

And still she sought excuses. 'Could he be ill? He says none of it happens and he really seems to believe it.' It was not an illness her doctor cared to consider.

'Get out,' he urged. 'Get the children out and come to me

as soon as you are ready to use this. It will all be here on my file.'

Ready? Would she ever be ready? She wanted to get out and with a new urgency. At first his attacks came at night. He would return home late, surly drunk or just nasty sober, from his job as investigative journalist on the gutter press. The smallest annoyance would trigger an attack. No use to hide from him, to go to bed before his return. He would appear beside the bed, looming over her in the darkness, and order her downstairs. With the children sleeping, she would follow him down to another beating.

He had all the power, and her need to protect the children from the truth dragged her further into his pit. He was omnipotent. The exact shirt he desired, even the exact pair of socks, must be laundered when he wanted them. His dinner must be waiting whenever he came home, his gin and tonic must come with ice and lemon, his toast cut in half, his apple washed and dried. He demanded a military precision in the house, which made no allowances for childhood. A word out of place, a discarded toy, fingermarks on the wallpaper, were grounds for cold fury. And always his castigation began, 'Just because your mother has no standards.'

Perhaps in a different marriage she would have had 'standards', have been more of a disciplinarian, but with his relentless bullying and unreasonable demands, how could she not soften their existence? The children were sanity in the midst of madness, loving, beautiful, bright. But while the need to protect them had held her in his grip, once they began to grow and become victims too she had to fight her way clear.

Life in those days was a constant schizophrenic rollercoaster. His two selves, their two homes, all love and laughter in his absence, frozen silence as his key turned in the lock. The nights of screaming quietly, cleaning up the blood before morning, gave way to constant vigilance, placing herself between him and them. When he started physically attacking them her stupor receded; now she must act, for the children. But how to escape? She could not endure watching him hold Josh, her firstborn, up by the throat for raising his eyes at a lecture, yanking Alex's hair out of his scalp when a window was broken by a football, knocking Sophie sprawling for talking during the radio news at breakfast.

One night, when he was sober and full of dinner she told him she wanted a divorce. He laughed. 'You will never divorce me, my love,' he said. 'I will see you in the gutter, without your children.' And the subject closed, he returned to watching the TV, a little smile dragging at the edges of his clipped moustache.

It would be one hell of a fight. She would need a good lawyer, the best. Then, when her father died, she put the money left, after buying his Jaguar and settling the bills, on deposit in her own name. He was quietly enraged, unconvinced by her explanation that she had placed it on deposit merely for the time being. It gave her a new independence, removed her from his total financial dominance. He began to circle her like a man-eating tiger who has discovered that his prey has acquired a loaded gun. It was the start of her fight to be free.

The decision to, at last, consult a solicitor, to start divorce proceedings, was forced on her one sunny Sunday afternoon. The kids were playing a silly, boisterous game in the garden, while he took cuttings from a heap of newspapers and yelled at them to shut up. She was upstairs sorting out clothes, when Sophie burst in howling, 'Mummy, Mummy, come quickly, Daddy's beating Josh with a stick.' She raced down to find the boy on the bottom of the staircase, defiantly braving the stick, which was descending in his lunatic father's fist.

She grappled with him for the stick, yelling, 'No, you will not do this. You will not do this in my house.' It was the worst thing she could have said.

'*Your* house? *Your* house?' Maddened, he turned on her, knocked her to the floor with the stick and threw himself on her, pounding, pummelling, grabbing her throat, spitting threats and saliva in her face. The children dragged at him, shouting. The boys tried to haul him off. Sophie sobbed. Eventually, he flung her aside. The children stood in front of her, shaking. 'Why don't you divorce Mummy?' Sophie yelled at him. 'You don't love her.'

He wiped the spit from his moustache, surveyed them all

for a moment and smiled. 'A divorce? She can have a divorce.' Then he looked at her challenging her. She would never have the strength, the guts. 'You can try it, my love. Just take care,' he warned her, 'that I don't have something on the judge.'

She had found a good lawyer, an old, well-respected war horse. He had given her the customary chat about reconciliation, about being certain that this was what she wanted. He had stressed the trauma of divorce, particularly when children were involved. In that first interview it was impossible to begin to tell of the trauma of her marriage.

'You are a writer,' he had observed, having taken down in her details that she freelanced for a national paper. 'So write it all down, everything. From the start of the marriage.'

She had written it all down, matter of fact, a revelation, even to herself, of how awful it was, had been from the start, and dropped it in at his reception desk. When she arrived home later, her solicitor had already phoned, leaving a message with Josh that she was to return his call the moment she got in.

'This is one of the worst cases I have dealt with,' he told her when she rang him. She felt strangely vindicated. 'We have to get him out,' he said.

And they did. Her barrister, who had told her how difficult such orders were to persuade a court to give, got an ouster order from a judge in the High Court, to which the judge, in his wisdom, added a non-molestation order. But that was merely the beginning. Everything was fought and contested in the High Court. Thousands of pounds drained from her deposit account into that of her lawyers. Days were spent in cavernous court-rooms, designed to strike the fear of God into murderers and hardened criminals. She donned her one respectable suit and trudged off to wait interminably in corridors, to play out a game in which the rules took no account of a malevolent respondent, with the money to invest in mischief.

At the time the Conservative lawyers were hawking a report on divorce being too easy, the place of women being in the home, their downfall feminist free-thinking. She had written a dispassionate reply in a 'quality' newspaper, giving the stark figures of women divorcing husbands for cruelty.

But it was easier to handle on paper than in life. Divorce was only easy if you were not divorcing a man intent on seeing you 'in the gutter without your children'. The reality was that divorcing a lunatic was practically impossible and, for all its talk of the interests of the children being paramount, the system wanted to draw a veil over terror. Once grounds were established, it had no interest in the degree of unreasonable behaviour, the degree of a parent's madness.

Once they decided it was over, the court pretended that the mad were sane, that brutal maniacs were caring parents, with whom a rewarding relationship with their children must be maintained.

Now, here they were, stuck in the traffic, snarled up around Green Park, inching their way towards conciliation at Somerset House. 'Will we have to tell them what we want in front of Dad?' Alex was white-faced as she looked at him in the rear-view mirror.

'I'm not saying a bloody word,' said Josh. 'They don't want to listen so I don't want to talk.'

Sophie was pulling at the hole in her tights. 'Mummy, this hole is enormous. We have to get some new tights,' she wailed.

Christ, she wanted to turn round and take them all home. 'I will ask for you all to speak separately and privately. You must simply tell them what you want and then it will be over.'

'Over?' laughed Josh. 'If you believe that you're mad. I never wanted to come out of school for this. Why can't they leave us alone?'

'It's all right for you.' Sophie was still tugging at her tights, trying to drag the hole up her leg and cover it with her school skirt. 'I feel like a freak. All my friends know. Sister Dominic just had to call me from class to her office and give me a little talk. Everyone was whispering about me, Mummy. I hate it.'

'Oh, shut up, will you.' Alex had hunched himself in the corner. 'It's bad enough without you all going on.'

'Right,' she said, trying to take control of the disintegrating situation. 'Let's all calm down. We're almost there.'

Of course, it was a Monday, his day off. He would have meticulously prepared his papers, organized his campaign. She had meticulously laundered the children's clothes, shone their shoes, tried to keep them calm. She had done the round-trip of the schools, picking them up. She had set out early, getting later and later in the traffic.

All of it, the whole damn business, was relentless. Every time you thought you had escaped the hand reached out, tenacious fingers tightened around your throat and dragged you back in. The system was as inescapable a tormentor as he had been.

What else had she expected – paternal protection, justice? No, the fallen were forever mighty, the meek inherited eternal persecution. In the end they held you as paralysed as he had and they turned black to white just as adroitly.

It was pouring down now as Nelson loomed ahead of them in the deluge. The pigeons had all taken cover. 'Lucky old Nelson,' she thought. 'No one's shitting on him today.' For her bad light never stopped play, the game was never rained off.

She had attended the funeral of her favourite uncle the week before. He was an avowed atheist, a wonderful, wise and gentle man. They had bestowed on him a proper Christian funeral and it had bucketed down. 'Too right, Uncle John,' she thought. 'Serves the buggers right.'

Mourners had muttered, 'What a dreadful day for a funeral.' What did they want, birds singing, sun shining, a perfect cloudless sky? It was bad enough that he was not here in the rain, but not here in the sunshine? Still, there was no good day for a funeral, no good day for a conciliation hearing either.

She could have done without the whole of London taking to their cars though. The Strand was at a total standstill. She looked at her watch. 'Hell!' They were definitely going to be late if it didn't move soon. A taxi cut her up at the lights and she leant on the horn. It squeaked pathetically and she crashed the gears.

'For God's sake, Mum,' Josh shouted. 'Don't smash the stupid car.'

No, calm down. They had enough problems without adding a road accident. 'Okay, okay,' she said. 'Nearly there. Start looking out for car park signs, will you?'

They parked in an underground car park several streets from their destination and emerged into the teeming rain. They had to run along the puddled pavements and arrived at the grand portals of Somerset House breathless, scared and sodden.

As they approached, he was stepping out of a taxi, in his Harrods suit, starched shirt and polished, oxblood city shoes. He held an executive briefcase in one hand, an umbrella in the other shielded his immaculate lady lawyer from the downpour. The children stopped dead in their tracks. At that moment her lovely, fatherly solicitor came forward from the entrance and shepherded the group quickly across the forecourt, into the building and up the stairs.

They arrived in an overlit corridor on an upper floor. It was all so unreal, a neon nightmare of human anguish. Ashen-faced kids sat silently on leather-backed chairs, stony-faced parents stood grimly at their sides. Lawyers lounged like gargoyles against the walls. A row was going on quietly in one corner. 'How long do we have to stay here?' growled Josh to her solicitor.

He had now appeared at the far end of the corridor, a cold smile twisting his already crooked moustache, as he peered at her over his solicitor's shoulder and pushed his gold-rimmed spectacles back up his nose. The kids gathered behind her soaked skirts.

She asked to see the court officer in charge of the proceedings and was taken to his office. He seemed a reasonable chap, bespectacled and bald-headed. She told him that the children were afraid to give honest preferences in public. She wanted them to be allowed to speak in confidence, separately, privately, so that neither parent would hear and no one could carry back tales. He nodded and agreed that it was a sensible course of action.

The children, thus assured, trooped off one by one, looking lost and afraid, to deliver their opinions in confidence. At last, she thought, the system was giving them a degree of protection. Each of them came back to stand steadfastly mute, staring down at their sodden shoes.

Then she had to face him. Those whom conciliation has brought together let no decree nisi put asunder. Her hair was dripping into the perspiration running down her forehead. She shrank back inside herself as he stood silhouetted against a window, a black spectre from her past, brought into her present and looming over her future.

They could agree nothing. He was his sane self, plausibly adamant. She was battle-weary, the farcical game playing on around her. 'Joshua has said . . .' The court officer's account of his interview with Josh shocked her back into consciousness. 'Sophie feels . . .' the grey-suited goon continued. 'Alexander really wants . . .'

Their confidential interviews hung in the air like little fragile ghosts. Her eyes grew round, incredulous. She looked from the court officer to her solicitor, who averted his gaze. They could still stun her into total disbelief. She gawped at the balding, bespectacled idiot. If these people were sane, then she must be raving mad.

And what was it all for, this gruesome charade? What did it achieve? Only the promise of more, of an imminent visit from the court welfare officer, that ultimate judge and jury. It was not over, Josh was right. It went on rolling over their lives, flattening them, and now it had handed them on a plate to the one person they most feared. The poor little bastards had not rallied to his cause.

Back in the ghastly glare of the endless corridor she reclaimed the children from a strained junior solicitor who was clearly glad to see the back of them. Her lawyer looked at her, all concern. 'All right?' he asked.

'I asked him not to . . .'

'I know,' he said.

'It's crazy . . .'

'I know,' he said.

The children were anxious to escape before their father and his lady lawyer finished conferring further down the passageway. 'Let's get out of here, Mum,' Josh urged and they fled back down the stairs.

'I'll phone you tomorrow,' her solicitor said, and stood watching them as they rushed out of the entrance and darted through the rain, across the road, out of reach, before he emerged.

In a side street she stopped for them all to catch their breath. 'Why did you tell him?' Sophie began. The accusations spilled out brokenly.

'You little shit, Alex.' Oh Christ, not only had the bloody man told her and their father everything they had said, he had repeated the children's confidences to the others.

Back in the underground car park they shrieked at each other as the car spluttered into life. All across London they yelled at each other, at her, and she yelled back at them. Outside the Victoria and Albert Museum she shouted, 'Stop! Enough! I've had enough.'

'You've had enough? Don't you think we've had enough?' Josh yelled. Sophie was howling behind her seat and she began to howl too. She couldn't see past the bloody batting wipers, she couldn't see out of her bloody bawling eyes. She reached a hand back and found Sophie's clenched fist; steering with one hand she hung on to it. 'Hang on,' she told herself. 'Hang on. Pick up the pieces of your children and put them together again.' Put them back together so that he and the system could carry on tearing them apart.

And so cometh the court welfare officer. Ah, beware the detached, professional smile of the lady in the sensible shoes and the Volkswagen Beetle. She comes not to find the truth but to bury it.

Before the appointed arrival how she had cleaned, polished, scrubbed and hoovered. The windows shone, the bedrooms were tidied and then strategically untidied with sensible toys. She fretted over whether to put fresh flowers in the vases, fruit in the bowl. Would it appear extravagant in a single parent? She bought them anyway. 'It's not to be eaten,' she warned the children, piling up fruit. 'Not until she's gone.'

The welfare officer was a Miss, how could she begin to understand? She watched her stalk up the garden path and wanted to slam the door in her face, shout, 'This is my home and I don't want you here.' But, of course, she couldn't. Instead she pinned on a welcoming smile, made coffee, tried to project calm reason, while she shook inside.

She told of the access visits he made to the home. How he screamed and threatened each time, until told to leave. How he announced to the children, 'I have to go or your mother will have me arrested' and roared off up the road in his Jaguar, leaving them tear-stained and shell-shocked on the pavement. All except Josh, who would emerge from his room asking, 'Has that bastard gone?' (Of course, she didn't tell her that.)

She told too of their staying visits to him, when they returned with tales of how he had broken a broom handle across Josh, bashed Sophie with what was left of it, how she had seen a hand print still on Alex's face when he came home. The children, questioned independently, told too of his continued attacks.

The welfare officer took notes, nodded, smiled her practised smile, went to interview him in his solitary London pad and submitted a report of 'two intelligent parents, who care deeply about their children'. No mention of the violence, no protection except for the status quo.

Her solicitor had been adamant. No, he would not allow her to challenge the report. The court would not like it and beside it was not disapproving of her. 'But it is not the truth!' she had yelled at him. The truth? Who cared about the bloody truth, who cared about the children, already frightened and battle-scarred, being sent off weekly until their destruction was complete?

And so, finally, the childen too were dragged off to the terrors of the High Court. She had tried to prevent that but was, as ever, impotent. He wanted them there, scared to tell the truth. He wanted them there to torment her. When the judge had said that the children must be brought to court she sat on in the bench to pull herself together and dry her tears. As she left, after all the others, he stepped out of the shadows, barring her way, triumph glinting in his eyes.

'May you burn in hell,' she told him and pushed her way out of the swinging doors.

Yet again she had to watch her frightened children as they trooped off one by one. Sophie had hung on to her hand until the door closed between them on the judge's chambers. The cloisters were stony cold and she shivered uncontrollably as she waited. He was standing, surrounded by his aides, on the other side of the gallery, watching the scene with ill-concealed satisfaction.

The children's interviews over, they were once again dispatched into the nervous care of the junior solicitor. Now it was back into court. She sat on, unwilling to face the rest of it. All the lawyers had gone into the courtroom; she rose reluctantly. There at the end of the gallery he stood, framed by the heavy wooden door, smiling, waiting.

She was once again in the hallway of their home, running for the front door. He stood before it, laughing his maniac laugh, cutting her off. She turned, fled back towards the kitchen, the back door. He caught her by the radiator, grabbed her by the hair and smashed her face into the hot metal. He stood, watching her dart across the kitchen, reeling against the cooker, grabbing at a cupboard for support. There on the cupboard lay a kitchen knife, pointed and sharp. She picked it up as he advanced. If only she could bring herself to use it. He stood before her, his thin lips peeled back over little teeth. 'Take a knife to me, would you?' he snarled, and whipped her across the head with his flattened hand, knocking her across the kitchen and the knife out of her grasp. It clattered across the quarry tiles.

He let her run back up the hallway, caught her at the stairs, flung her back across them and gripped her throat. 'No,' she choked. 'Don't kill me here. Not where the children will find me.'

Laughing, he hauled her up by the throat. 'Where would you like to die?' he giggled, before throwing her back on the staircase and tightening his grip on her neck. She struggled, kicked and gurgled, the blood pounded in her head. His smile swam before her eyes. The same smile froze her now in front of the courtroom door.

She opened her handbag, tissues spilled out, her make-up case fell to the floor, lipsticks rolled across the linoleum. As he stood, looking down at the mess, she gazed for a moment at the pointed, sharp kitchen knife lying at the bottom of her bag. He had not changed, but neither had she. She stooped down, collected up the debris and stuffed it back in over the knife. It was a beautiful, impossible fantasy.

Her solicitor appeared through the door, placed himself between them. Putting an arm around her shoulder, he drew her inside. 'Come on,' he said. 'The judge is on his way.'

They all stood while the judge proceeded to his lofty perch. As they settled down in the benches, he spread some papers in front of him, coughed, took a drink of water, and looked down over his subjects.

'This is a case in which,' the judge began as she bowed her head and closed her eyes. Her solicitor squeezed her arm. He ripped a corner of paper off a page, scrawled on it with his Parker pen and pushed it to her. 'You will win!' it said.

'I have listened to what each of the children has to say,' the judge continued. 'They are three fine, intelligent children. They have made their wishes quite clear to me.'

She held her breath, the judge was looking down, directly into her eyes. 'I know,' his look said. 'I know.' She began to shiver again.

'Please,' she prayed. 'Please.'

'I have no intention of repeating here what the children have told me,' the judge said. 'I have given them my word and do not intend to let them down.'

She had won, the game was over. The judge found for her. She was in a state of total delirious shock. They all left the court. She put her head down on her arms, exhausted. Sitting up at last, she opened her hand. There was her solicitor's note. She slipped it into her pocket and gathered up her belongings. Now she could see light at the end of the tunnel and for the first time it wasn't the headlights of an oncoming train.

Foolish, foolish, foolish. He was waiting in the shadows again. 'It's not finished, my love,' he leered. 'Never think that. I will see you at the appeal.'

There was nothing she wanted to say to him. She couldn't

improve on 'May you burn in hell', which she meant to be the last words he ever heard from her.

Outside, her ever-watchful solicitor was waiting. Again he stepped between them but now he allowed himself the indulgence of turning to look at her adversary with utter loathing. 'Come on, Mum,' he said to her, briskly. 'They've waited long enough.' Down the stone steps they went, to a back corridor, where the junior solicitor, unaccustomed to the role of babysitter, had wisely hidden the children. This time she actually said goodbye to them and smiled.

Her lawyer led them out of a rear exit. They stood for a moment under the cliff face of the court building. 'I'll phone you tomorrow,' he said. And quietly, so that the children would not hear, 'Don't worry, he may not get leave to appeal.' Then he stood, watching them disappear down the street.

The little band of survivors made their way back to the distant underground car park. They were daft happy now, like prisoners of war who had tunnelled under the wire and whose jubilation ignored the guns trained from watchtowers, the tracker dogs in the woods. They were grinning, linking arms. Anyone watching them would imagine they had been on a family day out. She stopped as they reached the car. 'Right, we're going to McDonald's for supper,' she announced.

'Can we afford it?' Sophie asked.

'No, but I'll worry about that tomorrow,' she said. That and the appeal, the legal aid certificate, the gas bill, the unpaid maintenance, the overdue mortgage.

They leapt into the car, Big Macs and Double Deckers beckoning. She turned the ignition key. Nothing. Life was finally extinct. They climbed back out of the dead Deux Chevaux. She wrote a note on the back of an envelope. 'Broken down. Will come tomorrow', and jammed it under the wiper. Her membership of the RAC had long since lapsed. She looked at the crestfallen kids. What the hell? 'Come on,' she declared. 'We'll take a taxi.'

'Mum, are you totally mad?' Josh gazed at her.

'Don't start worrying, my darlings,' she laughed, 'until they tell you I'm sane.'

A CRACK IN THE GLASS

Dr Frances Peck

Frances Peck was born in Jaffna, Sri Lanka. She qualified as a doctor in 1984 and worked as a psychiatrist before becoming a journalist, specializing in women's and children's health. This is her first piece of fiction and she is now working on a novel for children. Frances lives in London with her husband and Reuben the dog.

A CRACK IN THE GLASS

The room was warm, stuffy, pitch dark, the corridor light filtering under the door too feeble to make any difference. Muffled voices from outside bade good night, doors slammed, far too loudly considering the time, and the sleeping figure moaned a little and turned. Silence descended, and from somewhere in the room the dependable ticking of a clock emerged.

Suddenly the shrill, hysterical repetition of a bleep screamed into the darkness. The slumberer jerked up, her heart racing and pounding in her ears. 'Cardiac arrest on –' the alarm crackled, with all the clarity of a platform announcement on British Rail.

'Oh shit!' She fumbled in the dark for the phone and stabbed blindly at the zero.

It rang twice and then connected. 'Switchboard,' came the sing-song reply.

'It's Dr Lloyd' – the voice was thick and slightly slurred – 'Where's the arrest?'

'Mountjoy ward.'

'Thanks!' She put down the phone and swung her legs out of bed. *Hurry*. Her feet trawled in the darkness for her shoes and fumbled over her whiskered Fluffy Bunny slippers, a present from David. Not on your life! she muttered and groped for the light, sending something clattering to the floor as her hand found the switch.

Outside, a door opened and heavy, male footfalls went crashing through the hall. *Jonathan*. They had both been up just five minutes earlier. The blood still pounded sickeningly and her eyes ached in the sudden brilliance, but the urgency of his steps pulled her to her feet.

She snatched her white coat from the crushed, tired heap

of her clothes, threw it over her greens, shoved her feet into her shoes, grabbed her bleep from the bedside table and pushed on her glasses. *Four bloody a.m.!* But she was wrong about their last call. Mr Blackett had vomited well over an hour ago.

A minute had passed since the alert and she was running down the corridor, out of the doctors' quarters and down the stairs, straight into the bowels of the hospital's east wing. Everywhere there was the faint, persistent smell of disinfected floors, deserted now except for the distant, cockney voices of the porters and the edge of a crash trolley disappearing into a lift at the end of the passage. She kept on running, following them up by way of the stairs. At the top of the fourth flight she swung left.

Mountjoy ward was hushed and darkened, save for the illuminated circle of a lamp at the nurses' station, and the faint glow of a light coming from behind drawn curtains, towards the far end. She passed through the open doors and slowed to a half-run, trying not to let her shoes clack too loudly on the hard floor as she hurried past the dimly lit shapes, some on their sides, some half-sitting up against a mountain of pillows, their mouths slack and hanging.

Suddenly, an elderly lady in a bed to the right jerked out her hand. It might have been a threat or a greeting. Confused old dear, she thought, quickly looking away and wondering at the woman's bright blue hair.

By now she could see the backs of the crash team pushing against the curtains and the square silhouette of the cardiac arrest trolley parked in the middle. She neared and heard a quiet, urgent voice which she recognized as Sister Anne's and another, deeper voice responding to it.

'I can't find a vein,' the houseman was saying as she pushed back the curtains.

'Ah, Ceri. There you are,' Sister Anne said. Her calm voice betrayed relief. She was standing behind the patient's head, her left hand cupping a thick rubber mask over the woman's mouth, the right rhythmically squeezing the oxygen from the Ambu bag. At the same time, Jonathan was pushing down on the woman's chest with the palms of his hands, elbows straight, his face concentrated into timing his exertions to a count of five, mumbling the numbers, pausing and then starting again.

Ceri turned to the Sister. 'What's the story?' she asked, catching her breath, taking in the relentlessly flat trace on the monitor and the woman's puffy but still pink face. She didn't know her.

'She woke up complaining of severe chest pain, Ceri. She arrested as we went to bleep you.'

Ceri nodded, quickly moving over to help the houseman.

'She came in yesterday,' Sister Anne went on, her fingers continuing to push tirelessly into the bag. 'Her name's Ida Bates. Mrs. Sixty-two years old. Family history of hyperlipidaemia. She's in for query angina.'

'Mm . . .' Ceri slipped the needle into an invisible vein. Blood: dark, slow, lifeless, oozed down its shaft. 'Plug in the bicarb,' she said quickly. '8.4 per cent.' But already she could see the pink tinge beginning to fade from the woman's skin. 'How long's it been, Anne?'

Sister Anne turned the wrist of her cupped hand a fraction without letting go of the woman's chin and glanced at her watch. 'Coming up to – eight minutes.'

Their eyes met. 'God! That's just great. We're going to have to get a line into her.' Ceri snorted in frustration. 'Where the *hell's* the anaesthetist?'

'It's Mike Stone,' put in the houseman. 'We bleeped him. He should be here any minute now.'

'And who's he?' she demanded.

'He's new.'

Yeah. From Hicksville Hospital. The trace was still flat. *Well, I'll be damned if I'm doing his bloody job.* Her last central line had been a disaster. Made the man's neck swell like a football. *He could have died.*

She looked down at the woman on the bed, at the dead, open eyes, moving about like a doll's with every push on her chest. 'Look, I'll have to put the line in' – her voice seemed calm – 'since the anaesthetist's not here . . .'

Sister Anne nodded, handed the Ambu bag to the

houseman and began to prepare the instruments while the doctor pulled on a pair of gloves.

She glanced at the medical student still pushing on the woman's chest. Large, dark circles had formed under the arms of his shirt and an unmissable one inch of striped material hung disloyally from the edge of his left trouser leg. It made her smile, despite herself. She started swabbing the woman's neck with iodine and watched the yellow-brown stain gather and run down the creases of fat.

'Here's the needle, Ceri,' said Sister Anne.

'Right.' She took it, conscious of the listening silence all around her and beyond the curtains – thick and heavy, punctuated only by the clearing of a throat somewhere in the distance and here, beside her, the rhythmic efforts of both nurse and student to sustain a life. The doctor looked again at the stained, fat-creased skin of the woman's neck and drew her breath. 'Right . . .' she said again, to herself. *Here goes.*

Suddenly footsteps were heard. Not a run but a brisk, confident stride.

'Stone,' said the houseman.

And Stone it was. Poking his head between the curtains, he ran his smiling, bespectacled eyes over the proceedings. 'Sorry I'm late, team. RTA down in Cas – horrible mess. Had to intubate the poor sod.'

'No problem,' said Ceri. She wielded the needle in the air and smiled coolly. 'Would you like to do the honours?'

He shrugged, still hanging on to the curtains. 'Oh, you might as well do it . . . now you've started.' Then he stepped inside and bent to peer hard at the woman's mottled, fading face. 'Hmmm . . . the old girl looks a bit blue round the gills. I'll intubate her as soon as you've finished.'

Ceri stared for a moment at the top of his head and then said: 'I'd rather you did it.' Her face flushed.

But the anaesthetist just nodded to himself. 'Right then, let's give her a decent airway first.' He reached out for the plastic tube and inserted it down the throat, then pulled on a pair of size eight gloves and cleanly slipped the needle into the woman's neck. 'Atropine and adrenaline?' he enquired, as he threaded the central line down towards the heart.

Ceri looked up quickly and nodded, avoiding his eyes.

'Right then, here we go.'

Everyone stopped and stared at the screen as he began to push the drugs down the line.

And the seconds passed, seeming like minutes . . .

But nothing changed.

At once the regular *whoosh* of the Ambu bag resumed, the student began pushing again. And they all knew – felt the precious, desperate, life-holding moments slipping away.

Ceri looked at the anaesthetist's impassive profile, his eyes still on the screen. Her voice sounded tight: 'Let's give her another dose.'

'Yep, might as well.' Stone nodded, once again pushing the drugs down the line. 'Come on old girl,' he whispered.

But the woman couldn't hear. She wasn't listening.

'Come on, you old tart. Show us what you're made of.'

But Ida wouldn't. And in her heart Ceri knew then that the trace wouldn't change.

The anaesthetist shrugged, but Ceri could see the defeat in his face. 'Anne,' she said eventually, her hand rubbing her forehead, 'has she got any family?'

And then it caught her eye. Unbelievably, the line on the screen was beginning to fizz. Everyone stopped and stared, watched as the line suddenly exploded into huge, jagged, frenetic waves – waves spelling disaster of a different kind, but also hope.

'Get the pads on!' cried Dr Stone, almost shouting. Sister and Ceri were doing just that.

'Stand back!' Ceri commanded, running her eyes round the team to make sure everyone was clear of the bed. She pressed the electrodes on to the pads, just above the woman's huge, flat breasts, and fired the buttons.

The body jerked high into the air, jiggled obscenely against the pads, then fell away, lay flaccid, silent. Nothingness . . . A dead, empty shell. And then the woman began to splutter – little, pathetic coughs at first, then growing stronger, increasing in violence, rattling through her, until suddenly her whole body began to heave and shudder in urgent, uncontrollable spasms. Ida Bates was struggling with all her will for another chance at life.

For a moment no one moved, just stood looking back and forth at the spluttering woman and the near-regular waves of normality flowing across the screen.

And then the woman opened her eyes, gagged and ripped the tube from her throat. 'Fuckinell!' rasped the gloriously large Mrs Bates.

Suddenly smiles and grins broke all around. And Ceri laughed. It didn't matter how many times they failed or succeeded. For her, resuscitations were always the raw confrontation between life and death. And when they won she felt a pure, simple happiness.

She put her hand on the woman's shoulder and leaned down. 'Hello, Ida!'

The woman tried to speak again but coughed instead.

'Right,' said Dr Stone, smiling at Ceri. 'Let's suck her out and get her up to Coronary Care.'

Two hours later it was a new day. The clock radio came to life to the sounds of Simon Mayo and his chirpy sidekicks, giggling inconsiderately as seven million Radio 1 listeners tried desperately to stay asleep. Just then paradise to Ceri was the chance to turn the damned thing off, pull the covers round even tighter, and revel in the thought – sheer bliss! – that today was the one day she wouldn't have to get up.

But then this wasn't paradise. *Don't even think about it. Just get up.* She did and groaned.

There was Ida Bates to check on before handing her over to Dr Williams's team, and Mr Blackett and the other patients she had seen on the ward the previous evening.

And there was breakfast. Her insatiable insides were telling her that missing dinner the night before was a big disappointment.

But at least the room was warm and the carpet kind to her bare feet as she swung her legs out of bed. On the floor lay a small picture. It framed a carefree young man with his arm around her neck, both of them laughing, nearly pitching forward – his unruly hair and her round National Health glasses revealing just how old the picture was. Once in a while it went flying across the floor when she reached for the light, but the crack across the glass had happened more than a year ago. She put it back on the bedside table and reached sleepily for her towel. Then she washed and dressed, considered for a moment entering the daylight world with spectacles, capitulated immediately to vanity, and gingerly poked the hard, alien lenses into her baggy, bloodshot eyes.

Mr Blackett had had a reasonable night, considering his condition. And Ida Bates was stable. Physically drained, emotionally shaken, but the old ticker, in Ida's words, was not ready to give up yet. She hadn't recognized Dr Lloyd, but on realizing who she was, reached out for her hand and squeezed it hard, holding on till the doctor had to go.

The gesture compensated for the resentment Ceri felt at her deep exhaustion – and the awful, rubbery fried eggs which came later, their edges – as always – browned to extinction. She had spotted Jonathan in the hospital canteen, shovelling down a mountain of anonymous stodge into a rake-like body, as thin people so often seemed to do. She went over to join him.

'Morning,' she said, setting her plate down opposite him. 'I won't say good,' she added drily, 'because it isn't.'

He swallowed prematurely and looked concerned. 'Oh, what's wrong, Ceri?'

'No, no, there's nothing wrong,' she laughed. She pulled out the chair and sat down heavily. 'I just meant that mornings are never very good if you've only had three hours sleep.'

'Oh yeah,' he nodded, rolling his eyes, 'I'd agree with you there. I feel absolutely kna – whacked out.'

'Mmm . . . I feel knackered too.' She smiled mischievously. 'Of course, *feeling* like a wreck's not enough. You've got to *look* it! Yes, Mr Bloggs,' she began whispering in a funny voice, 'that there gravy stain on my shirt's the self-same one you saw Friday morning. Haven't had a chance to change it yet, you understand. But it is only Monday.'

Jonathan was laughing. 'You mean like this –' He ruffled

his gelled hair and pulled at his tie – very nice, but the only one he seemed to possess.

'Yes, that's *exactly* right. Especially at night,' she laughed. 'I'm sure you get more sympathy that way.'

They joked again and then fell into an easy silence as they ate their breakfasts.

'I suppose we'll go and see Mrs Bates this morning?' the medical student asked, after a time. But she didn't answer. He glanced up and saw she looked furious. 'Um, I mean –' he began to stammer, 'did I say something wrong?'

Ceri blinked. 'Oh God, no!' She broke into a frustrated laugh. 'It's these bloody eggs. They're just so awful. And this bacon . . . I don't think it's real! Sorry, Jonathan,' she laughed again. 'Mrs Bates is doing just fine this morning, but if this is what she gets to eat, I don't give much for her chances!'

'You've seen her already? I wish I'd come with you.' He looked down at his plate.

'Yes . . .' She made a face. 'Oh, I'm sorry. I didn't realize – I just thought that after the weekend on call and the rest of the day to get through, you might like to be let off the hook.'

He looked up and nodded. 'Yeah, you're right, it has been a bit gruelling. But even so I've really enjoyed this week.' He smiled at her. 'It's given meaning to all that boring textbook stuff I have to go back to tomorrow. Thanks to you. You've been brill.'

Ceri laughed, sounding embarrassed. 'I'm glad you've enjoyed it.'

'I have. I've also been meaning to ask you,' he went on, frowning slightly, 'you must get time off – sort of in lieu or something, don't you, for all these extra hours you do?'

'Maybe on Mars, but not in the NHS.' She pushed her plate away and sipped at the strong, lukewarm tea. 'Oh, they're talking about changes. But talk is cheap, as they say. They've been talking for a decade.'

'Oh . . .' He looked around at the canteen. A group of nurses nearby had been drinking coffee and were now stubbing out their cigarettes, getting ready to leave – all five of them smoked, he noticed. 'Then I guess you get used to the hours?'

'Some people do, but you're not looking at one of them.' She thumped her chest. 'This body don't take kindly to a ninety-six-hour week.' The expression was neutral, carefully concealing recent, uneasy memories. And then she remembered the phone call. 'Oh shit!'

'What's the matter?'

'David rang, yesterday *morning*. But we were so busy, I didn't have a chance to ring him all day.' Something in her voice made the young man pause and study her face. And then she laughed.

'Right, Dr Montgomery,' she said lightly, looking amused. 'Better sort out the old duffers who came in through Cas last night. We're lucky. Apparently there are only three. Two on Fitzsimmonds. And a woman on Mountjoy.'

'Right.' He hesitated. 'What about – making your phone call?'

She was in front of him, walking towards the door. She didn't turn around. 'Oh, I'll have to ring from the ward.'

Here we are again. The sun streamed through the long casement windows in shafts of light and dancing dust, touching everything and everyone with its pure, clean brilliance, warming them, defying them all to remember the surreal, uneasy scenes of life, death, and life again, played out the night before.

Sister Anne had gone home that morning. Today it was Sister Elizabeth in charge – 'Liz' only if she liked you. She nodded as Ceri and Jonathan entered the ward, accompanying the gesture with a perfunctory smile.

Ceri nodded back. 'Hello, Liz,' she said, holding Sister Elizabeth's stare until the woman looked away and began to matter-of-factly run through the nurses' card index.

She pulled out a card. 'Now,' she said, looking up from the notes at Jonathan. 'We've got a Mrs Edith Jones, admitted last night by Dr Waleski. Lady in bed number eight, on the right, in the pink dressing gown.'

Ceri's eyes travelled desultorily towards bed number eight.

Isn't that . . . ? My God, yes, it is! The lady with the bright blue hair.

'What's wrong with her?' Jonathan enquired.

'Looks to me like she needs a new head!' she sniggered. She just couldn't help it – straight into Sister Elizabeth's waiting jaws.

And Sister Elizabeth duly opened them. 'Edith Jones is a lovely woman,' she retorted, addressing the medical student in tones which somehow managed to convey admiration for the good lady and utter distaste for Dr Lloyd. 'Unfortunately,' she continued, 'she has chronic bronchitis and came in last night with an acute exacerbation.'

Exacerbation? Is that with one b or two, Sister?

Ceri smiled with a lightness she did not feel. 'Thank you, Liz. Well, Jonathan. We'd better look at her notes and then see the old dear.'

Five minutes later Sister Elizabeth had gone off to supervise a student nurse further down the ward and out of earshot. David would be at the office by now. Ceri left Jonathan poring over the notes and went over to the other desk to make the call.

How will he be?

'Oh hi, this is Ceri Lloyd – Ceri James. Is David there please?'

It was one of his colleagues, deep voice, vaguely familiar. 'Just a sec.' He put down the phone. She heard his steps as he walked away, heard him say, 'David, it's for you.'

Ceri bit on a nail. He was taking his time.

'Hello?' Same confident, city voice.

'Yes.'

'I'm afraid he's not around at the moment. He must have stepped out of the office.'

David, it's for you.

'Hello?'

'Yes . . . I'm still here.'

The anonymous voice waited, then coughed.

'Um . . . will you give him a message please . . . say his wife – you did catch my name?'

'Yes.'

'That I called . . . from the hospital.'

'Yes, of course. I'll tell him.' He said goodbye and rang off.

Two old voices cackled in the distance. Metal clanked on metal as nurses in the side room jostled bed pans, kidney dishes and other sundry bowls of human debris down the sluice. Jonathan answered the other phone. And demented Mary Hill, sitting in perfectly dry knickers, cried for the hundredth time, 'Nurse, I've shit myself!'

Ceri was holding the phone to her ear in a strange, loose way. Jonathan, still on the other line, was gesturing politely to catch her attention. She looked up suddenly.

'Your bleep went off,' he said, covering his receiver and whispering unnecessarily. 'It's Dr McAvoy. He wants to know when you can tell him about last night's new patients.'

'Soon,' she said dully, then caught his expression and put down the receiver. 'Half an hour, Jonathan. I'll give him a ring when we've seen the patients on Fitzsimmonds.'

Jonathan relayed her message and then came back. 'He says that's fine.'

She nodded and looked away. 'Better see this bronchitic, then.'

Jonathan could see Mrs Jones sitting up in bed in a pink quilted housecoat, a matching pink cotton nightie peeping out from underneath. She was talking, but not to anyone obvious in sight. His mouth twitched and he glanced at his registrar, but she wasn't looking.

As they approached, the old lady caught sight of them and whatever conversation she was having stopped dead. Her face lit up, her mouth dropped open and her eyes grew bigger. He couldn't help thinking she looked like a blue-rinsed Harpo Marx, minus the horn.

'And how are you feeling today, Mrs Jones?' Ceri said as they reached her bedside. She gave the old lady a smile and picked up the board at the end of the bed.

'Ah yes . . . I *thought* it was you last night, my dear!' It was a thready, elegant voice directed at Ceri.

The doctor smiled briefly and began to flick through the charts.

'Now come over here, where I can see you properly,' Mrs Jones persisted. 'It's been –' she began to choke. 'Oh dear . . . oh dear!' she spluttered, thumping hard on her chest with the side of her thin fist.

Ceri pulled out her stethoscope and stood waiting for the eruption to subside. *The chest infection is making her dotty.*

'There,' said the bizarre lady in pink, clearing her throat one more time. 'That's better. It's been ages. But then you don't remember, do you dear?' – this an observation, not a reproach.

Ceri was about to ask the babbling old lady to kindly listen for a moment and answer a few questions, when the woman said, 'Well, *I* could never forget *you* – my dear Dr Sherry Lloyd.' She smiled proudly, to herself.

Sherry. Recognition began to dawn. She looked at the features under the strange blue haze, saw the eyes blazing out from the wrinkled face, and felt again the strange impression of youth watching her from behind a mask. 'Edith . . .' she said, the tone betraying pleasure, guilt and disbelief.

'Yes, that's better,' the old lady smiled. 'I'm so glad you do remember after all, Sherry. It's such a treat to see you again.'

'For me too, Edith. But you've changed.' Ceri took a step back. 'I didn't recognize you because of your . . . um – hairstyle.'

'Oh that,' the old lady chuckled. 'It is rather a good disguise! Eileen – my hairdresser you know – was off sick, and the girl who did it was new to the salon and *very* young. It's just a shame I was feeling adventurous that day. Still, it does help that I don't have a mirror.' She laughed an old lady's crackly laugh and shrugged her shoulders as if she were hugging herself. Then she reached for the doctor – the skin of her frail hand smooth, transparent, mottled with the brown stains of old age – and surprised Ceri with the strength of her grip. 'You see, Sherry, I'm still alive!'

'Yes' – the doctor gave a laugh – 'of course you are.'

'Yes. Perhaps of course,' she mused whimsically. Then she

turned to the student. 'And who's this then – not a replacement for that young man I hope?' The old lady was grave and threw Jonathan a slow wink. He smiled and looked down at his shoes.

For a moment, Ceri stared oddly at her. 'This is Jonathan Montgomery. He's a medical student. You don't mind if he sits in with us?'

'Ah . . . so he's following in your footsteps. How do you do, Dr Montgomery.' She shook his hand delightedly. 'Has she told you,' she said, beaming at him, 'that she was the nicest doctor I ever met?'

'I can believe it,' he smiled, glancing at Ceri.

'And that she saved my life?'

'Oh, Edith, I certainly didn't do that!' Ceri laughed, shaking her head. 'I couldn't have. I was just a student.'

'Nonsense! I may have survived that wretched infection, but if it wasn't for you, I'd have died of fright.' She whispered at Jonathan from behind her hand, 'Hate being amongst all these crumbling old specimens. Makes you morbid.'

Jonathan nodded politely and looked embarrassed.

'Well,' Ceri broke in. 'I reckon you'll keep going for another century at least, Edith. Now, just tell me how you became ill again and then we'll look you over and check your chest.'

'Yes, dear, I suppose I'll have to. And then we can have one of our nice, long chats, like in the old days.' She looked at Jonathan again and tittered. 'In the old days. Just listen to me!'

'Dr Waleski took down the details yesterday evening,' Ceri went on, 'but we'll just run through them again. From looking at you, though, the drugs you've had during the night seem to have worked wonders. You'll still get a lot of coughing for a while, but your temperature's down and you're not breathless.'

'Yes, I do feel better. I'm so glad it shows.'

'So am I, Edith. Now, where were we?'

Jonathan looked expectantly at Ceri, hoping she would ask him to do the questioning as usual. But she did it herself; quickly, expertly, with that clever skill of getting the patient to answer briefly and to the point, without seeming blunt. She made some notes and then got up to adjust the pillows behind the old lady's back. At once Edith Jones turned to Jonathan and began again in her high, dotty voice: 'Now Dr Lloyd and I first met – oh, it must have been at least – now let me see . . .'

'Five or six years ago, Edith,' said Ceri, pulling her stethoscope out of her pocket.

'Yes . . . that's right, dear, it would be, wouldn't it? Well, when Dr Lloyd and I first met she told me she was determined to become a *consultant physician* – you know, not an ordinary doctor, but a specialist. Of course, she knew it would be hard work, but she was *quite* determined that wouldn't stop her.' A wide, satisfied smile spread across her face. 'And I see it hasn't, has it, dear?'

Ceri smiled into the air, lifted up Mrs Jones's nightdress, tapped with her fingers all over her chest, then stopped to warm the cold metal of the stethoscope against her hand.

'And David . . . did he qualify as a chartered accountant?' Mrs Jones enquired, as Ceri placed the stethoscope on her bony chest. 'You said he was such a clever young man.'

'Yes, he did. Now just take deep breaths in and out for me.' Ceri listened carefully all over her chest and was about to straighten up when the woman reached out and touched her ringed finger. 'And when did you get married, my dear? You and David were planning to, as soon as you qualified,' she said with certainty. 'I remember your engagement ring. It's not unlike mine – poor George, bless his soul. And I see you've kept your maiden name.' She turned to Jonathan. 'Women's lib,' she said, and chuckled. 'But how long has it been, Sherry dear?'

'Four years. Now I have to listen to your chest at the back.'

'Of course, dear.' She leaned forward to expose her back and asked knowingly: 'And are there any – little ones by now?'

'No, there aren't.'

'Ah, then –' Mrs Jones began to cough again, a wet, crackling noise from deep down inside her chest. She heaved for a while and then the eruption gradually subsided. 'Oh dear!

Coughing does so take it out of you.' She looked at Jonathan and continued triumphantly: 'They decided they wouldn't have children until Dr Lloyd had established her career. Now that's dedication for you, young man. And I tell you, you have a hard act to follow.'

Ceri looked down for a moment. And then she said briskly: 'Edith, your chest sounds a bit wheezy and crackly, which is why you're still coughing, but you haven't got a temperature. And you're on all the right drugs now to clear the chest infection and open up the airways, so you should soon be on the mend.' She began gathering up her notes. 'It's been such a lovely surprise to see you again. We've got a few other patients to see, but we'll come round and see how you're getting on tomorrow. Do take care.'

The old lady's smile faltered a little. 'I see, dear,' she said, looking away. 'Of course, you must be very busy these days.'

Ceri flushed. 'It's just that we've been on duty since Friday morning and everything's such a rush at the moment. Not like when you're a student, Edith.'

'Of course not, dear.'

'We'll see you tomorrow for sure.'

'Yes, dear.'

'You take care.'

'Yes, dear, I will.'

An ordinary patient politely answering an ordinary doctor.

Jonathan was very quiet as they walked away. She glanced at him and bit her lip. 'Go and see the old dear,' she said casually. 'Take on where I left off – six years ago.' She sounded bitter.

'Sure.' They had reached the nurses' station. There was no one there. He began to put the notes away in the trolley. 'You can't spread yourself too thin, Ceri,' he said. He was still looking down at the trolley.

Touched by kindness, welling up uncontrollably, the hidden pain of everything threatening to spill over, through her eyes. *Oh David* . . . The pain broke through. Hot and stinging. Ceri fled.

*

Her finger touched his laughing face through the cracked glass. *How happy we look*. It was six o'clock. The light coming through the windows was all but gone, the sky beginning to change from dark, brilliant blue to an inky black. All her things were packed and Dr Harding, on duty tonight, had already left his belongings in a corner of the room. Ceri put the picture away in the side pocket of her travel bag. The weekend on call was finally over.

She drove home listening to Mark Goodier on the radio, a reckless, dangerous driver, drunk with tiredness. The traffic was moderate. She was glad it was this disc jockey. She liked the stuff he played. She could listen to it and not think.

On a Monday evening it took just thirty-five minutes to get home. The lights were on in the house. The car was in the drive. She parked on the road, left the radio playing, stared from the house to her husband's car and thought about getting out of her own.

Eventually she walked to the front door, stood for a moment, then pushed the key in slowly, wanting to become invisible as the door swung open. She could see his briefcase in its usual place under the stairs. She let the door shut hard and stood there in the darkened hallway, holding her bags. But he didn't come.

She walked down the hall, into the sitting room, the kitchen. The lights were on. She heard a noise upstairs and gazed at the light burning on the landing and began to feel angry. *I'm not going to call him*. Her bags were starting to pull at her arms and as she bent to put them down saw the light flashing on the answerphone. Suddenly she knew he wasn't in the house and her heart began to thump. She hesitated, then pressed the button.

The tape hissed for a few seconds and then the message came on: 'Hi Ceri, it's me-eee!' Ceri looked round in bewilderment. Her friend, Alice. The dizzy voice went on insanely. 'Josh and I would love to have you both round for dinner, Saturday next. That is, if you're not busy saving lives. Tony and Sue are coming. Anyway, darling, give us a buzz and let us know. Bye-eee!' She stared at the machine, heard it hiss again then click several times before rewinding. That was it.

She began running up the stairs. 'David!' she cried, his name catching in her throat.

She rushed into the bedroom, saw his suit flung over the clotheshorse, the door of his cupboard open, half his clothes gone. And then she saw it on the bed. She looked away and bit her lip. But she could still see it in the window, reflected clearly against the blackness outside. And eventually she turned and picked it up, and read it, over and over, until the words began to blur.

Outside, a car pulled up softly across the road. Doors opened, then slammed shut, children chattered loudly and someone – Mr Robinson – laughed. A front door slammed. The handwriting was messy, but neat for him. He hadn't signed it.

Once again the high, shrill sound of the bleep exploded into her dreams, wrenched her from sleep, drove out her hand to grope for the phone. It wasn't there. Her eyes snapped open, saw the clock and beyond, the walls of her room. She silenced the alarm.

It was 7 o'clock and still dark outside, the song of a single sparrow the only sound. For a moment she looked at the empty pillow beside her; then, with an effort, she lifted herself up and out of bed, into the cool bedroom air, shivered a little, pulled on her Fluffy Bunny slippers and her dressing gown, and put her hands up to her throbbing temples. Then she padded downstairs, habit making her avoid the parts that creaked.

I need some paracetamol and a cup of tea. But the phone was waiting for her. She picked it up and dialled the number. Her stomach churned. She had never done this before.

'St Andrew's Hospital,' an indifferent male voice on switchboard announced.

'Yes,' she croaked. 'Could I speak to Dr Alistair Simms please.'

If the operator heard, he didn't have the courtesy to acknowledge it. She seemed to be waiting a very long time for someone to answer. *Perhaps he's sussed me out and cut me dead.*

But at last a voice came on the line. 'Hello, Casualty, Sister Julie speaking.'

Her heart thumped. 'Oh hello, Sister. Is Dr Alistair Simms around? I bleeped him.'

'The medical reg?'

'Yes.'

'Who is this?'

'It's Dr Lloyd.'

'Just a minute, I'll see if I can get him to the phone.'

She hung on nervously, could hear an old man's coughing, words spoken, some near, some far, and then the nasal voice of Dr Simms.

'Alistair?'

'Yes.'

'It's Ceri Lloyd.' Her thick, just got-up-in-the-morning voice sounded suitably ill.

'Right.' He sounded short.

He must know what's coming. 'Are you first on call?'

'Mm.'

'I'm afraid I'm not going to be able to come in today –' she thought she heard a snort but pressed on, 'I'm supposed to take over from you, but – I've had diarrhoea and vomiting all night.' Unconsciously she clutched her stomach. 'I think it was from a takeaway we got last night. My husband's got it too. Could you please ask admin to get a locum when they come in. Is that OK?'

'That's bloody great.' He sounded furious.

'Sorry?'

'There are another seven patients to be seen down here. It's a complete madhouse. The houseman and I are working flat out. And they won't get a locum until the evening – if they get one at all, knowing how bloody tight they are. And now you're not coming. Fucking marvellous.'

'Oh God, Alistair, I'm really sorry.'

'Yeah, right.'

'Look . . .' she said, hesitating. She shut her eyes. *I'll see you at ten tomorrow, if you're there.* But he hadn't signed it.

'I'll –' She drew her breath. 'I'll drag myself in, Alistair.

It's settled a bit in the last hour. I might be a bit late – just give me a bit of time to get ready. OK?'

'I'm sorry to do this to you.' But he sounded relieved.

'It's OK,' she said, her heart sinking. 'Bye.'

The little girl pushed back the curtain and watched the woman opposite close the front door and stand on the step. 'Doctor,' she murmured to herself, and then she stared curiously because the woman stood for ages with her eyes closed before going to the car.

Ironically, because the traffic was light, she got in slightly earlier than usual. It was ten minutes to nine as she went to the reception to pick up her bleep. The porter, a large young chap, was sitting behind the desk poring over a copy of *The Daily Star*.

'Yes, love?'

'Bleep 467 please, Steve.'

He put the paper down on the desk, started to get up, then suddenly leaned towards her, reeking of cigarette smoke. 'Don't worry, love,' he whispered in her face, 'it might never 'appen!'

'No,' she said, jerking her head up with a short laugh.

He looked at her with a half-knowing, half-reproachful smile and turned away towards the rack of bleeps. Another doctor came up to the desk. Ceri smiled distractedly and said hello.

'Now, let me see,' the porter continued. '467 . . . 467. Yep, here it is.' He turned round and handed it to her, holding on to it for a second longer, saying: 'Now, mind 'ow you go.'

She nodded and pushed the bleep into the top pocket of her white coat, vaguely bewildered at his perceptiveness. Then she walked off down the corridor, considered snatching a coffee in the mess, rejected the idea and headed towards Casualty.

Halfway there her bleep went off. *David?* The nearest corridor phone was just behind her. She dialled zero, her fingers tingling, an emptiness in the pit of her stomach. Switchboard replied. 'Hello. I'm answering bleep 467.'

'Hold on, dear.' The operator connected the call.

'Ceri?' Her heart sank. It wasn't him.

'Yes. Alistair?'

'Uhuh. I'm glad you're in. I'm just going to see a chap who'll need admitting from the sounds of it, but there's an old duffer called Newby – think he's had an MI –'

She cut in: 'Actually, Alistair, I was on my way down. I'll deal with him when I get there.' She felt irritated; it was only just nine o'clock.

'Great. See you in a minute.'

'Yeah.' She hung up. *Pillock. I'm feeling fine, thanks for asking.*

Two minutes later she reached Casualty, chaotic and overflowing as he'd described. Dr Simms emerged from a cubicle, calling out to one of the nurses. He caught sight of Ceri coming through the doors. 'My God, Ceri, you look like you've been through the wringer,' a trace of compunction in his voice, 'or is it the glasses?'

'Oh, definitely the glasses,' she said shortly. 'Where's Mr Newby?'

He motioned to the third cubicle along. 'The Cas Officer's notes are on the desk. Mary Wilkins was the one who saw him. He's had bloods taken and a shot of diamorph.'

She nodded indifferently, picked up the notes, quickly ran her eyes over them, then pushed through the half-drawn curtains of the third cubicle and went inside.

An oldish man – the notes said sixty-six, lay on the bed in a hospital gown, his eyes closed, his upper body raised against pillows, chest and limb leads connected to a monitor. An elderly woman sat next to him, holding his hand. She looked up as Ceri came in, her face haggard.

'Mrs Newby?' Dr Lloyd enquired, her fingers already on the man's wrist, feeling his pulse.

'Yes, Doctor.' Her husband's eyes flickered slightly but remained closed. The woman looked at him, whispering: 'Harry, Harry,' and then suddenly she grabbed the doctor's arm, her eyes starting to fill with tears. 'We've been together nearly forty years, Doctor.'

Dr Lloyd nodded understandingly.

'And I know we've had our ups and downs. But it's only

now when it's – it's now I realize what it's all about. What he really means to me . . .' The woman was pleading. 'I'm not going to lose him . . . am I, Doctor?'

Ever so slowly, the doctor turned and stared at the woman. She had heard the words a hundred times before, from other Mrs Newbys in other cubicles, but these were different.

'Am I, Doctor?'

The doctor pressed the grabbing hand and tried to smile. 'No, no . . .' her voice sounded far away. 'You're not going to lose him . . . not if I can help it.'

LIFE WITH THE FARMERS

Lesley Tilling

Lesley Tilling was born and brought up in Walton-on-Thames. She studied History and Politics at Birmingham University and has travelled extensively. She lives in Fife with her husband, where she works as a secretary.

LIFE WITH THE FARMERS

John Farmer was sent to our school when he was fourteen, which is unusually late to enter a boarding school for the first time. He was brought by his mother on his first day and they walked around the honey-coloured stone buildings in bright autumn sunshine. Mrs Farmer was wearing a peasant-style outfit with a flowered skirt and white lace petticoats. She was tall, blonde, tanned and smiling – a very striking woman; I've never forgotten the first time I saw her.

John stomped composedly along beside her. If he was nervous or doubtful it didn't show, but I think it must have been hard for him to be sent away from home for the first time. His class all knew each other and he knew no one.

His mother tried hard not to upstage other parents or staff. She was well-known both as an actress and as a painter, and the parents would have known her face from the Sunday magazines where her two careers were reviewed with the launch of some of the projects she was involved in. It was widely known – my mother knew, for example, from her glossy magazines – that Penelope Farmer was a widow, and had five children. Her fame had begun with a TV series in which she played the faithful wife of a cheating husband. Her real-life pregnancy had been worked into the plot. She acted infrequently and led an idyllic life in the country where she developed her talent as a painter. Her paintings went on exhibition in London at the time she herself went on exhibition, in a new West End play, and the publicity for both was doubled. The pictures were good; even without the interest of her name on them they would have sold because they were the kind of pictures most people can live with: sunlit interiors, cats on rugs, views of trees through a window, a breakfast table with a bored lone breakfaster. They were bright, harmonious scenes, and she used colour with great relish. I believe that the first exhibition made her wealthy. She went back to the husband and children in the country, intending to devote herself to painting. Not long afterwards the husband died of a heart attack. He was apparently shy and home-loving, an actuary, the perfect contrast to his glamorous, artistic wife.

I saw Mrs Farmer taking leave of her son and was impressed by her intensity, which I thought of as 'actressy'. Rather than giving John a quick hug and kiss on the cheek, as was usual, she pulled him close to her side with one arm, and with the fingers of the other hand she stroked his face, gazing at him, then she bent and whispered in his ear. When she left she seemed to be in tears.

This was an autumn in the early seventies, the last years of prosperity and boom. One looks back and is surprised by the mood of optimism that prevailed. The young were indulged as never before. Even at a middle-rank old-established boarding school like ours unprecedented freedoms were obtained in what the boys were allowed to do and where we were allowed to go. I look at the photographs and am astonished by our hair, for example, which we wore flopping around our ears looking chewed at the ends, or bushing out unevenly – young people today are sensibly less happy with a state of nature. There was talk of abolishing uniform – a step we never took – but the rules concerning out-of-school wear were relaxed, and everyone took to wearing frayed jeans and ordinary tennis shoes. With our freedom of movement and lack of identifying uniform we managed to find ways of smoking cigarettes and drinking alcohol and, in the sixth form, we smoked grass regularly. It was a good time for the young.

So there was John Farmer, at fourteen, in a grey pullover and striped blazer, among many others, completely unremarkable. His hair was brown and his skin was sallow. He was good at games. As the weeks passed it became apparent that he was good at everything. And he was liked. He had some quality that marked him out. It was something to do with his unquestioning acceptance of things and people which made him a reassuring presence. John was calm and accepting of people and they liked to have him around. In the space of two terms he became one of the most popular boys in the house. He retained an air of detachment that some people copied – it drew the attention by understatement, which is an interesting skill. It became quite the style of the house, in fact, to make all facial expressions as subtle as possible; to acknowledge others with half-closed eyes and a sleepy smile. I adopted the habit myself before I realized that I was imitating John Farmer, because I rarely saw him, then one day I happened to see his signal to a friend during prayers.

He was older than me and it was natural for the younger boys to imitate the older ones, but the John Farmer style became adopted throughout the whole school, including the sixth. He himself was included in activities usually guarded by older years. He was given a better part in the play, for example, than seniority demanded, and he was picked for house rugby teams in which he was the smallest player. He never disgraced himself. In the play he moved about the stage easily and seemed to speak completely naturally, but he was not the star of the show, who got all the laughs. In rugby games he could show courage and resilience such as would leave you gasping, and he never fumbled, he was reliable – but was not the fastest mover. His thing was: he inspired the others. You felt his presence, and he was calm, and this gave you a definite surge of confidence.

It was the custom at our school to have older boys coach the slower younger ones in certain subjects. At this time I discovered that mathematics was no longer within my comprehension. It was something of a relief when Mr Thompson discovered at last that I could not follow the examples he worked, let alone work examples in prep for myself. (I copied friends' prep – this was how I managed to hide my incapacity for some weeks.) Mr Thompson quickly grew exasperated by my blank expression when he tutored me and assigned John Farmer to go through my prep with me three evenings a week.

John accepted his role as a teacher as impassively as ever. He took a pencil in his square fist and painstakingly explained his method through a problem.

'Now do you see?' he asked.

I hated having to tell him that I did not.

'What is it you don't understand?' – he was puzzled.

'That value there.' I pointed hesitantly. 'You said you didn't know what it was.'

'It's a complex number,' he said. 'Square root of minus one.'

'But if you don't know what it is,' I asked in high embarrassment, 'why is it in this problem? Why are we mucking about with it? Maybe it doesn't really exist at all in, um, mathematical terms.'

'Just think of it as X the unknown,' suggested John. 'It's really just another kind of X.'

'I can deal with X,' I told him. 'But I can't understand this one.' I pointed to X squared.

'Why?'

'Because we don't know what it is, right? So why bother putting that it's squared. Isn't it just as unknown?'

'Because that's how to solve the problem. Listen. Don't look at the figures so hard. You're looking all the way through them. You don't have to hold the values in your head as concepts. They exist without you understanding them. All you have to do is solve the puzzles. You just learn the rules and go through the puzzle and get the answer. You might enjoy it. I enjoy maths sometimes.'

This was a big breakthrough for me. It took some patience on John's part before I caught up with what I had missed because we had to go back and solve simpler problems, but John was not short of patience. He gave me the ability to look at calculations without getting entangled with them. I felt as relieved and grateful as if I had been rescued from torture, and one day I made some uncharacteristically flippant remark to him out of my euphoria – to which he commented:

'Oh God, you sound like my brother Stan.'

After three weeks of intermittent coaching I was back to standard in maths and John Farmer started spending the evenings at cricket practice.

*

In the following autumn Anthony Farmer joined our class. He was immediately accepted, being the brother of the popular John. We found that he was more than younger brother, he was also John's close friend. John would come in search of him in a seemingly absent-minded manner.

'Ah, where's, um, Stan?'

They would go off together to play football or chess or talk. They seemed to be perfectly equal, and loyal to each other.

Stan was never like John, nor did he ever try to be. They did not look much alike. John's face was perfectly proportioned, his features all neat. Stan's cheeks were hollow and his nose tended to beak, his brow was higher and his hair was lanker. His limbs were rangy, John's were compact. Where John was calm, Stan was excitable. Where John cultivated a politic acceptance, Stan argued. Where John had no enemies, Stan had several, of whom he was quite fond. Stan had a generous spirit and a ruthless rationality. He brought to school a whole set of leftist attitudes which had him labelled a 'communist' (at our school the word meant 'traitor' to the majority) and he was sufficiently sceptical of ideology to refute the label. Our classroom discussions on every subject were suddenly heated debates. The masters started to find us 'challenging and rewarding to teach'. Stan had opinions on everything and some of us made it a point of honour to always take the opposite stance.

Stan's hero was Bertrand Russell, whose short polemical books had been recommended to him by his mother. I had read Russell's *Autobiography* which had impressed me deeply, and I happily recounted to Stan the details I could remember of the philosopher's early life and the development of his opinions.

I never had much self-confidence, and I admired that, as I admired many things in Stan. Our friendship started as an unequal partnership. I was an only child, and had spent much time in the company of adults; I had lived abroad, and I had read a great deal. These were not attributes which carried much weight, on the whole, but with Stan they did. Which was strange. Stan smoked, swore habitually (often within the hearing of masters), always played his records too loudly, did great impersonations of Mick Jagger, and used his great charm to make himself the pet of the kitchen staff – he ate like a horse.

On the face of it we were unalike, but we were both at bottom deeply serious – I suppose rather pretentious – and we immediately got on well. When you are still at school your experience is limited, and your friendships can encompass all of it. Perhaps it is not possible to be so close to someone ever again, outside of marriage, and perhaps not even then.

John Farmer was quick to appreciate that his relationship with his brother must now change. They still sometimes practised sport together but otherwise John withdrew, only his manner indicating his affection for Stan, while he was to me as accepting and detached as ever. Not having a brother myself I was jealous of Stan. I admired John enormously – I would have hated anyone to know how much. I also hated to think that John might feel in some way superseded by me in Stan's friendship. Showing this kind of emotion would not have been in John's nature, but I imagined how he might feel, and was uneasy on the occasions when our paths crossed.

When Stan asked me to stay with his family in the Easter holidays I was pleased and accepted happily, but later I wondered if John would be as happy about the arrangement.

But the experience was a great pleasure for me and worked well for the Farmers. Stan and Mrs Farmer came to meet me at the station, and Mrs Farmer made me feel wonderfully at home, apologizing for and making fun of the ancient Land-Rover she drove. She had – she has still – great charm, a way of looking at you and attending to you that makes you feel very alive. My parents were even then elderly; when I'm with them I have always had to change down a few gears. Penny Farmer (she made me call her Penny) was quite the other way – you had a feeling that she was always two jumps ahead.

She said that Anthony had told her that I had lived in Kenya, and that she had been brought up there herself.

'I have such happy memories of my childhood,' she said, and sighed. I could not think how to describe my own childhood, which seemed to have ended when I was sent to prep school in England, at seven.

Mrs Farmer asked after my parents, at home in Kensington, and I told her that my father was an accountant and that my parents were interested in visiting old churches and fine art exhibitions, and that their other main hobby was playing bridge. In response to her enquiry I had to say that they did not take much interest in gardening.

'Stan's father used to grow fruit and veg,' she said. 'We have enough land to be productive so I try to keep the kitchen garden ticking over. It needs quite a bit of work but it's also a hobby. We have a couple of enclosures and we keep a donkey called Wilbur.'

'Why do you keep a donkey?'

'The girls insisted I adopt a poor old donkey and give him a tranquil retirement home.'

'He lives in a sea of mud and brays his head off,' Stan said rather nastily.

'It's a lovely calming mud bath and he brays with joy,' Penny told me firmly, and smiled. 'The manure is useful too.'

Stan and I were sent out on bikes to 'get the lie of the land' as Penny put it. I think she realized that I might find the whole family together rather alarming at first. Let me be specific: there were twin girls younger than Stan and I who seemed to be as composed and graceful as girls could ever be. It didn't help that they were so alike you thought you were seeing double, both having dark eyes, long dark hair and full lips. Their names were Tommo (Thomasin) and Dora (Theodora). (They also had a younger brother called Arthur, who had all the brattish, attention-seeking habits I found annoying in children. He was about ten. Luckily he spent most of his time with another brat who lived nearby. He doesn't figure much in this story.)

We rode the bikes down country lanes and tracks until we found a track that followed the brow of a hill, which would give us the view Stan wanted. From its small summit we saw the vast exposed tract of land that is Salisbury Plain, with the clouds darkening and lowering over it. Stan produced his baccy and we rolled cigarettes. We leaned against a gate, and

Stan pointed out the nearest town to the house, the nearest pub, and finally the house itself. He looked possessively at the landscape.

'I love it here,' he said. 'When my father died my worst fear was that Mum would want to move to some bloody suburb of some city. I suppose it is quite lonely here. But it's better than living in a crowd. Mum decided on balance that being isolated would help her to concentrate on work.'

I did find the family overwhelming at first. Dora started arguing with Stan as soon as she saw him. They would argue about anything, and keep it up for hours. Together they were too alike, too much of a good thing. I gradually sorted out the differences between the girls. Dora was slender and had more bounce, whereas Tommo was about half a stone heavier, and moved with a calm, sensual grace.

Penny said that she didn't want to work much in the boys' holiday, she wanted to see as much of them as possible. In fact we were all outdoors most of the time, wearing gumboots, jeans and thick sweaters. There were plenty of chores to be done, and John, Stan and I were set to digging a vegetable plot in trenches one day, and the girls planted beans, and another day Stan and I sprayed the fruit trees. We were also bribed to clean all the windows of the house. It was not that there was no money to hire window-cleaners, just that the house was far off the beaten track and no one else would do them. I enjoyed it all – it was all fun because it was so novel. I asked Stan one day why his mother didn't marry again. It was when we were in the vegetable plot.

'She doesn't need to because she's got us to do all the worst jobs,' said Stan cynically. John was digging energetically, his sweater discarded and his hair smeared across his sweaty brow, but he laughed at this.

'Do you want a stepfather, Stanley?' he said.

'Fuck off,' said Stan.

'Then keep digging.'

Although all the house looked old, only the centre of it was original sixteenth century, and there were steps up and down between the rooms, as is the case with most old houses which have been built on to. The sitting room was the oldest room, and it was quite small. It contained a piano which Dora played excellently, and Tommo and John pretty well. Penny could play just a little, but she liked to sing. Otherwise the room contained chairs and books – including some beautiful art books – and a rectangular table around which we played cards and other games, like the Dictionary Game. I played John at chess twice since no one else would, because he always won.

The cooking part of the kitchen was very clean and tidy (Penny did employ a woman to clean and iron and so forth) and was quite a new addition. The old part of the kitchen functioned more as a living room. All down one end was a wide shelf, which amongst the clutter held Penny's home-made wine (we were allowed a glass with our meals), seeds germinating in trays, some bicycle parts belonging to Arthur, and a pile of sketchbooks belonging to Penny. Dividing the two ends was a kitchen table at which we usually ate. We also gathered around it before dinner, if we were not watching TV in the girls' room. (John and Stan also shared a bedroom.)

On the second day of my visit Penny took me to see her studio which was a cottage she rented in the village. She was doing still life studies and experimenting with abstractionism. I really knew nothing about art and could say little except that I liked the colours which were her usual range, light, bright, and happy. John was unusually animated and interested. He seemed to have a better understanding than Stan or I, and Penny treated him like an adult. She asked him if he wanted to paint during the holiday, and he seemed keen.

Penny showed me her work from previous years; she had painted portraits of all her children and they looked out from their frames full of life and individuality. John's portrait showed him looking over a book to his mother with a small, reserved smile – completely characteristic – while Stan had been painted playing his guitar; and the shape of the instrument contrasted wonderfully with his angular body. His face was full of the fierce concentration that was Stan trying to master something. Penny commented that sitting still had been a real challenge to Stan. She showed me a sketch she had made of him flailing his arm like Pete Townsend, which made me laugh, it was so typical of Stan. The girls had been painted as ballet dancers, in beautiful many-coloured dresses. Penny said that they didn't dance any more.

'Ridiculously contrived form of expression,' said Dora. 'And it takes so much time.'

'Lazy pair,' said Penny. 'All that time I spent dragging you to classes when you were small . . .'

Arthur was simply Arthur, but Penny had somehow managed to give him a very hopeful expression, which I suppose was how she saw him.

I enjoyed being with them so much, I loved the arguments that were nonchalantly refereed by Penny.

'I think you've made that point already, Dora,' she would say, draining the vegetables at the sink. Or, 'Stan, you ruin your case by overstating it.' John sometimes played the referee role as he had an instinctive idea of what was fair. I have said that Penny treated John as an adult. The result was that when he was with her he seemed to assume adulthood. She would work at amusing him, telling us stories of things that had happened to her, and of the eccentric neighbours – she could imitate the Wiltshire accent perfectly, and she would also imitate other actresses, and to amuse us, but particularly John, she would clown around, bursting into a song-and-dance act in the kitchen. John would sit at the kitchen table smiling at her like a cat basking in the sun – he was never more relaxed.

One evening when John was reading out crossword clues to her, Penny came over to look at the newspaper over his shoulder. Her hands, resting on his shoulders, absent-mindedly began to massage the muscles in his back and neck. John leaned back delightedly. Stan watched with narrowed eyes. Finally, he reached over to his mother, tapped her hand, and said, 'Me next, Mum.'

'Then me,' said Tommo.

'And me,' said Dora.

'And me,' said Arthur.

Stan turned to me and said, 'What about you?'

Penny said, 'Oh, sorry' and laughed. She put her hands

back lightly on John's shoulders and frowned over the puzzle until she had solved a clue.

Penny liked people to be expressive; she enjoyed Stan's volubility and the emphasis the girls gave to their speech – 'Oh, Mum, we *can't*, he's the vilest *toad*' – and she would mimic them, showing her amusement and her pleasure in them. But John refused to be impulsive in speech, he remained reserved, and by his reserve he held her fascinated. She encouraged him to paint because she thought he would reveal himself in that way, but John's art was spartan and geometric, interesting but impersonal. Stan and I returned from a fishing trip one day and called in at the cottage, when John and his mother were painting. The atmosphere inside was dense with concentration.

Once when we were alone I asked Stan if his mother had any boyfriends.

'No,' he said. 'Lots of friends, some of them men.'

'Sometimes she seems to treat John a bit like a boyfriend,' I observed.

'Mum *knows* she does it.' Stan's eyes were wide and he nodded at me. 'When Dad was alive it was much easier because he had time for everyone, whereas Mum gets wrapped up in her work. Mum wants to be fair, and when we all told her that she seemed to favour John all the time she talked it over with him and they decided he should go to boarding school, but it was a big wrench, you know. Then I got the benefit of Mum's attention for a year, which seemed to even things up a bit. But I asked to go to boarding school. I like going away to school and I like coming home.

'Mum knows the girls need her too. But in the holidays she still spoils John too much. She really ought to have a man, I suppose . . . But it would be so difficult to fit someone else in around here.'

Back at school I saw John Farmer in a slightly changed light – no longer as the entirely self-possessed distant hero, but rather as someone whose thoughts and affections were far away, someone who was exercising patience, or doing a penance; marking time.

Stan's guitar-playing improved, and I managed to get a set of drums from my parents, on the understanding that I would not practise on them at home. John occasionally came to hear our band practice, and Stan prevailed on him to play the keyboard synthesizer – a primitive model. John, used to the subtleties of a piano, quickly bored of it. Stan and I were dreaming of becoming rock-and-roll stars. The pounding, sweating and strutting of rock music provided an excellent outlet for the frustrations of adolescence. Like all creative activities it is absorbing, and the mutual inspirations and frictions inside the band – five of us, usually – became all the world to us for months at a time.

Stan and I booked a sailing course and went to stay at Cowes for a fortnight during the summer holiday. Penny, on a whim, filled in for another actress in a play that was touring, and left the house in the charge of a Swedish au pair called Helena. Stan's accounts of Helena's body rendered me simultaneously jealous and disbelieving. She sounded like a Barbie doll, and was, according to Stan, totally uninhibited.

'Sunbathes nude in the garden,' Stan reported, his eyes gleaming. 'Poor John doesn't know where to put himself.'

When the play Penny was in came to Chichester, Stan and I took a break from the sailing school and hitched over to see it. We had supper with Penny afterwards and were introduced to the rest of the cast. Penny looked lovely in a bright green dress and silver bangles, and was obviously delighted to see Stan, admiring his suntanned face, touching him frequently as we ate. Unfortunately we had forgotten to arrange anywhere to stay overnight, and Penny had to ask around for us. A kind and very camp colleague of hers allowed us to stay with him. We found it highly embarrassing and in the morning, laughed hysterically all the way back to Portsmouth.

We were fifteen and John was sixteen, as naive as it is possible to be at that age, having been so thoroughly and expensively protected. Stan, although able to take care of himself, suddenly developed a reluctance to grow up. The death of his father had marked him, mixing his natural rebelliousness with a strong sense of responsibility. At this time he shed a little of both. Far more than I was, he was conscious of being happy, and, being pessimistic in outlook, he wanted simply for everything to remain the same.

Stan returned to the house in Wiltshire to find John was sleeping with Helena in his mother's bed. John, it seemed, had at last found the outlet for expression he had needed for so long. Helena had made love to him as a diversion, then had fallen in love with his responsiveness. His devotion to Helena was total – and she was fascinated by the power she had over him. She also liked being associated with his artistic family, because she considered herself to be an artistic talent. She was interested in photography, and had some prints to prove it. However, these were nearly all nude studies of her ex-boyfriend, and Stan suggested to her that she should keep them to herself.

Helena also claimed to be a talented actress. John had been so suddenly knocked off his feet that he could hardly see straight. He told Stan that he thought Helena would become a better actress than their mother, and perhaps as good an artist.

Stan despaired of John's madness.

'She's a pretty girl, she's got lovely big tits and a nice arse, her accent is incredibly attractive, but she's not what John thinks she is, at all! He thinks she's Greta Garbo and Van Gogh rolled into one. For fuck's sake! She's not a dumb blonde, but . . .'

Stan's major complaint against Helena was that she had no sense of humour, and to make the point he would go to absurd lengths of nonsense with her. She saw what he was trying to do.

'My sense of humour is very good,' she told him coldly. 'Your jokes are stupid.'

When Penny was eventually told of the affair she seemed unsurprised, in spite of the two-year age difference between them. Stan felt that she over-romanticized it. He reported that Dora and Tommo were unhappy at losing a brother, and were always uncomfortable when the inseparable couple were in the same room.

The affair did not end with the school holidays. Penny went to see our headmaster and explained the situation to him. She took John's view that he should not be denied the time he needed to spend with Helena so that they could continue their relationship. If he were, he said that he would leave school immediately. The fact that John was academically highly gifted (and good at sports) weighed strongly in his favour. Helena had a car and picked John up from school two evenings a week. We became used to the sight of Helena waiting to see John, sitting in her car, or lounging on its bonnet, her breasts bouncing about under her T-shirt when she moved. John went out to her like a dog with its tail down. He loved her but he was also owned by her, entirely in her possession. And he suffered, knowing that she had the upper hand.

Helena was very conscious of her desirable appearance. She habitually seemed to be posing before spectators. I heard that she could not model clothes because her figure was too voluptuous for clothes to sit well on her, so she signed up with an agency that dealt in bikini models and topless models. For some months she was never short of work. She despised this work, although it was very lucrative, and when we talked to her, one winter's day when she came to watch John playing rugby, she seemed to be in a sultry sulk about it. She was wearing a grey fur coat over her jeans, and expensive boots. She smiled contemptuously at the boys who brought glossy pictures of her flesh for her to autograph.

'This is not *me*,' she told Stan, holding up a copy of *Mayfair*. 'This is some pink object a man has made. It is all a big lie, a big joke. Where is my sexuality? Not represented. A woman's sexuality is *never* shown because it is a threat.'

She looked for a while over at John, mud-spattered and panting, catching his breath in the field, and her face softened. She turned to the owner of *Mayfair* and said: 'Maybe a woman will love you, maybe not love you. In this case or that you will see that these pictures are a silly object, a boy's toy, nothing like what a woman is. Maybe this is a consolation for you if you can't have a pretty girl in your bed. That is all. It is not me.'

The fans looked stunned, and drifted away.

'If you feel like that about it,' Stan challenged her, 'why do you do it?'

Helena made a wry face. She was quite fascinating to watch, her expressions so pouting and childish. It wasn't true that she was humourless, she simply liked her own kind of humour.

'I dream a movie director will see my picture and say, "I must have her for my big new movie." Then I will be an actress. But it is difficult. In Sweden, in America maybe I get better chances, but I stay here because of John.'

It was impossible not to be jealous of John, especially when Helena said, scornfully, 'You can't have a pretty girl in your bed' – which hit the mark – and at the same time you knew that John was getting it all, not as often as he wanted, probably, but often enough. After that rugby match they drove off together – John learned to drive in Helena's car – and she returned him to school after dinner. I saw him come in and was envious enough to ask him where he had been.

'Helena's flat in the town.' He looked nervous at being questioned, and defensive. His face was very pale against the dark wood of the hallway. I understood that something had happened to upset him. He smiled slightly.

'Did I miss anything?'

'No chance of that.'

'Ah, good.' He thought for a moment.

'Like a game of chess?'

Helena had somehow confused him, and chess relaxed his mind. The familiarity of the school study, the chess pieces, me . . . and later Stan, when he came in and sat quietly playing his guitar and singing; these things were all soothing to John. By the time I went to bed I had forgotten my envy of him, I simply felt pleased that he had sought our company.

Helena got her movie chance quite soon after that day. She went away for a term, to film on location in Fiji while John, supposedly, concentrated on studying. He had promised his mother that he would take 'A' levels, which meant that he would stay at school for another year. He could hardly avoid working, and was by nature conscientious. He did a fair amount of mooching about, and played the piano much more often than he had before. Sometimes, late in the evening, he requested that Stan sing his favourite: 'More Fool Me'. Stan's voice was never more tender than when he sang for John:

And you'd be the one who was laughing,
Giving me something I don't need
You know I'd always hold you
And keep you warm
Oh! More fool me

But when it comes
round to you and me
I ask myself do I really believe
In your love?

Yes, I'm sure it will work out alright.

About twice a term there were parties where we met girls from neighbouring schools – and much snogging went on. We looked forward to these parties for weeks beforehand, planning strategies to 'trap' the most attractive girls for an evening's ultimately frustrating but sweetly erotic encounter. It all looked ridiculous, though, compared with John's experiences with a highly-paid sexy model and movie star who talked about 'exploring' her sexuality. John, although he was prompted frequently, would not elucidate on these explorations. He was utterly discreet, the 'man of honour' we joked about but nevertheless idolized.

Stan, reacting to this circumstance, refused to enter into the excitement over these parties, and never demeaned himself by declaring a preference for any girl, or kissing any of them. He would react aggressively and offensively to the more attractive girls, and ask those who sought his attention questions such as 'Why should I entrust my chaste body to your faithless arms?' Quickly boring himself with this tactic, he pretended to be gay. I found this very embarrassing.

Helena returned from the film-making and took John for

a summer holiday in Monte Carlo. Stan, Penny and the girls made several excursions to London for cultural refuelling, where I joined them. Penny was as charming as ever, but wistful, bereft. She said of John:

'I didn't want to let him go, ever, and I knew I was far too possessive, so now I've got my punishment – he has grown up and gone away before I'm ready for him to be grown up. Ah well, perhaps the time always comes too soon for us mothers! Soon Anthony will do the same, won't you, darling, and then the girls – I shall keep little Arthur for a little while yet, though.'

We were all eating a sandwich lunch in the Tate Gallery café. Penny fiddled with her beads and sipped her coffee. She sighed.

'When I employed Helena as temporary nanny I thought that the boys would be more helpful to her because she was such a pretty girl. I thought she was such a find as a nanny. And now! I can't say I approve of the way she makes her money. Does that sound stupid? I really don't think that doing the work she does is good for her. Or anyone.'

Penny sat back, brooding, and the girls tried to distract her with comments about the exhibition.

As we toured the gallery it seemed to me that Stan, by his mother's side, was commenting just as John used to – even copying John's voice. Penny seemed entirely engrossed in the pictures and noticed nothing unusual. I had to ask Tommo if I was imagining it.

'Why is Stan pretending to be John?' I whispered.

She smiled at me with a reserved charm second only to John's, and whispered back, 'To help Mum. She misses him. She can't work. That's why we keep coming to town.'

I didn't mind at all.

John, in his 'A' level year, continued to be obsessed with Helena, although he saw her less frequently because of the demands of her modelling work. Eventually her film was produced and John saw previews of it which he described as 'beautiful'. It was released when he was actually too young to be admitted to watch it, as it was 'X' certificate, a story of a lesbian love affair, shot mainly with a sepia tint. It was titillating rather than pornographic, although I suppose this is arguable. Those films were very popular then, and you can still get them on video. As a student I saw it at a crummy flea-pit with a girl who found it very shocking, although really it was quite innocent – the sequence where they strip each other was very sexy, and the massage, but the sex itself was very badly done, as though the director had suddenly been incapacitated by his scruples. It was probably just badly cut by the censors. Helena's performance was entirely convincing and she looked, as John said, beautiful.

To publicize the film she was photographed by *Playboy* in erotic poses, with her lover. John's face was hidden as he was pictured from behind. John didn't intend anyone at school to know about it, but of course, someone was sure to get hold of *Playboy* if Helena's picture was in it. In no time the thing blew up from an embarrassment to a scandal. John was suspended from school and allowed to return only for his exams. He was very embarrassed but was not convinced that he had done anything wrong, claiming the pictures were merely a rendition of the theme of Rodin's 'The Kiss'. He argued that the photography constituted poor, cheap art, but was still art.

John was paid rather well for posing in these pictures, and spent some of the money on a gold bracelet for his mother. Penny very sweetly refused his gift. It was John's first insight into Penny's state of mind. He accepted Helena's interpretation of Penny's action, which was that his mother resented his absence, having relied on him too much before. Stan told John that Penny's real concern was over his 'immoral earnings'.

Stan thought that John had done nothing wrong, but worried over him having been cast out. Stan did not expect the rest of the world to see the pictures as innocuous. His argument was merely that most jobs required a wilful blinding to iniquities and inequalities, and that it was therefore impossible to say what were 'immoral earnings, for fuck's sake!'

Immediately after the first film there were plans for

Helena's second film. Because she was a 'hot property' and could not afford to wait for the right script to turn up, she demanded a degree of control in making her second film, her main objective now being to make a film that would appeal to women as well as men: 'beautiful sexual images that any woman can happily respond to' was her way of putting it.

Helena felt that she could not celebrate sexuality without John, and after making a brief reappearance at school for the exams, he spent the rest of the summer in the film studios. In the name of what she was sure was art, he could not refuse. Perhaps he was afraid that the alternative was that he would see her on screen making love with someone else. The pair were inseparable. It was impossible for anyone to talk to John about the possible implications of making a pornographic film without Helena being there to laugh at 'Victorian ideas' and point to the timeless quality of erotic art.

In the midst of all this Penny decided to exhibit her paintings. Stan assisted her in any way he could, discussing which pictures she should show and what order they should be hung in. Stan often came to stay with me in London before and during the exhibition, and we 'cased the opposition' as he put it. My parents enjoyed him enormously for his vitality and humour, but he found our house middle-aged and dull, which it was. Peculiarly, he envied me for our matched sets of books, which he seemed to think better than the Farmers' higgledy-piggledy heaps of paperbacks. He borrowed all the volumes of the *Barchester Chronicles*, and for a few days of the exhibition we called in at the gallery to see how it was going, then roamed the streets of London, dropping by the wayside to drink cappuccino and devour another few chapters of Trollope. Stan was fiercely supportive of his mother at this time. He knew that John had caused her great anguish and that she needed some success. He phoned her every day when he was not with her, and made sure that he did not stay away from her longer than a few days at a time.

The exhibition was a great success. For the first time Penelope Farmer received serious critical acclaim, not just as a painter of nice, commercial pictures, but as an important entity in the art world. Most of the pictures were semi-abstract. (One of them was entirely abstract; I recognized it as a working-up of one of John's designs.) There was a sombre mood to many of them, a threatening element intruding, as in the picture of a carrion bird rising out of a field of daisies, and the stream, pictured at the top of the painting cheerful and blue in daylight, and at the bottom inkily poisonous under the sinisterly twisted trees. All the pictures that were for sale were sold for enormous sums, which made Stan widen his eyes in a kind of horror, and after it was over the whole thing sent him into a gloom.

John failed to attend the preview, but he did congratulate his mother on the opening day when he turned up with Helena, who looked wonderful, but rather as though she had just spent a fortune in Harrods on a classy black dress and black stiletto shoes for the sole purpose of putting Penny in the shade. She held John's arm tightly and dragged him away after his first tour of the walls. This disappointed Penny greatly as she had intended to take John and Helena out to lunch to congratulate him on passing his 'A' levels. He had been offered a place at Durham University to study maths, and he had deferred it.

Stan cheered up when we returned to school. We enjoyed our studies and our music. I learned to drive a car. Stan was not interested in driving, he claimed to prefer hitch-hiking. Our band performed concerts at school and we were very popular – that is, of course, on our own territory, where we could be sure of a friendly reaction. Stan's mind occasionally went blank when he was on stage and he used to sing the same verse of a song three times, forgetting what had gone before and what came next. However, the audience forgave us, shouting out prompts to help Stan along. They called him 'Forget-the-words-Farmer'. He was very funny on stage, leering down at the faces he knew, leaping and skipping about, turning to me in mock panic when he forgot the words . . .

Penny's children were now all away at school. The twins went to an international school in Switzerland and Arthur went to a co-educational school that Penny had been recommended. (She thought that our all-male school might have been partly responsible for the way John had become infatuated with Helena.) The change enabled her to accept a film role – her first. She was thrilled to have the opportunity to act in a film. The director was an admirer of her painting: and he claimed that the mood of the movie was so like the mood of her pictures that he had had her in mind for the main part as soon as he had read the script. *The Hermit and the Soul of Martha Hutchins* was a turning point in Penny's life. As the heroine, the saintly medieval woman who is racked with temptation, she turned in an unforgettable performance. It is an extraordinary, overwrought film. Which is not surprising, considering what was going on while it was being made.

When the filming was completed on *Sex Without Sin* John broke up with Helena. He wrote to Stan giving him the news and arranging to meet him in town – he didn't want to be seen in school.

I was more concerned about John than Stan was.

'I wonder why she's finished with him?'

'She's probably found a bloke with a fatter wallet and a bigger dick.'

Stan came back from their meeting and reported that John was devastated.

'Drinking like a newsreader, or a doctor, for fuck's sake.' (They had met in a pub, which was theoretically against the rules.)

'He's really gone to pieces. He said they should never have met, they should never have got involved – he's telling me! – and that he was always too young for her and he only realizes it now. Poor old John. He really needs friends right now – but where can he go? His old friends are all over the place; universities, America, Australia; and we're locked up in here. I should really be with him now, I ought to tuck him up at eleven o'clock and kiss him goodnight like a nanny. Mum should talk to him. She's got more sympathy than I have. I don't know what to say except, "You'll get over it old chap." But if he says, "How do you know?" I'm buggered.'

I saw what he meant.

'Where does he live?'

'With some other Swedish bird who is a friend of Helena's. Just a temporary arrangement. He's thinking of going home but our house is being house-sat by some friends-of-some-friends of Mum's.'

'Can't he go and see your mother?'

'Filming in some boggy part of Ireland . . . yes . . .' Stan seemed very doubtful. 'There are two things about that. One is: Mum is fucking angry with John about doing that film, and even he, now, will admit that it's a dirty film, arty or not. Secondly: she's involved with the director, fucking darling brilliant Hugo. And I mean,' Stan smiled humourlessly at his lack of taste, 'literally.'

'They could make it up now, though, can't they? Your mother and John?'

'I don't know. I don't know. I can write to her and John can write to her. I feel as though I should just get on the road and hitch to London and look after him. What the fuck am I doing here?'

It was not necessary for Stan to go anywhere, because Penny called him from Ireland later in the evening. She was trying to find out where John was, having received a scribbled letter from him along the lines of 'Why did you let me do it?' She was desperate to talk to him. Stan was sure that his mother would find a means of dealing with John's heartbreak, and he became quite optimistic, looking forward to a reversion to the old days, before Helena.

John went to Ireland and talked to his mother. I imagine that when they were together she tried to make him laugh, as before, and that she discussed her work with him, also as before, but that they discovered that the close tie had finally been broken. Her great capacity for concentration was being taken up by her film role, and her need for approval, which John had often supplied, had been fulfilled by her involvement with Hugo Seaton. If she had been at home, painting and gardening, perhaps it would have been different.

Penny suggested that John go touring Europe until the filming was over, when she would join him for a holiday. She suggested they go to India together. John was enthusiastic about India, but saw no amusement in travelling in Europe. He wanted to go home to Wiltshire, and this he did.

First he came to see Stan and me, and we met him, again, in a pub. John drank quickly. He wanted to talk, and being naturally reserved, he needed the alcohol to loosen his tongue. He went to the bar and downed a double Scotch when Stan wasn't watching.

John told us that Helena's obsession with the film they made together had destroyed their relationship. Performing in steamy scenes before the cameras required an intrusion into his personality that had frightened him.

'Sex, you know. We had a remarkably tolerant, permissive upbringing, for British people. Our parents were open about it. They didn't tell us you can have too much of it.

'Helena and I used each other up until I loathed her. I hated her and she knew it, and we kept hanging on, thinking it would all go good again. It was a good love to start with. We ruined it. We made it dirty and disgusting, you know, until neither of us wanted it anymore.'

'I always thought Helena was greedy,' remarked Stan.

'You mean, greedy for admiration. That's true. She needs so much worshipping! And I feel – exhausted with it. But I loved her. I was mad. She's got no sense of . . . privacy.'

John turned his face away. His profile was dark, stricken with regret and pain, his mouth twisted.

Stan said, 'When is the film coming out?'

John didn't know. He supposed it would be soon. He was appalled that the people who knew him would see it, and the thought that his mother might see it was unbearable. For a minute he buried his head in his hands.

I looked at his square, practical hands in the unfocused way that means you've drunk quite a bit, and I remembered things I'd seen them do. I remembered John dealing cards to a ring of friends. I remembered watching his hand's deliberate placing of a chess piece. I remembered him playing the piano. I had a memory of him on the rugby field, gripping a team-mate's sweaty shoulder to encourage him, and I remembered clearly the afternoon when he had picked up a pencil in his square fist and demonstrated the working of a simultaneous equation. I knew that something had gone forever, the strong feeling of calm he had given out. It had been shattered, and when John lifted his head and reached for his glass I noticed that his fingers trembled.

John said: 'I made Mum promise never to see it. And I want you two to promise, too. Word of honour, Stanley.'

'Nothing could make me watch it,' Stan told him, his eyes big with emotion. 'If I was given the genius of Eric Clapton as a reward, I wouldn't. Right now, I tell you honestly, I'd rather die.'

I promised too, and so I am unable to tell you what *Sex Without Sin* would have done for me. It was in a different vein to the usual blue film because it was more explicit, and claimed to show genuine sexual responses. It heavily exploited the scandal-value of John's youth, and sincerity, among other things, and confirmed Helena's instincts by appealing strongly to women. My theory is this: that women are excited by images that render men powerless just as much as men are by images exploiting women, but the difference is: for women nakedness is nakedness, not power. For women, a man's emotion equals power. That is why men are often angry with women.

John went back to Wiltshire, where he pottered about. As he seemed to wish them elsewhere, the house-sitters packed up and left him to look after the place. He trimmed hedges and pruned trees. He fed and watered the donkey and repaired its shed. He read some thrillers. He planted seeds in trays. A friend came to visit him from university for a few days, and they drank many, many bottles of elderberry wine. John started to consume the apple wine. He painted a small, strange, sad picture which he called 'The Fool'. One night, needing company, he drove to a pub in the local town. On the way back he cornered Penny's ropey old Land-Rover too fast, and overturned it into a ditch. He broke his neck, and died instantly.

Stan's first thoughts were for his mother. Penny went on as though it wasn't true. When she was at last forced to accept it she was hysterical. She blamed herself for not being there when John needed her. No one would have expected her to have sacrificed the film for a headstrong adult son, but hindsight seemed to indicate that she should have done. Hugo Seaton provided the shoulder Penny cried on, and Stan ended up being grateful for him. Stan coped by blinkering himself to everything but work until the exams were over. He couldn't bear the intense sad circle of Dora, Tommo and Arthur.

I cried at the funeral. Afterwards Stan asked me why.

'Fuck all good crying for John,' he said callously. He seemed, in a peculiar way, to be happy.

Stan went into a state of delayed shock, I think. All the weeks we spent busking around Europe singing the Paul Simon Songbook in unreliable falsettos have vanished from Stan's memory. Every night we found some way of getting high, until Stan had a paranoid fit in Paris and nearly threw himself through a third-floor window. We fought. His late-night face looked horrible to me, like a gargoyle. The next day we seemed to have done each other little damage, and made it up over one of our interminable breakfasts of coffee and rolls. We decided that we couldn't bear to sing 'The Sound of Silence' at all that day.

We went to a big store and wandered around the record department. The salesman at the counter took one look at us latter-day hippies and played a Pink Floyd track for us: 'Wish You Were Here'. Stan started to cry and continued for days. I can never go back to Paris. All I think of Paris is grief; grief in the Notre Dame, grief by the Seine, grief in the fucking Galeries Lafayette. All Stan could say was 'How I wish you were here'. He said it endlessly, through streaming red eyes and shivering sobs, and each time he said it I saw John in my mind's eye, as he must have been in his final days, battling with hedges in the mud, healing his heart in the cold spring landscape. I miss him still.

When I see the newspapers enjoying a scandal, like the kind that accompanied the launch of John's film and the news of his death, I wonder if there is a further story to be told, like this one.

Penny sold the house in Wiltshire and married Hugo Seaton. They have a place in California and a place in London. They are both very busy and successful.

So is Stan. People are often surprised that we are friends. I know he is ruthless in business. It is his way not to give in to fate. His financial success is his form of revenge. When he comes to stay on our smallholding he finds it hard to relax. Tommo and I struggle very hard to stay on top of things, and children seem to make it ten times as complicated. We hardly know how to react when Stan turns up in his XJS and says he envies us.

NIGHT SHIFT

Patricia Tyrrell

Patricia Tyrrell was born and educated in Norfolk and she holds dual British/American citizenship. She has had various jobs in England and the U.S.A. including civil servant, cook/housekeeper, hospital nurse and flea market stallholder. A scribbler since childhood, she began to write seriously in 1985 and since then several of her short stories have been published in magazines and she has won several prizes. Patricia is currently working on a novel.

NIGHT SHIFT

11 p.m. A new patient just admitted, which broke into report-time. Sal (the evening nurse) and I (the arriving night nurse) check him together; the stretcher leaves with a thin creak, scarlet ambulance blankets tangled amid Casualty's. Wish I were leaving too; there's lots more fun places than this. However.

So we check him. History sudden onset left-sided pain, query cardiac query epigastric. Man about forty – tall? Everyone looks tall lying in bed, but I'd bet he's a sixfooter. Pressure 140 over 90 – a bit high, pulse 100 (fast), temperature normal. Colour – ouch! Then I realize he's thickly greasepainted; meanwhile a friend of his has sneaked in and is telling Sal in loud whispers how the guy's an actor, leader of a London company now touring us. The name means nothing; Sal and I aren't into theatre. Try us on heavy-metal rock or callisthenics or new cuisines, anything except opera and theatre. The guy moves well in the bed, seems vigorous, no present complaint of pain. Sal goes to call the house officer who'll need to do a routine admitting exam; at the guy's request I hand him a box of tissues and he scrubs at the greasepaint; a normal-looking man emerges. Handsome like a cliff, not my type. A bit pale, but his fingernails and lips look normal-coloured (this is my sixth night – I almost forget where normal's at). He hands me the tissues and says, 'Sorry to have messed the pillow.' A resonant, rather stagey actorish voice; he plonks out each word as if he'd just carved it.

'That's OK.' Faintly from across the hall comes Sal's voice phoning; patients in the ward snore or mumble (he's in the little room opposite Sister's, in case he'll need special watching). I throw the tissues at a wastebasket and by a miracle they plop in. He cranes to see; we grin together.

'Not bad,' he says, then all the worries of the world descend on him; I worked a year in Washington once, and his worries look like vultures descending to roost on a warm apartment-house chimney. 'Hey,' he says, raising up on an elbow, 'I've got to get out of here – things to do –' Pain suddenly ambushes his face; I watch its tracer-fire as he flops down again. Pressure and pulse steady (I recheck them) but his skin now is slippery under my fingers. Sweating – there's probably *something* then. Might even turn out to be one of those quote emergency unquote admissions which are really rather urgent. Sal's finished talking, she comes back into the little room and he says (with a slight feebleness which might be stagey actorish or genuine), 'Has anyone told Helen?'

Sal mouths at me. I ask him, 'How's the pain?' The vultures have obviously lifted; they might be hiding behind a chimney but for the moment they're out of sight.

'What pain?' he says and laughs, the sort of total laugh you can't manage if you're hurting. 'Heck of a fraud I am,' he says, and twists around in the bed to prove it. Sal mouths some more, and I take her point. The rest of the ward is waiting: thirty-one other patients. And her off-duty time approaches, my time on. Thirty-one other beds to check by midnight, measure intravenous bottle levels, give midnight medicines. Check blood-pressure of a few shaky types; might be iller than this man; who knows? Can't prove anything on him yet, and anyway one pair of hands must cover everything. And the take-over report isn't finished, because his hurtling arrival interrupted it. I nod to Sal, check his vital signs again and into his questioning eyes say, 'Stable as a rock' (which they are); I follow Sal out and across the hall. 'The house officer's coming?' I ask her, hanging up my stethoscope.

She nods and we sit down to finish the report. I interrupt her recital of patients' names, operations, medicines, with, 'Who's house officer tonight?'

Without breaking stride she neatly inserts the nickname between two patients' diagnoses. 'The Beast.'

'Oh lor!' Resigned despair is the only possible reaction.

While Sal flicks on through the Kardex I scribble a note to the waiting night aide, a hefty ochre woman. Please go sit with him across the hall (the note says) till we finish report, tell me if he gets any more pain. I hand the note to her, she reads it and those huge chocolate eyes roll. Telepathy between us has reached a fine art during the past year: I shake my head No, he's not dying. Just . . . I don't like to leave him alone – not yet, anyway. Vital signs stable, but still . . . Something about that sheen of sweat and the flicker of pain's dark wing behind a phantom chimney – *something* about the guy worries me. Not acutely and for obvious reasons, not all my alarm bells jangling at a catastrophic gasp or a continual slide, but a tiny worry in my head, more like a slight tingle than words. An itchy scratchy unrelaxed feel, the sort of sensation you learn not to ignore, blast it. So I send the aide to him.

Sal flips the Kardex shut; report's finished. For an instant I see against the glittering metal cover the words, Did anyone tell Helen? His friends or touring-company are still around; their low-voiced conversation drifts from the waiting-room near the lift. I'll mention it to one of them when there's a chance. Idly I wonder who Helen is – wife, girlfriend, former leading-lady . . . Sal pulls on boots, coat, woolly hat; she looks twelve years old. She hesitates, says, 'You'll be OK? One nurse isn't many.'

I carry the Kardex to the medicine cabinet and start to fix midnight doses. 'When was there any more?' I grin (you acquire this automatic front of confidence and behind it you storm, question, worry, while the calm hands and cool voice do whatever must be done). 'Snow's deep out there,' I tell her, 'and cold – but, hell! you'll be too warm to care.' She's two months married and at my guess about two months pregnant – she's got that abstracted glow – but canny Sal's not saying yet, so I don't ask. I chuckle at the tender neatness of it – the fact shines out all over her, but she with her buttoned lips thinks it's *secret*? I chuckle, fixing medicines and watching her rush away. The lift clangs; she's gone. The floor is suddenly very quiet.

*

12 midnight. The Beast (who's just finished examining the new patient) sits at Sister's desk drumming his fingers in an irritated small rhythm. Bonk-bonk, bonk-*bonk*-bonk. That could get to a person. At least he hasn't hurled anything around or busted up any hospital equipment tonight. Not yet.

He gets his nickname from a series of hectoring thuggish demands made by him on other staff – nurses or doctors – always at the most inconvenient time and without regard for whatever else may be going on. A do-it-yesterday sort. Last week on this ward he threw an intravenous armboard when he got angry – missed nurses and the window, but broke the armboard. Now he sits growling; I guess at the growl's meaning and hand him the list of consultants' phone numbers. He dials; I eavesdrop (this is the only way to find out anything from him, and I've now made fast rounds on the other patients). The aide moves about her own errands: startlingly noiseless for one so large, she fills water jugs and piles clean linen for the morning. In five minutes I'll recheck the actor's vital signs, then perhaps I can relax about him. Five minutes in which to eavesdrop.

No, the house officer is saying, he seems stable. The Beast then clamps his mouth shut, scribbles, makes faces; so do I at his growing list of immediate orders. But that's OK if they'll keep the actor safe and quieten the alarmed little buzz in my head. He hangs up and shoves the scribbled sheet at me. All these orders are Rush, he says with a ferocious grin. I take the list, make phone calls, fill in request slips; then pick up a stethoscope ready for the next check.

The house officer frowns deeper, but not at me. I dangle the stethoscope and wait; something hangs invisible in the air between the Beast's brain and mine. By the most careful, the most acute of divinations, I realize that he's wondering whether to communicate something to this nurse, this anonymous body who jiggles a stethoscope and says nothing. The Beast preparing to communicate is an unusual sight; the worried alarm in my head buzzes louder and I try to make my silence receptive. It must work, for he says (like issuing another order, but maybe he can't mellow his tone), 'His doctor'll be in. Half an hour – and he'll want the results of all this urgent stuff.'

'OK.' The first of my phone calls achieves tangible results: a lab technician arrives with his tray of little tubes. He'll only take a moment, then I'll check the blood pressure before the cardiogram technician, whose rattle sounds in the far distance, arrives. A machine rattle which by the time it arrives at our ward will be loud enough to wake the other thirty-one patients. Rose the night aide looks at me and glares. All this damned noise! But the tiny alarm which buzzes in my head obviously isn't sounding in hers; she's at ease about the new patient. He looks fine, he's moving around in bed, talking, doing all the healthy things; so why worry? Rose, I don't know. But if the doctors hadn't ordered all these tests I'd be *profoundly* unhappy.

The lab guy leaves; I sneak past the bang-crash of the approaching cardiogram and check the patient over. Colour – probably the same as it was the last time; these low-voltage lights are really something. Pulse 104, a mite faster than before; that's not too bad. Pressure 140 over 80 . . . Um. A shade lower; would be a nice reasonably normal pressure in most people, but . . .

A voice proceeding from the little warning buzz in my head asks the guy, 'Do you usually have high blood pressure?'

The buzz is unsurprised when he grins and says, 'Oh Christ, yes! I should have warned you –'

My calm fingers stay automatic on his wrist as if I were still pulse-counting, but every alive part of me is probing him; my eyes sharply interrogate. 'How high?' asks the calm nurse's voice. 'Do you have any idea?'

He grins wider and says, 'Why? Is it off the top? Wouldn't be surprised.'

'No,' says the calm voice, 'but I just wondered –'

Her face must reveal something (though, believe me, damned little) because he sobers and gazes reflectively at her. 'You want figures? Let's see. One-ninety over one-ten, does that sound right?'

His pulse is steady but couldn't it – shouldn't it – beat stronger? Not a heart problem – there's no faulting the regularity, the evenness – but . . . The ECG girl slams her machine into the room – I'd swear they give those technicians a special course in how to move noisily. 'One ninety over one-ten, eh?' I say, and watch the clearcut face, the firm lips, the watching-me eyes.

'Yeah, I'm sure. And that was – oh, a week ago, ten days. Before we came on tour.'

The cardiogram machine crashes into my ankles where I stand beside the bed; I fight it off and ask, 'Do you take medicine for your pressure?'

He grins wider, the charming handsome male-lead grin. 'When I remember to. You know how life is?' I say nothing and he gets serious. 'Is it much higher than that now – or wouldn't you tell me?'

'No.' I smile back, a professional-nurse smile but it tries to get his confidence; that might be important with this patient. 'No, it's not much higher.'

'Good.' He sinks down relieved; is my imagination twitching or is he getting paler? The cardiogram machine reaches out and enfolds him in its tentacles, inflicting another bash on my shins as it nuzzles beside the bed. The technician and I stare at each other; she gives a faint shrug as if the octopus really isn't under her control. Past the coils I tell the patient there'll be X-rays as soon as this is over. 'Jee-sus!' he says, awed. 'The *works*!'

The technician anoints the air, him, me (accidentally?) with gloop so that the leads will stay in place for long enough. The house officer had started an intravenous on him; I check its drip – perfect; he's got good veins. Then I turn away; as I'm about to leave the room he says past the gloopy coils – says it as if everything that had happened and been said till now were totally irrelevant – 'How about Helen, is she coming?' The undertone of his voice runs like a ripsaw.

'If your friends –' I begin.

'Ask them, would you?' Not belligerent but accustomed to giving orders. The technician tells him to stay still and silent or her performance will take longer. I swiftly appraise the strip appearing from the machine; it looks fine. Not cardiac then . . .

'I'll ask them,' I say, and go to find his friends before I forget. On the way I tell the house officer the blood-pressure history; he says, 'What's the pressure now?'; I tell him that too. Our eyes meet and for an instant we are a single thinking, fearing, intelligence.

Quickly I check intravenous bottles in the ward, and the sickest patients, then out to the waiting-room. The cardiogram machine, leaving, grinds past; the portable X-ray machine clanks in approach. Rose is busily checking the remaining patients, most of whom are now awake from the noise. As I walk across the waiting-room area beside the lift, the Night Sister steps from the lift and heads toward our wing; any attempts by us at arm-twisting to get extra help rarely achieve it, but tonight I'll have to try.

The patient's friends cluster round me – men with chiselled faces and well-groomed women; a good-looking bunch. 'How is he?' they ask. 'Can we do anything?' That actorish intonation – a slight over-emphasis of words and emotions – would probably colour their talk however much they might try to squash it. I find an official answer; there's no grounds for committing any of us to anything more at this stage. 'He's resting comfortably.' I don't want to sound brutal, so I don't add (though it's true) that they might as well go home and get their rest tonight; whatever happens or doesn't happen with him tonight, they'll have to exist tomorrow. But no doubt they'll soon realize this and leave. 'They're running some tests,' I say. Beyond these people the lift clangs; the consultant has arrived. I must get back; the doctors will want me for ten thousand things – and perhaps the other patients will too. But I must ask one question, since it bothers him so. 'He was asking,' I say, 'about – uh – someone called Helen. Wondered if she'd been told.'

They glance at each other, all with a sort of lurch as if a lift had got stuck between floors. Then one of the men – tall, with a massive jaw and mop of grey hair – says generally, 'Helen's in California now, isn't she?' Nods, murmurs of agreement; they know who he means. Somewhere in the group a half-smile begins; it spreads among them. The X-ray machine clanks to the lift – that technician's as fast as a whistle. He calls to me, 'Doc's going downstairs to look at the wet plates.' I say, 'Right,' and turn back to the group; the answer to my next question might be as important to the patient as any of the tests we're running. 'He asked if she'd be coming to visit him.' Or, if she's overseas, phone. I wait, deliberately, for an answer.

Their smiles get smothered; feet shuffle; a woman laughs, then apparently regrets it. 'But,' she says, 'that's – isn't it?'

'Yes,' says the grey-haired man to her and the group, 'all over with, right?' Nods and agreement spread again; he tells me, 'No, she won't be coming. Or getting in touch. That's definite.'

Definite but . . . I'd hate having to tell the patient so. Nor do I think anyone should tell him this at present; I hope the group will leave. They stand in a solid phalanx facing me; Helen has armoured them against any more intrusive questions. After a jerky laugh one of the women says, 'If there's no more you need us for tonight –'

'No. Thank you very much.' The women all now have a bright defensive glitter which the name of Helen put there. I bet she's beautiful. Perhaps she's bitchy – or perhaps not – but beautiful anyway. And the men now act protective towards their women, concerned; you can sort out the couples in the group. And the lone men lean protective over the lone women; all since the name of Helen cropped up. She must be quite a person.

They start to move towards the lift. Because it's possible that some of them feel affection for the man, I'm unhappy about not telling them, He could die tonight. But the grey-haired man salves my conscience (and perhaps the rest of them didn't want to hear such words spoken). He hangs back and runs his fingers through his springy hair; in a tone too low for the others to hear he says, 'Is there any danger?'

'Yes,' I say (glad to give an honest truth, it's like a surgical lancing), 'yes, I believe there is.'

He nods and seems unsurprised. The rest of the group, at the lift, chatter about sending flowers, about understudies; I hear Helen's name again and a stifled laugh from the young blonde. The grey-haired man leans close to my ear and says,

'He's got no children – you could say the theatre is his closest relation. An elderly parent somewhere, but we'd take care of that. We'd want to be told first. And – oh yes. I'll phone Helen tonight and let her know, but she won't be getting in touch with him. That's for certain.'

I remember that on admission this man's name was given as next of kin; all the forms are in order. The grey-haired man and I stare into each other's eyes; his are grey with tiny black flecks and calm, calm as a peaceful sea. While the lift hauls itself up and its door jerks open, I search the grey-haired man's eyes for what you'd expect to find when a friend is ill, but I don't find it. Business acquaintance perhaps, but no more than that. Never judge, nurse, never jump to conclusions; but so help me . . . Nothing.

He nods brusquely, turns and joins the others; the lift swishes them away. I walk back along the hall and meet the clanking X-ray machine leaving. At our desk is only Night Sister; the consultant and house officer must still be with the patient. This woman has the skin and shaped bones of some East African goddess, and a mind like a medical encyclopedia streaked through with compassion. Now she raises an eyebrow at me; she and I understand each other's silent nocturnal language, a strange bleak talk. She says, 'How are things?'

I'm already fixing the next intravenous bottles for a couple of other patients: adding medicines, writing the labels. The desk sprawls with sheets of paper and the actor's gutted chart-cover. 'As you see.' The intravenous are ready; I glance at my watch – 12.50 a.m. I start fixing 1 a.m. medicines.

'Too bad,' she murmurs in that musical brown-goddess voice, 'that I've no help to send you.' This is her stock refusal, although usually she waits until the request has been made. I raise both eyebrows at her across the tray of medicines; she grins, mildly shamefaced, and says, 'This new admission – is he stable?'

I bang a bottle on the floor to loosen its stuck cap. 'Not exactly.'

She riffles the spread pages of his chart. 'You're awaiting the results of –'

'Everything.' While I speak the phone rings, its muted

night-time buzz; I grab it. In the ward Rose pads on noiseless rounds, cajoling patients back to sleep. Meanwhile my hand pulls lab slips from their rack and I note down results; the lab technician at the other end of the phone is a disembodied whispering voice. '*What?*' I say to him sharply as the results become wildly abnormal. 'Are you sure about that one?' But yes, he rechecked it himself. And the next result and the next; the technician gives each result loud and firm now; I repeat them and write them down; the Night Sister answers her bleeper and watches me.

With the last result I hang up the phone and instantly become a three-handed dervish: one hand chucks the second-carbon of the results across to the Night Sister, another hand assembles first-carbons on the desk – to be filed in the chart later – and the third hand grabs the top copies. Before the last carbons hit the desk, my feet are travelling; across the hall the consultant and house officer stroll from the actor's room. 'The hemoglobin and hematocrit,' I say, and show them the figures. As if these were an electrical charge, the air around the three of us pulsates with tension.

The consultant flips through the other slips and says, 'How many units of blood did you type him for?'

'Total of four,' I answer, 'two to be available right away and two more on hold.'

'Run three into him now and get him typed for eight more.' He hands the slips back to me. 'Don't run them in too fast – we mustn't overload his circulation. You'll need to check his vital signs frequently.'

Yes indeed; the line between overload and letting the patient bleed to death can be a thin one. Night Sister (who's been called to another floor), you *must* get me some help. I grab the phone and tell the lab to line up the extra units at once – yes, from wherever you can get them. (Of course the actor isn't a common blood type – not the most uncommon, but the sort you have to hunt around for.) I haul Rose from where she's giving an insomniac a backrub and send her downstairs to pick up the first unit of blood from the lab; they won't normally give us more than one unit at a time because it needs to stay temperature-controlled in their fancy refrigerator until it's hung. While Rose is gone I change intravenous bottles on two other patients and check dressings on a post-operative woman – a fast five minutes. The house officer slumps on a chair in Sister's room; poor man, he looks tired more than Beast tonight. 'The guy's bleeding,' he says (and a lank strip of hair hangs across his face), 'but where the hell from?' He scrunches his weary eyes upward till they meet mine. 'He hasn't vomited since admission?' I shake my head. 'No stools either?' I start to shake the head again, picking up a stethoscope for another check; promptly at this cue the patient's call-light goes on. A split-second journey; the house officer and I reach the bedside together.

The patient, lying there calm, stares at panting us. 'If someone could help me into a bathroom?' he asks politely. 'I'd take myself there, but this damned tubing makes the journey difficult.'

The house officer's eyes flick mine and I know how to answer. 'We'd rather you stayed in bed for the time being,' I tell the patient. 'How about trying a bedpan for size?' I'm already sliding it into place.

'Oh Christ!' he says with unusual peevishness, grimaces briefly as he uses the pan, then relaxes and says, 'All done now.'

In the bathroom I transfer some of the grossly-black liquid to a specimen-container. The house officer peeks over my shoulder and once again our eyes flicker in accord; the blood content of this stool must be as high as the heavens. Rose enters with the unit of blood; I take it and hand her the specimen-container. 'To the lab *now*?' she asks in disbelief. I tell her, Right now; the house officer calls after her, 'Bring the second unit back with you.' And I wouldn't quarrel with that.

My hands fly like fast birds; hook up a saline drip to the intravenous which is already running, flush it through the whole tubing, hang the bag of blood. The house officer and I perform the essential check of bag label against the lab slip which came with the blood, then I start the blood running; it pearls and slithers through the saline, then the tubing runs all red; we're in business. Thanks be that the guy's veins are holding up OK. As I start to take his pressure the house officer asks him, 'Any pain now?' The guy answers, in a voice which sounds surprised at its fading tone, 'No *pain*, just a bit woozy.' A game type – he attempts a joke. '*Should* I have pain?' He gives that wide grin to show he's fooling.

'Maybe not,' says the house officer. (With an understanding which warms my heart he answers, quiet and considering, the seeking eyes rather than the joking words.) He adds, 'We think you might have an ulcer that's started bleeding.' Now I realize where the consultant disappeared to – went downstairs to look at those X-ray plates.

'That's likely,' says the guy, 'that certainly is likely. There's been enough reason for it lately . . .' His voice fades out again and this time he doesn't try to haul it back, he just lies there watching us. 'Blast and damn the woman,' he says after a while; the eyes glare venomous but the voice holds no strength.

Pressure 100 over 60, pulse 120; I scrawl the figures on a scrap of paper and show it to the house officer along with the reading on admission. Our eyes lock and a sliver of my mind says: Sex doesn't bring this closeness, marriage comes nowhere near it . . . 'Yes,' the house officer says to me under his breath, 'yes, I see.' He leaves the room – gone to chase the consultant – but reappears almost instantly with the second unit of blood. The two of us check it, then he leans past me to open up the valve on the tubing and let the remains of the first unit zip straight in. Under his breath again he tells me, 'When you hang the second unit, run it this fast.' I nod – this patient's losing blood so fast, there's no danger of overloading him – and the house officer leaves. Behind me Rose shuffles; she's getting mulish; I know the signs. She's a rock, a fortress, when she understands the necessity; but there's been no time tonight to keep her in touch. I touch her arm and show her those terrible blood-pressure figures along with the previous ones; she stares, nods solemnly, stares now at the patient (it's fortunate that his eyes are shut at present; Rose's stare is so full of eloquent concern for him). She nods at me; she understands the emergency and will last the night. She tells me under her breath that the other patients are fine.

That's good, but I can't leave them to her checking for ever. The first unit of blood finishes, I hang the second and leave Rose to watch the man while I hurtle across the hall to the phone and page the Night Sister. An urgent page, the sort I almost never use, but this time it's justified; she may not like it but it'll get her fast.

And it does – the phone rings instantly. I am (I tell her) virtually doing private duty, and am going to be; this man won't get stable soon. If at all. Yes, she says, yes (her thoughts click almost audibly and I can read them, I know her difficulties; but I know mine, the doctors' and the patients', too. Above all, the patients'). All right, she says finally, I'll find someone for you. It won't be a registered nurse, there simply isn't a spare available, but – someone. I thank her tersely; some other floor will be short and curse us, but that's unavoidable. She says, 'In the morning there'll be plenty of staff on duty, we can pretty much give him his own nurse then.' I thank her hollowly for that; we both know that by morning the bed might be empty. I replace the phone and race across the hall to relieve Rose; behind me sounds the tromp-tromp of the returning house officer and consultant. Why do all doctors walk like trampling elephants? Especially at night. As we meet the house officer tells me, 'Big gastric ulcer – perforated.' I nod thanks for the information; past my hurrying back the consultant says to the house officer, '. . . *if* we can get him stable enough.' So the man needs an operation, but there's no knowing if they can stabilize him sufficiently. Rose sticks her head out of his door to tell me he's vomiting; I arrive instantly. 'Oh Christ!' he says, sweating between heaves, 'nurse, I'm so sorry –'

He's sorry? My calm hands and cool brain work while my heart aches and pounds for him; all the alarm bells in creation jangle inside me. Because the vomit is bright red. I hold the basin for him and zip the blood valve open to its fastest, but nothing's going to help with a loss like this. I'm chained to his side, so I press the call-light for Rose and ask her to send the doctors in pronto. Tell her quietly, so that perhaps the patient won't hear; in case he does, my voice holds an icy coolness. I *hate* my tranquil voice, my steady hands.

The house officer and consultant enter, the former carrying a big bowl of ice like a delicacy for some grotesque feast. I yank the nasal tube from its transparent wrapping; between us the house officer and I persuade it through the patient's nose, down into his stomach, while my voice makes polite explanations to the patient. Then the house officer picks up a big syringe and begins to shove ice-water in through the tube, sucks ice-water and blood out. Shove in, suck out . . . I hold the guy's hand and explain that he won't vomit any more now that the tube is down, and that the ice-water is just to settle his stomach (the hell it is). He lies with closed eyes but his hand on mine is firm, he nods in answer to my explanations; so he's still with us. The consultant watches him alertly but looks grey with fatigue. Shove in, suck out . . . Now the water is only pink-tinged; the house officer pauses to catch his breath. I recheck the vital signs. Pressure 96 over 60, still dropping; pulse 124. Not good, not good at all. Slightly worse than the last lot – and *that* was before we started pouring in fluids which ought to raise the pressure and slow the pulse. The consultant orders more blood tests; I thankfully leave the room for a moment to phone the lab. Beside the phone a girl in a white uniform is picking up a stethoscope – she's not a registered nurse but the best of the licensed ones; Night Sister has done us proud. 'If,' I say to her between lab talk, 'you can keep an eye on the rest of the ward –' She nods, takes my scribbled worksheet and begins her rounds – a load removed from me. I'll need to do the intravenous and medicines, but even so . . . I quickly check all the intravenous; they're running well, thanks be! No more medications due till 4 a.m.; it's now – oops! 3.30. Into the patient's room; for the next half-hour I hope to be all his.

More blood to run in; Rose hurries to the lab and back. She moves amazingly fast when it's necessary. I check his vital signs again; they're a bit better than the last time. Sighs of relief all around; I wonder what the patient himself is thinking. Some patient-reassurance would be in order, if the doctors weren't hanging over him. They read my mind and shift to just outside the door; now I must talk to cover their not-quite-low-enough voices. 'How're you doing?' I say chattily to his quiet body and open eyes.

He squinches his face into an extraordinary expression and we both chuckle. He's a tough one, a valiant fighter; my heart warms to him. He abruptly lets go of the expression and says direct into my eyes, 'Are you married?'

'No.' And I hope he won't enquire further about my love-life; a recently-cracked-apart romance and subsequent period of celibacy don't make for the most stimulating tale. Anyway he's a patient; there are limits beyond which one doesn't become unofficial and divulge anything. And into the bargain he's very ill, not to be perturbed or perplexed or worried about *anything*. Yet this man – as no other patient ever has – suddenly pierces through my official front and says direct into the centre of me, 'But I really *want* to know; I'm not being impertinent.'

'You shouldn't be talking,' I say, and smile to remove any sting. The suction hooked to his stomach tube burbles peacefully; it's true he should save his strength, but . . . what if he's got no future? If this is the last night he'll be talking to anyone ever? He underlines my thought by saying with surprising strength, 'The hell with that! if a man can't talk *now* –'

I meet his gaze and say gently, 'Talk if you want to.'

'Not married, eh?' he says, and a small grin plays around on that too-pale face. 'Nor living-with either? And *that* question,' he adds, 'strictly isn't any of my business.'

I meet the engaging smile, the steady eyes. 'Not living-with. Not right now.' A unit of blood finishes running; I flush the intravenous tube through with saline and hang the next unit.

He stares up at it and says with that startling force, 'Helen won't show up.' His gaze switches to me. 'They thought it was amusing, didn't they, when you asked? Nice people, but . . . a cuckold is always fair game. Just a bagful of laughs.'

What I ought to say is, Rest now, give your body a chance, even if it's a tiny one. We can't do anything about Helen for you; the only field in which we might be able to exercise power is the blood running in, the cessation of blood running out. And maybe we can't even control that. But what I *want* to say is something strictly unprofessional: Talk if it makes you easier; who knows how much time you've got left? Talk at me if you want, since Helen isn't here and even if she were on her way you mightn't be able to wait for her coming. Use me as a surrogate: rant and plead and make love to me as you would to her; I'll understand. However, it's not possible to say any of these things, so I try to warm my eyes and my smile to exactly the right point between strict discipline and a loving anarchy, and I say, 'You know you shouldn't be talking, but I don't have a doctor's order to tape your mouth shut.'

He laughs and looks human, almost healthy. Only almost, but the house officer sticks his head around the door and seems reassured; I make a cautious signal to him, out of the patient's sight, to indicate that things are holding steady at present. By how small a margin, we both know. He nods and seems vastly relieved (but mortally tired too – this past hour he's been rushing to and fro on calls elsewhere in the hospital); his head disappears again. The patient studies my face point by point and says, 'You look a bit like her. Not a lot but a bit – something about the eyes.'

He shuts his eyes and I – official mother-hen – say, 'Try to rest now.'

'The hell with that.' He reopens his eyes and sounds genuinely angry at me. He says, 'If you remind me of Helen, and I want to talk about her, what's the odds to you?'

'Nothing.' I fiddle with the intravenous tubing. 'No relevance at all. Only –'

'She used to be a sweetie.' Then he glares. 'Of course, if you've something better to do – I forgot you had other duties.'

Thanks be that he doesn't realize he's ill enough to keep me chained here. I shake my head and then remember those 4 a.m. medicines; nothing urgent there but it's 4.10 already. I check his vital signs again; halleluia, they're stable. Rose will sit with him two minutes while I attend to those other duties. 'Well –' I begin.

'I'm an oaf,' he mutters with his head turned away, 'keeping you here – and you responsible for the rest of the ward –'

This is all wrong; patients aren't supposed to guess or care about other ill people. Especially patients as ill as this one aren't. 'Oh no!' I say, warmer than I intended. 'Just a couple of tiny things, then I can stay.'

'You've got help?' he insists. His thoughtfulness for me, an unknown nurse, gets behind my reserve and I curse the absent Helen; how could she walk out on a man so considerate? I'm thankful to be able to answer truthfully.

'Yes, we've got extra help tonight.' And again my tone is warm because he must be convinced, on account of both his ill state and his caring. It works; he grunts in acceptance and says, 'You've got two *tiny* other things to do?' Despite his actor's skill the wistfulness gets through. I nod, reassure him again, fly out and set Rose in position with him, hang the two other intravenous medicines and check with the licensed nurse who seems to me made out of solid gold. 'Everyone else OK?' I ask. She produces facts and figures; she's got this ward at her fingertips in the two hours she's been up here. A gem.

The consultant has disappeared but the house officer still lounges on one of our hard chairs, his torso sprawled across the desk; without moving he says in my direction, 'The big shot's gone to grab some sleep downstairs – he's got a heavy operating schedule today. If this one stabilizes, we'll squeeze him in before the others; but there's no point in getting him on the table and having him go as soon as we start to open him up.' I nod; there's no point in jeopardizing the chances of all those can-get-wells either. I show the house officer the latest vital signs; he grunts and orders more blood. 'He seems fairly stable now,' I say, wishful-thinking, dubious, and get the expected answer. 'Could blow at any time – and barely stable, with the intravenous and blood wide open?' His stubbled face glares up into mine. 'How long d'you think he'd last on the table, in that shape?' Angry, but not armboard-smashing angry; and this time I've merited it. I say, 'I take your point.'

The house officer (who to my knowledge also has a tough operating-room schedule in the morning) looks so exhausted that I venture – although knowing again what the answer will be – 'If you want to go downstairs and rest in your room, I could call you –'

The expected answer comes; this guy is conscientious. 'Nah, I'll stick around.' His head droops but the eyes are still awake, seemingly by pure willpower. He forces his neck straight and says, 'The X-ray – you should *see* the size of that hole.'

'Um.' Those must be the words I least wanted to hear, but a nurse needs to know. As I start to head back towards his room, the desk phone rings. It mustn't be Night Sister withdrawing our helper . . . I pick up the receiver.

No, it's an unfamiliar voice, but with that careful rounding of syllables which tells me at once what the speaker's occupation is. One of the women who visited earlier? At least two of them were young enough. It exudes professional charm, but isn't there a ragged *something* underneath? She asks how he's doing.

'Well,' I say – there's professional caution but equally there's a professional duty to make sure that any near-one understands the gravity – 'he's been having rather a bad time, but at the moment –'

Her catch of breath sounds stagey but could well be genuine; a voice and personality this carefully controlled would have difficulty in making a drowner's cry for help sound spontaneous. 'I knew it,' she says. 'I couldn't sleep and I was sure . . .' Then she says with renewed energy but more carefully than ever, 'Has he been asking about his wife?'

Whose business is that? but it's certainly not yours, nurse. Level-voiced I say, 'Her name would be – oh yes. Yes, he has mentioned her, but I think he understands that she's not coming.'

'No, nor phoning either. Helen is the original bitch and he never deserved . . .' She attempts a light laugh and adds, 'Though he's not the easiest to get along with.'

Chitter-chat; soothing the patient is one thing, but listening to the convoluted reasonings of all his girlfriends is not my job. 'If you'll excuse me –' I say. The house officer, listening silently past my ear to the distinct voice, mouths at me: They're a bitchery. Yes, they are. And Helen no doubt is just such another chattering unfathomable bad-mouthing type.

'Yes, of course,' says the disembodied voice, with all raggedness now gone or hidden. Maybe I'm maligning her, maybe not; either way she's not my problem. She adds, 'I mustn't keep you.' Then, out of the blue, clear and detached and without a quiver in the voice, she says, 'Is he going to die?'

'We don't know.' It's a vast relief to speak so honestly. And they must be told; the risk is so great.

'I rather thought he would.' Then a fast goodbye, a click as she hangs up.

'Bitchery bitchery bitchery,' says the house officer, letting his neck sag again; his voice expresses total contempt for all designing females everywhere. But I'm not so sure about her; how can you catalogue these anonymous people? The house officer lets his hand fall emphatically flat on the desk as if to say, From a woman – any woman – what else could you expect? He glares as if he expects me to turn rabid feminist and slay him; I wonder if some of his usual belligerence is because he fears a world full of bully-nurses? I say smiling into his stiff face, 'The trouble with you is, you've got too much imagination.' His face thaws startled, but I can't stay badinaging any longer, can only take an occasional moment like this one; these smiling moments are vital for the sanity of any hurrying nurse. So I head back from the thawing disconcerted house officer to the patient's room.

Vital signs still stable, though they remain low; I hang the next blood unit. But something . . . I don't know. Can't put a finger on it, but my mind feels that those dangerous vultures I'd almost forgotten have poked their heads out from behind a chimney and said, Aha! we know a thing or two you doctors and nurses never will. Foreknowledge, that's what you lack. Then the vultures flip out of sight, but I'm strung now, wholly alert; I'd swear that down in the basement of catastrophe someone is getting ready to light the boiler. The vultures know this for sure, they've poked their heads down there and seen, but I can only sense. And yet, for now, everything checks out OK.

'No,' the patient tells me suddenly, 'you're not really like

Helen. You've got a gentle face.' He adds with extraordinary force, like a well person riding an obsession, 'Don't ever marry – you hear me? Or live with anyone on a long-term basis.' I want to play the cool professional and say nothing, but he's waiting for my answer.

'That's a recipe for celibacy,' I say at last, and am disconcerted to hear my own voice almost as angry as his. Most inappropriate to a nurse; I smooth it down. 'For sterility, for aridity, for –' I fumble with the ancient cliché. 'A person's got to get involved, even if it hurts.'

His expressive hand at his abdomen asks, Like *this*? Do you think the game is worth *this* result? We stare at each other, his face grows warm and soft, and an absurd voice in my head says, We could have loved each other. Probably too late now unless a miracle happens, but we could have. And I'm sure he's thinking this too. Too late, too late, unless . . . He says nakedly into my naked self, 'Why did your last one break up?' He smiles, not actorish at all, but a smile of such sweetness . . .

'Jeff found someone more exciting.' Into his receptive face I explain, 'He'd always wanted to be free to play the field, never made any secret that he meant to keep his options open, and when an interesting opportunity came up, why –' My spread hands complete the explanation.

'Young fool,' he says. Then, 'Would you like to see a photo of Helen? I owe you that at least.' His smile deepens the words' meaning.

I can't very well say No, her face is already firmly fixed in my mind, thank you. A hard-featured glitzy bitch; you and the others have made that clear. So I stare dumb while he jerks his head towards the cupboard and says, 'In the wallet – my inner jacket pocket.'

I don't bother to wonder why he's still carrying around a picture of the woman he hates so much; I find the wallet, hang his next blood unit and check his vital signs one more time before I open the wallet; my hands tremble. His signs are stable, low but as before. Perhaps my premonition was wrong, perhaps the vultures have shifted to a more likely home? Finally I open the wallet.

There's only one photo in it; no mistaking. He says in a tone of quiet hatred, 'Yes, that's her.' I make my own face unrevealing, then I look at the photo. And stare incredulous.

Because she's the exact opposite of what I'd expected, of what he made her sound. 'She's not an actress?' I ask, and am not surprised when he answers No, she's not, she doesn't even care much for the theatre. No, she wouldn't – with a wide-open gauche face like that. The bony young body, the startled gaze, the shy half-smile . . . could these coexist with treachery, deceit, harshness? I fold away the photo without comment.

'She *quit* me!' he says, still strongly astonished. 'She'd been messing around all over the place, but I didn't discover that till she'd *quit* me!' Because of our present nurse/patient status I can't say to him, Let me try to heal that injury; although I long to say it. Can't say to him either (though the words ring in my head since I saw the photo), Are you sure about what she did, about why she left you? With a face like hers, it seems there must have been some reason. And – which I couldn't say in any circumstances to him; only embraces speak this language – Are you sure there wasn't fault on your side as well as on hers? For one wild moment, as I watch his strongly-moving head, his alert eyes, I believe there'll be some possible chance one day for the two of us. Just for one wild moment.

Then, as he begins some conventional cheery remark about the decor of this room, the vulture swoops in full roaring flight; the guy twists on the bed, clutches his stomach and groans as if some towering dockside crane, undermined, were crashing. I jab the call-light on and send the intravenous racing in; my stethoscope searches for the beats which – as I now know – won't keep on sounding. Already they trail in a series of disjointed dots, there's no calling them back . . .

The house officer beside me starts another intravenous, though his eyes on mine say it's hopeless; he calls for more blood and more. The licensed nurse scurries away and is back in no time at all, her hands stuffed with blood bags. I hang the first, the second, wide open and pouring in; but the trickling fading pulse, the ebbing pressure, seep away from us.

The stomach tube gushes scarlet and keeps on doing so; our six hands work while our six eyes confront the clawing vulture.

And lose to it, of course; perhaps there was never a chance of anything else. I ask the consultant, 'You want the resuscitation cart?' in a hurry as the last pulse-beats, the last unconscious breaths, begin. He shakes his head and the house officer says, 'What would be the use? We might get another heartbeat or two that way but we'll never manage to hold on to him.' He droops, a young man defeated. Doctors hate death – a personal enemy; the consultant beside him seems aged by twenty years, watching. It finishes; hasn't taken long.

I walk back across the hall with the licensed nurse and hear the consultant ahead of us say to the house officer, '. . . nothing I hate worse than a massive bleedout like this – you feel so darned *helpless*.' He's trying to rationalize his own unhappiness and make the house officer feel better; young doctors hate death more than most, because it strikes at the root of their training. I talk with the licensed nurse, trying to comfort her; but she's a rock, she understands.

7.30 a.m. Shift finishes. All intravenous checked and running OK, medicines given (this last lot were on time, there was nothing to delay them), all necessary blood-pressures taken and stable. Outside the window there's a grey rainy dawn; I wonder where Helen of the pure expectant face is, what she's doing, if she really has found someone else. And who'll tell her this news, and how tactfully or otherwise they'll tell it. Nurse, that's not your business. I thank Rose and the licensed nurse profusely; where would any of us be without them? Rose and I performed the last quiet duties in that room half an hour ago; the morgue stretcher has come and gone; the belongings are packed and await collection by the next-of-kin; the room is stripped and ready for cleaning. I give report to the Day Sister and her crew, mentioning only briefly the patient who died because all they'll want to know is the fact that he came and went, the bed's empty. They have no responsibility, no ties, in respect of him. I pull on my coat and boots, I travel down in the lift and trudge out of the back door towards the nurses' car park.

I walk across the slushy park to my car; walking, I watch the grey heavy sky and I start to shiver. A shiver that rises from the deepest centre of me and expands to fill the world; the shiver grips and clenches so that I can't break free of it.

I shiver shiver shiver, because I realize I'm alive.

About the Awards

'These Awards are like no other awards. They are not an accolade for an already established writer; instead they are the opening of a door to all of those who aspire to become professional writers.' So said Ian St James at the very first Awards ceremony in September 1989.

This has been the ethos of the Awards since their inception – to open a door for twelve new authors every year and to help them take that all important step in a literary career. The reward for the twelve winners is not just a share of the annual prize fund of £33,500 but ultimately more important – to gain access to the world of publishing. Access to literary agents and editorial directors, in short to the very people who can help them realize their ambitions to become full-time professional authors.

Past winners are already making the most of that access. Elizabeth Harris, one of the winners of the Awards in 1989, has had her first novel, *The Herb Gatherers*, published by both British and American publishers. Her second novel, *The Egyptian Years*, will be published in 1992. Other past winners are hot on her heels . . . all positive proof of the value of the Awards.

For entrants to the Awards, the challenge is to write a short story of not less than 5,000 words and not more than 10,000 words. The story can be on any subject of the author's choice except stories for children.

Entry forms for the 1992 Awards will be available from all good bookshops from September 1991 and the closing date for entries is January 31st 1992. A full list of the rules of entry is contained within the entry form. Anyone unable to obtain an entry form from their local bookshop, or seeking further information about the Ian St James Awards, please write (enclosing an SAE) to the Ian St James Trust, PO Box 1371, London W5 2PN.